W9-BFC-128

'I may not be the perfect husband that you dreamt of, but married we are, and I, for one, intend to make the best of it!'

Julia stared at Falk for a long moment. Her voice was a mere whisper. ''Tis not a perfect husband I seek, but—'

'Tell me.' His dark eyes sought hers as she tried to avoid his gaze, and he had to hold her chin with his fingers. 'What manner of a husband do you want?'

'One that I may honour, and respect.'

'And I am lacking both?'

'You—' Julia bit her lip, stamping down on the twinge of pain that flickered in her heart. 'You are Norman…'

Catherine March was born in Zimbabwe and her love of the written word began when she was ten years old and her English teacher gave her *Lorna Doone* to read. Encouraged by her mother, Catherine began writing stories while a teenager. Over the years her employment has varied from barmaid to bank clerk to legal secretary. Her favourite hobbies are watching rugby, walking by the sea, exploring castles and reading. She lives in England, very near to the site of the Battle of Hastings.

Catherine March is a vibrant new voice in Mills & Boon® Historical Romance™

MY LADY ENGLISH

Catherine March

WITHDRAWN

LP
F
M 315.3 my

MILLS & BOON®

All the characters in this book have no existence outside the imagination of the author, and have no relation whatsoever to anyone bearing the same name or names. They are not even distantly inspired by any individual known or unknown to the author, and all the incidents are pure invention.

All Rights Reserved including the right of reproduction in whole or in part in any form. This edition is published by arrangement with Harlequin Enterprises II B.V. The text of this publication or any part thereof may not be reproduced or transmitted in any form or by any means, electronic or mechanical, including photocopying, recording, storage in an information retrieval system, or otherwise, without the written permission of the publisher.

MILLS & BOON and MILLS & BOON with the Rose Device are registered trademarks of the publisher.

First published in Great Britain 2004
Large Print edition 2004
Harlequin Mills & Boon Limited,
Eton House, 18-24 Paradise Road, Richmond, Surrey TW9 1SR

© Catherine March 2004

ISBN 0 263 18193 6

Set in Times Roman 15¼ on 16½ pt.
42-0804-74945

Printed and bound in Great Britain
by Antony Rowe Ltd, Chippenham, Wiltshire

To my father, Mannie de Araujo,
I will always hold you in my heart.

Chapter One

October 1066

'My lady!'

Julia turned at the sound of Ulric's shout, her fingers tight and firm on the reins as she brought her horse to a halt. The mare's white legs danced and the nostrils of her soft grey nose flared as she champed impatiently at the bit, politely opposing Julia's tight hold, eager to be gone from the salty wind and the stinging sand that tore up from the seashore.

Julia waited while her bailiff struggled up the steep slope, his gruff voice urging the two lads Ham and Chester to hurry. They staggered along bearing four wicker pots dripping wet from the sea, crammed with fresh shellfish they hoped Cook would make into several good suppers. She took one hand off the reins to rescue her cloak from the snatch of the wind and secure it more firmly beneath her thigh, sitting easily astride and bareback as Snow shifted restlessly from one foot to the other.

'What is it?' Julia called out, just as keen to be on her way home, flinching from the first sharp, cold spit of rain and realising that the grey light of the autumn afternoon was fading quickly.

Ulric reached his mistress, panting, one hand clutching at her dangling foot and the other raised to point at the far horizon, murky with cobalt clouds.

Her eyes narrowed, a puzzled frown creasing the fine arch of her brows. Then they widened and Julia exclaimed with shock. Ham and Chester also turned back to gaze and, like Lot's wife, the sight that met their astonished eyes paralysed them. Only a loud bark from Ulric roused them from their horrified stupor, and they continued to stumble up the slope in the wake of Snow's heels and the dirt her hooves tossed up. The lads flung their pots into the back of a cart, but Julia would not let them board.

'Run on and warn the village!' she shouted. 'Tell them to hide their valuables and douse their fires!'

'But, my lady—' Ham looked up at her, a question on his broad, plain face '—we cannot leave you.'

'Do as our lady bids!' roared Ulric, giving the boy a shove. 'I will bring her safe home.'

'And I will bring Ulric safe home! Go now! Quickly!'

As though the devil himself snapped at their heels, the two serfs ran off on long, lumbering legs.

'And say nothing to Master Randal!' Julia called after them, 'Hurry, Ulric!' She swung Snow around to stare once again at the distant ships that now crowded the horizon, drawing so slowly, but surely, ever nearer to England's shores. 'I have never seen so many sails! There must be a hundred ships out there. Is it the Danes? Or Tostig come with his Vikings?'

'Nay, my lady,' muttered Ulric darkly as he urged the ox forward and the cart jolted on its way, ''tis William come from Normandy. And 'tis more like a thousand ships he brings, for he will need a great army if he plans to take England's crown from Harold and place it on his bastard head, and...' Ulric looked back over his shoulder, swore and spat '...I think he has one!'

'Where will they land, Ulric?'

'Not here, my lady. My guess is that William will pick a quiet spot, further down the coast mayhap, where he can unload hundreds of horses and thousands of men unhindered.'

Julia pondered on this thought as a curtain of rain tore down from the dark sky, obliterating their view of the sea. Then she said, 'The only place I can think of is Pevensey, and that's a good fifteen miles from here.'

'Aye...' Ulric nodded in agreement. '...we don't want the Bastard on our doorstep. Not just yet, God have mercy.'

They turned inland, following a narrow track that led up from the seashore and over a wooded hill to the banks of the River Bourne. Snow put her head down, ears twitching, tail flashing, as Julia urged her mare down the muddy bank and into the rushing green waters. After weeks of constant rain the river had risen high and the hem of Julia's gown was quickly soaked.

Emerging out of the water, she touched her heel to Snow's dripping flank, after glancing back to make sure that Ulric was having no trouble bringing the cart through the river. He waved her on and gave the ox an encouraging shout and a poke of his staff.

Panting hard with excitement, the swift ride, and just a tiny frisson of fear, Julia wondered if a message could be relayed to her father. Lord Osbert had been away to the north these two months past, with her youngest brother, Wynstan the Red, and most of their men at arms and hearth-knights. He marched with Harold Godwinson—Earl of Wessex and now King of England since the death of Edward in the new year—to defend the kingdom against Harold's very own brother, Tostig, whose allies were none other than the fearsome Vikings.

As she turned Snow around and galloped home Julia thought it was futile to even attempt sending a message but decided to send Wulfnoth, one of her serfs, anyway.

A lazy drift of smoke guided Julia to the keep and, as she slowed to a canter across the meadow to the west, she realised how vulnerable was Foxbourne. The stone-and-thatched keep had no protecting moat and only one small tower, a recent and very expensive addition. All they could do, thought Julia, chewing worriedly at her lower lip, was smother the fires tonight and place the great oak beam across the main door, a flimsy barricade to bar an invading army.

Slowing to a trot, Julia took Snow around to the stables at the back, scattering hens and barking dogs, who jostled eagerly to greet her return. At the forefront stood her own massive hound, a tar-black Great Dane who shoved his nose into her hand as she slid down from her horse.

'Hello, Kenward, have you missed me?' Julia murmured, handing her reins to a stable boy, then telling Wulfnoth to go and warn the villagers before making her way across the muddy yard to the kitchen door, surrounded by several jostling hounds as they vied for her attention.

Etheldred the cook looked up expectantly as her mistress came in the door, her beefy forearms flexing while her huge hands kneaded a cushion of dough, soon to be baked into fresh loaves of bread.

'Well?' demanded Etheldred.

Julia stared at her for a moment, all thoughts of their catch from the sea gone and replaced with far darker and frightening thoughts. Shaking her head, Julia patted the cook's broad back and promised her that Ulric was on his way with the fish.

'Humph,' grunted Etheldred. 'There not be much in the larder, my lady, if we're to keep the pork for salting.'

''Twill be fish stew for the next few days then, Etheldred.' Julia smiled and stole a fresh honey cake from a batch cooling by the hearth, laughing at the cook's half-hearted shout and dodging out of her reach behind the wooden screen that divided the cooking area from the hall.

It took a moment for Julia's eyes to accustom to the gloom of the great hall, and, holding her cake in one hand, she went to greet her mother as she sat with a pile of mending by the fire. But before she reached the hearth a shout halted Julia in her tracks, her back stiffening and her expression suddenly still and wary.

'Where have you been, you lazy slut?' roared a deep voice, the words slurred together.

Kenward, his very name meaning 'brave protector', growled a low warning and Julia looked up as her brother Randal approached. His face was florid with the rosy hue of a heavy drinker, his red hair a wild, untamed mass and his mouth a porcine gash buried in the thick bush of his ginger beard.

'I have been—'

The blow struck before her explanation could leave her mouth, his fist on the side of her head knocking Julia to the ground. She lay on the stone flags in a crumpled heap, stunned, gasping, curled up as she waited for the kick that would certainly follow. Sure enough it came, Randal's boot exploding pain deep into her hip. Kenward barked, furious at this treatment of his beloved mistress, and for his trouble he was rewarded with a punch across his tender snout that knocked the hound sideways, whimpering.

The others in the hall bent their heads more attentively to their chores. Her mother squinted at her sewing, the maids Hilda and Gytha swept at the rushes more diligently, everyone pretending they had noticed nothing.

'Ham says you have sent Wulfnoth on an errand,' barked Randal, a little breathless from his efforts. 'I wanted the whoreson to take out the falcons this afternoon. Where is he? Fetch him at once!'

'Nay, Randal...' slowly, gasping, Julia struggled up on to her knees, then slowly to her feet, looking up with wary defiance at Randal as he loomed over her slight frame '...he has gone to the village. We...Ulric and I...have seen many ships... approaching across...the Narrow Sea. I have sent Wulfnoth with a message of warning.'

'And why did you not come to me first? Am I not the master of this house in our father's absence? You take much upon you, sister, in giving orders as though you are lord of the manor!'

Julia stared at him with ill-concealed loathing, for it was well known and often bragged upon by Randal that his sister would not inherit so much as a grain of salt at Foxbourne. Of the three children, Julia, Randal and Wynstan, she was the eldest, but she was female and Lord Osbert would not consider for a moment leaving his estate to a girl.

It was always in the faint hope of winning her father's approval that Julia strived to be useful, taking upon herself duties and responsibilities that Randal was too drunk most of the time, and too stupid all of the time, to shoulder.

Swallowing painfully, tossing her dishevelled hair over one shoulder, Julia spoke through pursed lips and clenched jaw. 'I advise that we bar the door and douse the fires. With the river rising mayhap the invaders will pass us by for the moment.'

'You advise!' scoffed Randal with a scathing tone to his rough voice. 'Nay, we shall not cower in the dark with a cold supper.'

'Randal, for the love of God, have some sense! When William reaches our kingdom he will come to take everything in his path. He will not ask us kindly, nor will he care if the price he pays is our blood upon his sword!'

His answer took no one by surprise. 'Get you from my sight, wench!'

Julia retreated. Her cake lay crumbled amongst the rushes on the floor, scoffed up by the dogs, but her regret was not for an empty stomach as she climbed the shallow flight of steps that led to the chamber she shared with her mother.

Before sunset many of the villagers came up to the hall to seek refuge. Randal turned them away and Julia watched from her chamber window as they straggled back to the village beyond the trees, armed with pitchforks and scythes against an unknown enemy and pathetic in their attempts to protect their vulnerable families. She blinked away the tears that threatened to overflow, a renewed surge of hatred for Randal and his mean ways sweeping over her in a hot, red tide. Even their own people, within the walls of Foxbourne, were anxious, but knew very well they could not look to the 'master' for reassurance. It was to Julia they came, sending

Ulric as spokesman, but all that she could offer him, and the others, was a suggestion for prayers of deliverance.

The serfs tiptoed around the great hall all evening, while Randal lounged at the dinner table, ate and drank his fill with his customary disregard for good manners and a civil tongue. As Julia silently forced a few morsels down her throat, she wondered if an invasion was truly to be feared, if it would rid them of Randal. But she very much doubted that he would latch on his sword and go out to fight the invaders; much more likely, she thought with a wry glance at her brother as he stuffed himself with sweetmeats, that he would turn tail and run faster than a hunted deer into the great and dense forest to the north of Foxbourne known as the Ringwald—a mysterious place that some said was haunted, but, being so deep and so dark, no one had ever ventured right the way through it.

After supper Julia retired to her chamber and sat close to the meagre heat of a brazier. Her work for the day was not done, and the sharp scratching of her quill on parchment etched into the silence, accompanied by the soft, restless snuffling of Kenward as he kept her small feet warm with his chin.

Julia strained her eyes in the dim light of a tallow candle while she penned the estate accounts in her neat hand; besides Father Ambrose, she was the only person now left at Foxbourne able to scribe and count intelligently. Carefully, but with little patience as her fears made her jump at every little sound, she kept a record of all matters that would be of interest to her father upon his return and, of course, be invaluable in her dealings with the revenue officers of the new king, Harold. She had no doubt that it would fall upon her, again, to deal with the reeve.

Julia paused in her labours, her thoughts wandering and worrying over the welfare of her family. How they fared no one knew, for no messenger, or travellers bearing news, had passed this way for over three weeks. Ulric had tried to ride out once, last week, and had returned to say the river was in full flow from the recent heavy rains and he had been unable to cross and make his way to the village of Broadoak. Indeed, the weather had been foul for ten days or more, with violent storms, heavy rain and wind that howled and tore at every nook and cranny of the keep. Julia now hoped and prayed that the river would flood and protect them from any advancing foreign army, even if only for tonight.

Kenward stirred and lifted his great black head from her ankles. Julia followed his gaze with her own and looked askance at the oak boards of the closed door. She murmured softly to him, but was unable to reassure him that there was no trouble abroad, and she caressed his warm, velvet black shoulder before returning to her task. However, she was so beset with anxiety that she could not continue. Her eyes stung with weariness and she kneaded the tight, tired muscles of her neck. Her hip ached from Randal's beating and she was vexed that another bruise would flower purple and ugly just as the others were beginning to fade.

It had been a long day. At this time of year there was much to do in readiness for the coming winter. She had been on her feet from dawn, supervising the salting of pork and beef; the preserving and pickling of apples, pears and plums; hanging garlands of onions and garlic to dry from the store-room rafters; setting the maids to carding and spinning the summer wool shorn from the sheep. It still had to be dyed and she had to make time somewhere, somehow, to collect the nettles needed for the green dye and peel onion skins for yellow.

Julia sighed and her glance lifted from the parchment on which she wrote and fell upon the sleeping mound of her mother, who had been snoring contentedly these several hours past. Julia wondered if she dared entrust the gathering of the precious herbs, so vital to their health, to her mother, whom she loved dearly but whom she acknowledged to be a timid creature at the best of times. Randal was not the only one handy with his fists—indeed, that particular vice had been inherited from their father—and Julia feared that long ago her mother had been broken, leaving a sad shadow who talked in whispers and sought refuge in solitude.

Perhaps she would send young Edwin along to assist; the nine-year-old page, fostered to them at the age of seven by his father, Lord Leofwine of Mercia and brother to the king, had ably proved himself capable of hard work and good sense. There was no one else. No man other than Ulric— who would be well occupied—that she could depend upon.

Long ago, when she had first come to womanhood at the age of thirteen, Julia had dreamed of making a good marriage, to escape the tyranny of her father's violent household and be lady of her own more tranquil domain, with a gentle knight who would love her kindly and honour her.

But over the years it had gradually become apparent that her father would not provide a dowry tempting enough. Prospective suitors had fallen by the wayside, each year fewer than the one before; now, at the age of twenty-two and no one having showed an interest in her hand for three years past, Julia had come to accept her lot in life. She would never marry.

Laying aside her pen, she bowed to the aching weariness of her body. The keys bunched on to her girdle chinked as she stumbled to the bed and she was glad to be relieved of their weight, setting them beneath the safety of her pillow.

Slipping off her girdle and pulling her kirtle over her head, Julia removed her soft leather shoes and woollen hose, blew out the sputtering tallow light and climbed into her parents' great tester bed. She snuggled with a sigh against the warm bovine bulk of her mother's back.

For some moments Julia lay awake in the dark, listening to the wind rushing through the trees— the yard would be full of leaves come morn—and listening to Kenward pace restlessly. Something disturbed the dog, for he was rarely so restless. Her heart beat faster, but she could hear and see nothing untoward. If William and his army were out there, she prayed that they too would need a good night's sleep.

Just as she was drifting off Julia was startled by the vicious screams of foxes, her shoulders jerking with fright, their noisy fighting in the meadow beyond the keep's walls an eerie disturbance, their screams uncannily human. Julia shuddered to think of an invading army landing on their shores, and burrowed more deeply under the covers. What could she do against armed soldiers, with a house full of women and children and old men? How she wished that she had a husband of her own, who would defend and protect her, and her people.

Five days after their sighting of the ships Julia rose, on an eerily calm morning, before the first mass of Prime at daybreak, combed her long red-blonde hair into a semblance of order and donned her chilled clothes. Then she woke her mother gently and Edwin with a shake of his shoulder and lit the remains of the tallow light to guide her from the chamber down the spiral stairs to the great hall, Kenward padding behind her in the hope of being let out.

Julia was content to see that there were no slug-a-beds this morn and she had no need to take a broom to backsides reluctant to depart from the warmth of their bedrolls; except for Randal and he was best left alone. Their fears had largely faded and the serfs gossiped that mayhap the ships had been heading for a different destination, Ireland or Denmark.

She gave a cheerful goodmorn to Etheldred, who was slicing bacon, and the two serving girls, Hilda and Gytha, as they chopped cabbages and turnips. Ulric gave her a nod as he warmed his gnarled hands before the fire. She opened the door to let the dogs out and watched for a moment as Kenward bounded away into the frosty meadow, cavorting with a joyful grin, his great pink tongue lolling to one side as he cast back a grateful glance to Julia with his warm brown eyes.

The morning passed quickly after mass. Julia broke her fast on honey-cured bacon and warm bread, a small slice of sweet curd-cheese tart, all washed down with a mugful of ale, which her father had fetched from Hastings in the spring. There were only four barrels left and she wondered what to do when they ran dry. Indeed, she must do something long before that, but to make the journey all the way to Hastings was not a prospect she relished without the protection and aid of her father and his knights. And she would not dare entrust her father's precious coin to servants, even to one as honest and loyal as Ulric.

Before the mid-day meal Julia escaped from the activities of the kitchen to her herb garden at the rear of the keep. She knelt to pull up weeds, then set about the task of plucking those herbs that were suitable for drying. The rosemary and fennel were all but gone, the lavender too, but she reaped what she could of yarrow and St John's Wort, tansy and marigold and mugwort.

It was a beautiful day, calm and bright, the sky a clear blue that mirrored the colour of her eyes as she glanced up. On such a day, thought Julia, the saddest person could feel hope, even joy. How she longed for Wynstan to come home and on such a day faint hope stirred and blossomed within her heart. She was just leaning back against the cold but sunny wall and wiping her brow, thinking about the welcome she would give Wynstan and the merry feast they would enjoy on his return, when a shout made her sit up.

'My lady!' shouted young Edwin, bounding along the stone paths on his spindly legs and waving his arms in great excitement and agitation. 'Oh, my lady, come quickly!'

'What is it, scamp?' she asked quietly, trying to keep the irritation from her voice at being disturbed, and a slight smile from her lips as she surveyed his earnest little face.

'Soldiers! A great party of men, my lady, fast approaching on the Hastings road!'

Julia felt a quick stab of alarm in her chest and rose quickly, rinsing her earthstained fingers in a bucket of water, taking a moment to control her expression and the sudden flood of alarm that coursed like a river of needles through her veins. Then she picked up her skirts and ran across the garden, with Edwin and Kenward close on her heels.

The maids were in the hall, setting up trestle tables for the midday meal, and looked upon their mistress with perplexed faces as her feet drummed across the flags—and up the narrow dark stairs that brought her out upon the square ramparts of Foxbourne's single tower.

Behind her Edwin and Kenward pounded with youthful enthusiasm, barging into her slim back as she halted to face Ulric and her mother, who already looked out anxiously at the horizon.

Taking care to remain sheltered behind the stone battlements, Julia followed the aim of Ulric's pointing finger, with eyes narrowed against the sun, searching beyond the meadow of green grass to the distant track that led to a vast world beyond the wooded hills that sheltered Foxbourne.

Sunlight glinted off the steel armour and raised spears of a cavalcade of mounted men, wearing helms and shields of a shape she had never seen before. They carried bright banners, one of them three leopards on a black background, but she did not recognise this or any of the other devices.

At the head of the troop rode a knight on a destrier as pitch-black as her own dear Kenward, who now thrust his nose inquisitively through the battlements and sniffed at the scent of strangers on the wind. A growl rumbled deep in his throat and Julia laid a warning hand on his head and pressed him to her thigh as she whispered for silence.

The fact that these mounted knights were dressed in full battle armour alarmed her even more, and she turned questioningly to Ulric, a frown creasing the fine arch of her brows.

Ulric cleared his throat and responded, 'My lady, I fear our time of waiting is over. They are Normans.'

Julia's gasp was echoed tenfold by her mother, and even young Edwin choked on his excitement and now gurgled with fear.

'Then your fears are well founded, Ulric!' exclaimed Julia. 'William of Normandy has come to take England's crown. What do we do?'

'Why, milady, what can we do? Surrender is our only option. It would at least buy us time and mayhap King Harold will return from the north to challenge William and free us.'

'Mayhap.' But doubt was evident in her voice as she turned back to survey the approaching soldiers. 'Where is my brother?'

Ulric shifted uneasily from foot to foot, his eyes unwilling to meet with hers, for he had seen Randal hive off into the barn with a lass from the village, an unwilling lass who no doubt would be lucky if all she bore from his sport were a few bruises.

'He…um…' Ulric cleared his throat '…be down in the byre.'

Julia thought hard for a moment. She could not send a serf out to the barn to warn Randal. It was too great a risk. Making up her mind quickly, she said, 'I will run and fetch him home.'

'Nay, my lady, you will not!' exclaimed Ulric. Even her timid mother voiced a soft protest. ''Tis too dangerous by far,' pressed Ulric. 'Besides, Randal will have heard, if not seen, the approach of so many horses. Chances are he is already legging it halfway to the Ringwald.'

'Very well,' said Julia, 'get everyone else in and bar the doors! Hurry, Ulric! For they ride swiftly upon us!'

Ulric went off to do her bidding, returning just as the cavalcade crested the far hill and entered the meadow bordering Foxbourne.

As they waited upon the advancing soldiers, movement to her right caught Julia's eye and she spotted a small band of foot-soldiers as they ran from the shadows of Foxbourne Wood and towards the inviting, if doubtful, safety of the keep. They were Saxon, possibly members of King Harold's ffyrd and armed with swords and bows, the latter slung over their backs and clearly useless as they appeared to have no arrows. Julia's party gave voice to varying cries of alarm and confusion as they watched the men run desperately for their lives.

But it was too late. The Normans had spotted them. The massive black destrier leapt forwards, its rider accompanied by two other knights mounted on great warhorses the like of which they had never seen before—powerful, armoured beasts, trained to warfare as surely as any soldier.

Julia watched silently. With ruthless efficiency the Normans ran down the fleeing Saxons. She hoped that her countrymen would be sensible and surrender their arms, but they did not. Their shouts and cries of war were belligerent as they turned and raised their swords.

The Normans did not flinch before this challenge. Their leader, the one all in black upon his black horse—the Black Knight Julia dubbed him in her mind—swung his broadsword as though it was a mere wooden toy. She knew great strength was required to wield such a weapon, as she had hardly been able to lift her father's sword.

Before her startled eyes, the Black Knight sliced the head from a Saxon shoulder and the body toppled to the ground, gushing blood. Her hand flew to her mouth, to stifle the cry of horror that sprang from her throat, her other hand gripping the cold stone crenellation behind which she sheltered.

They watched the scene of carnage with fascinated revulsion, the dismembered bodies, which only moments ago had been living, breathing, fearful men, grotesque as they littered the greensward.

Giving vent to a snarl of rage, her voice flooded with a fury that made her eyes snap like lightning, Julia commanded the page, 'Bring me my bow!'

'My lady,' cautioned Ulric anxiously behind her, knowing his young mistress's temper that on many a day had matched the suddenness and ferocity of her father's, his liege, Lord Obsert, 'it is not wise to provoke the Normans.'

'Oh, dear!' exclaimed Lady Fredeswide, her hands clasped despairingly to her bosom, as though that ample structure would provide her with succour.

The Normans now surveyed their handiwork and the Black Knight wiped his bloodied sword upon his saddlecloth. He sheathed the mighty weapon with grim satisfaction and paused to speak with his lieutenant before preparing to wheel his horse and return to lead his men.

As he gathered the reins in his gloved hands he heard a familiar, yet entirely unexpected, sound and exclaimed with shock as an arrow struck and bounced off the shield tied to his saddle. His head jerked towards the tower of the insignificant keep upon which they were marching, a small household of women and unarmed retainers and serfs— or so he had been told. The taking of Foxbourne Keep had been anticipated as a mopping-up chore and not a military exercise of danger or importance.

The Norman knight glanced down at the arrow, now lying harmlessly on the green grass, and realised that it had been fired without due force and been mainly spent of its venom by the time it had travelled the distance between archer and knight.

With fearless, or perhaps foolish, daring the Norman urged his snorting, wary, prancing destrier towards the keep; his eyes sharply scanned the tower ramparts for the bowman who had dared to fire upon the Duke of Normandy's man. He was astonished to glimpse the figure of a girl, with red-blonde hair fluttering on the breeze, even now nocking a fresh arrow and raising her bow, sighting with nose and practised eye in his direction.

She would not dare! He heard the twang of bow-string followed swiftly by a whoosh of fast-flying arrow as it sped on its way…far too close… With a jangling thrust of spurs and fierce rein-pulling he attempted to retreat, but was too late.

The knight flinched as he was struck, releasing an ear-splitting bellow of pain that grew ever louder as anger followed. With shock he surveyed the shaft protruding from his calf, in that vulnerable spot below the hem of his chainmail hauberk, protected only by the leather of his chausses. Muttering succinct French curses, he leaned down, with one hand grasped the arrow's shaft and tested to see how deep the head had penetrated.

Fortunately, he considered, it had not pierced his flesh more than a thumb's width and he clenched his teeth as he removed the offending point with one swift jerk. He had no doubt that had the archer been a full-grown, broad-shouldered man the damage would have been far greater. Blood seeped a small trickle, to merge with the dirt and the dark maroon of Saxon blood that already stained him.

He glared up at the far-off figure, the glint of bright hair and the pale oval of her face just visible, and he silently vowed to teach the *esprit malin* a lesson for her insolence.

Spurring his horse, he galloped across the meadow to the head of his party. He was met by the guffaws of his comrades. Some regaled him with amused laughter, others, more loyal, expressed their rage at this insult that he, who had wielded his sword and fought to the death in many battles under the banner of Duke William, had been wounded by a Saxon wench!

'God's teeth, mistress, that was foolhardy! Seek thee to bring destruction upon this household?'

Edwin was jumping around in gleeful circles, hugging Julia at her success and even Kenward thumped his tail and grinned.

'My apologies, dear Ulric—' Julia was sober beneath his wrathful glare '—I had not expected my aim to be so true!' Indeed, Julia had hesitated a moment, aware that death lay before her door. She had felt sickened then, and adjusted her aim so that her arrow would be a warning shot only, not intended to reach its mark. It was fate, or the wind, that had caused her arrow to find its target in the Norman's leg.

Their discussion was interrupted by a commanding shout. The ground trembled as the Norman force halted before the barred doors of the hall.

'Ho, Lord of Foxbourne, we come in peace!'

'Why,' exclaimed Julia, leaning recklessly from the battlements, 'the devil speaks our tongue!'

'Hold fast your own tongue, milady—' Ulric dragged her back '—if you wish to see the morrow with your pretty head still upon your shoulders.'

'They would not dare harm us,' said Julia, a contemptuous sneer curling her lip. 'Why, we are kin of the Godwinson and who would be unwise enough to harm the kin of England's king?'

'What do they want?' asked Lady Fredeswide, as they crowded together to hear what the Black Knight was now shouting in his roughly accented English.

'In the name of William, Duke of Normandy and conqueror of England, surrender to his banner and no harm shall come to this house!'

'What!' cried Julia. 'Is the cur mad in his head?'

'M'lady, how do we know what events have occurred these days past? Mayhap William is now ruler of England and, besides, whoever now rules our kingdom, we are faced with a party of some twenty men who could slay us all in a moment and burn Foxbourne to the ground should they so choose. Do you not see the bodies of slaughtered Saxons before our very gates?'

Ulric's words brought a small chill to Julia's heart and she surveyed the scene with narrowed blue eyes. She shrank from looking at the terrible sight of those corpses abandoned on the meadow, all too aware of how swiftly death could be dealt with a single stroke of the sword.

'It does not sit well with me,' she answered slowly, 'to so tamely give us up into the hands of these…these…' She waved her hand in the direction of the Normans, unable to find the right words to describe them and loath to admit to any truth in the Black Knight's words; had he really said 'Conqueror of England'? Could this be true?

'Milady,' counselled Ulric, patient, but with a note of desperation in his voice, 'there is truly naught we can do. Tomorrow is another day, yet only if we still live.'

'Very well.' Julia sighed, after a long moment of thoughtful silence. 'I bow to thee, dear Ulric, and thy greater wisdom. I will gather the household in the hall and anon inform yonder knights that we surrender.'

Ulric bowed to his mistress and watched as she swept down the stairs with her mother, young Edwin and Kenward following closely in her wake. His eyes then fell upon Lady Julia's bow and quiver of arrows and, finding a suitable niche, he hid them in the stone ramparts of the tower.

'Ho, Knights of William,' shouted Ulric, in his deep booming voice, leaning outwards, 'my Lady of Foxbourne surrenders, on condition that no harm shall come to her or anyone in this keep.'

'We do not stand here to parley, Saxon,' came the swift reply. 'Open your doors now or we will break them down and lay waste to everything in our path!'

'Nay, sir, hold fast! We shall open and let there be peace between us.'

'Very well. Open your doors!' shouted the Black Knight impatiently, muttering under his breath, 'This ''devil'' seeks an audience with her ladyship!'

Chapter Two

Julia gathered her household in the main hall. It had been no easy task either, as she had descended from the tower to find pandemonium. The serfs were running about shouting and screaming, convinced that they would not live to see the sunset.

'Be quiet!' shouted Julia above the uproar. 'Listen to me! No harm shall come to us, but for the love of God, hold thy tongues!'

Their terrified shrieks and running about in mindless confusion came to a halt and, one by one, muttering and murmuring prayers and grave misgivings, the household gathered about her like frightened chicks seeking shelter beneath the wings of their mother hen. She had promised them that no harm would come to them, but as the pounding of the Normans on the barred door increased, shaking the rafters and echoing through the hall like the worst thunder she had ever heard, she bit her lip in fear, not at all sure if her promise could be kept.

'Quiet now,' she urged, as their terrified wittering grated on her own frayed nerves. 'Edwin, come stand by me.'

The page was quick to do her bidding and Julia resisted the urge to kiss his soft cheeks and whisper her comfort, merely contenting herself with gripping his narrow little shoulders and holding him firmly in front of her, as though it were he who were protecting his mistress, and not the other way about.

Ulric descended from the tower, and, accompanied by Ham and the young kitchen scullion, Alfred, crossed the hall on his way to unbar the main door. But then he paused and returned, his bushy grey brows drawn in a worried frown, tugging at his beard as he came to stand before Julia.

'Milady,' he spoke with considerable graveness, 'I beg thee to cover thy hair.'

Defensively Julia's hand went to touch that bright glory and silently her serfs eyed their mistress, all agog. Lady Fredeswide and young Edwin were equally speculative in their glance, but with greater reason. Then Edwin turned and ran to the kitchen behind the screens at the far end of the hall and returned a few moments later, with a swift patter of his small feet, bearing a linen wimple and an apron for good measure.

As an unwed maiden Julia was entitled to wear her hair unbound, flowing free in all its beauty, but now, given her rash actions, she did not argue. She hurried to don the wimple and cover her kirtle of good quality, mulberry-coloured wool that singled her out as a noblewoman. Assisted by Hilda and her mother, she urged them to hurry as the pounding on the door and the shouts of the waiting Normans grew louder and more threatening.

Again Ulric went to the door, glancing over his shoulder, watching as every last red-blonde tendril was tucked away and then, with a consenting nod from Julia, he lifted down the solid oak plank that barred the main door from the outside world.

The Normans had already dismounted and all at once, led by the Black Knight, they shouldered aside the double doors and surged into the hall, bristling with the menace of drawn swords, armour clanking and ringing, the ground shaking to the pounding of their leather boots. Their steel helms were of an unusual design, with a long nasal bar covering the centre of their faces, and even stout-hearted Julia felt quelled by these strange-looking giants who now surrounded them, as she stood with fast-beating heart, clutching young Edwin's bony shoulders to her breast.

Their stench too, was quite overwhelming and she resisted the urge to hold her hand over her nose, her eyes perusing their blackened and dented armour, confirming her suspicion that their foul stink was not just that of male sweat and dirt, but of death. These men, she felt sure, had fought a hard battle and very recently.

Several of the Norman knights swarmed up the solar steps, three more ascended to the tower. No quarter was given until the Normans had satisfied themselves that those gathered in the hall, a paltry group of ten people, were indeed the entire and surrendered household of Foxbourne.

Their captors came to a halt. The commander ceased his barking of orders, and now surveyed them as an uneasy hush fell. Kenward growled his dislike of their invasion of his territory, nudging himself protectively to Julia's side. The Black Knight's deep voice rang out again, loud enough to be well heard but far lacking from anything as uncontrolled as a shout.

At his command the Normans rushed in and grabbed at all the men present, separating them from the women, even young Edwin and Alfred who were scarcely little more than boys. Following briskly barked orders, the men—Ulric, Edwin, Alfred, and the two lads who tended to the livestock, Ham and Chester—were forced to kneel down and their hands were tied behind their backs with harsh rope, swift kicks and vicious arm-pulling. Swords were then held tip-pointed at their naked necks.

Julia made to dart forwards and opened her mouth to make protest, but her mother's quick hand on her waist checked her and Etheldred, a massive woman, jostled her back with a warning frown on her meaty brows. Now was not the time for foolish heroics, seemed to be the message that was glared her way by both her mother and the serfs, united one and all as powerless Saxons before these unpredictable foreign soldiers.

The Black Knight strode towards the group of women pressed together in a tight bunch in the middle of the hall. He circled them slowly, his eyes narrowed in speculation, his boots crunching on the rushes and his chainmail hauberk chinking at every step. Then he stopped, just behind young Gytha. He reached out and quickly yanked the wimple from her head. The serving maid gave a little startled cry, which she stifled with her apron, half-glancing up over her shoulder at the tall, powerfully built Norman knight as he eyed her greasy, mouse-brown locks.

Then he turned away, ignoring the terrified gasps of the girl, and again he circled the group with slow, predatory care. With the point of his sword and a silent jerk of his head, he indicated that Etheldred and Lady Fredeswide should step aside and when they had moved several steps away, he considered the two maids remaining.

No one could mistake Hilda for Julia, for she was a buxom peasant lass with broad, ruddy cheeks and lank dark hair, standing head and shoulders over her young mistress.

With a slow, satisfied smile the Black Knight pushed Hilda to one side with the flat of his sword and then he came to stand before his quarry.

Julia could not still the frantic beat of her heart as the Norman knight stood just inches away from her. She kept her eyes lowered and saw upon the floor the shadow of his hand as he reached out and snatched the concealing linen wimple from her head. At once her magnificent mane of hair tumbled down and her eyes flew, furious, to his face.

One of the other Norman knights now spoke, in his own tongue, unintelligible to Julia. ''Tis the red-haired bitch that wounded you, commander. What vengeance shall you seek? If 'tis rape, then be generous to your comrades and let us have our turn before you hang her from the nearest tree!'

Throaty Norman laughter applauded this suggestion, for the bloodlust of battle was still hot in their veins, but the Black Knight himself remained silent. He towered over Julia. She felt her knees begin to shake but, defiantly, she raised her gaze and met his stare. It took a mighty effort not to quail before the blackest pair of eyes she had ever seen, observing her with cold calculation.

Lady Fredeswide now made a move and clutched at Julia's arm, placing her bulk between her daughter and the tall, dark threat of the Norman knight—silent, fearful, yet belligerent as she, who had failed so often, now sought to protect her child.

'Fear not, Mother,' said Julia gently, amazed at her timid mother's show of courage, and tossing a sidelong, defiant glance at the Normans, 'our kinsman, good King Harold, will not fail to come to our aid.'

At her words the hard line of the Black Knight's mouth relaxed into a faint smile, and he translated them to his comrades. More laughter and Julia frowned, glaring at dark eyes in a dirty face that so insolently examined her.

He observed Julia's pale skin, unmarked by pox or scurvy, her blue eyes boldly bright, the hair that fell in exuberant waves to her knees and the slenderness of her body. Her words now arrested his previous train of thought and it occurred to him that if she were indeed kin to Harold Godwinson then she might be of some value to William; a hostage for ransom, or mayhap a pawn of some kind, but that only the Duke could decide. He turned his attention then to the mother, instinctively finding the weakest member of this odd household.

'*Parlez-vous français?*' When he was met with a blank stare he realised that he had the advantage of his captives, in that he could speak their language, but they could not understand his. Gruffly he asked aloud, in English, his next question, 'Is your daughter married?'

Julia felt a flush sting her cheeks, but she bit back an angry retort. Lady Fredeswide trembled, her arm clutched about Julia's waist as she answered in a whisper, 'Nay. She is unwed, and untouched.'

His eyes narrowed thoughtfully. This was good news; no husband was about to come charging out of the woodwork, and a virgin noblewoman was a valuable chattel in the marriage market, which William traded in without hesitation. Even his own daughters, sisters and cousins were bartered to strengthen his ambition. Then his voice rang out in a French command and his squire, a young man who had removed his helm to reveal Danish-blond hair, sprang forwards. At his commander's request he grabbed Julia and forced her arms behind her back.

At once, Kenward, misliking this rough handling of his mistress and eager to show his mettle, bared his teeth with an ominous growl and loosed a bark as loud as a trumpet blast, forcing the squire to leap warily to one side, and to look askance at his lord.

The tip of the Black Knight's sword drew level with Kenward's throat. 'If you wish your…cur… to live, then order him down.'

She glared at the Norman knight, but her soft whisper was for Kenward. Obediently, but casting Julia a chagrined glance, Kenward lowered his haunches to the floor, his tongue lolling as he panted.

Now satisfied that no part of his anatomy was about to be claimed by the dog's teeth, the squire continued with his bidden task. He lashed Julia's wrists together with a long leather cord, looped it around her neck like a collar and the remaining length, effectively a leash, handed to the Black Knight.

He smiled grimly, satisfied with his squire's handiwork. He jerked the lead until Julia was forced to stumble towards him. With her arms tied behind her back the cloth of her kirtle was stretched taut across her bosom and this vision went not unnoticed by several of the knights, who gave voice to lewd comments and suggestions as to how their commander should now proceed.

But he had his own ideas and he was not rightfully named commander for no reason. He jerked the lead hard and with a small cry Julia lost her balance and fell to her knees before him. He raised his sword in a singing arc, the sharp blade shining as it cut through the air.

'My lord, nay!' shouted Ulric, leaping rashly to Julia's defence and instantly dragged back at swordpoint by several Normans, his neck pricked a small trickle of blood for his trouble. 'I beg thee to show mercy. She is but a foolish girl. Do not slay her!'

'Please, my lord,' pleaded Lady Fredeswide, 'take your pleasure of her, but do not take her life!'

Julia kept as still as she could, her head bowed, huddled over like a frightened little mouse, her knees pressed painfully against the knobbly rushes covering the cold stone floor.

'What say thee, my lady archer?' enquired the Norman knight softly and he knelt down to raise Julia's face, first removing his leather gauntlets and taking her chin firmly between thumb and forefinger.

He expected tearful pleadings, but the face she raised to him was bright with proud and angry defiance. The beauty of her eyes, sparkling with unyielding bravado, astonished him. The softness of her warm skin against the roughened tips of his fingers stirred some long-denied emotion deep within him. At that moment he would admit to no man how so much death and blood as had engulfed him the day before had left him weary and anguished. The shouts and screams of dying men and horses, the clash of steel on steel, still rang in his ears. He had no intention of slaughtering a helpless wench, but his pride had been wounded before those he must lead and for that she must pay his price.

Swiftly, tiring of this particular sport, he tossed his gauntlets one by one to his squire. Then he stood up and, leaning over her back, he grasped the lovely mane of Julia's hair. Between his callused fingers he felt silken softness, and heard the startled, fearful cries of her family and the hoarse encouragement of his own men crowded into the hall.

For a moment his eyes fell upon her neck, pale, naked and...vulnerable. Leaning so close, he could smell the female scent of her body and he saw her shoulders tremble. He knew this Saxon wench not at all before this afternoon, not even her name, and yet he felt within him recognition, as if some part of him had harboured her image always and only now held up her reflection for him to see.

Before an eye could blink his sword sliced through the air and, with a well-aimed swipe, he cut off the mane of Julia's beautiful hair, just below her shoulders. Her family and serfs, who thought to see her head roll upon the floor, uttered cries of shock and horror that congealed into something only slightly less as the Norman knight held up his booty, to the thunderous roar of triumph and approval from his men. Then, tucking the two-foot skein of still-warm hair into his belt, he sheathed his sword and removed his helm before he sank, with a weary groan, into a chair beside the fire flickering in the great stone hearth.

Whilst the other knights took this as a signal to ease their own exhaustion and remove their helms, their commander jerked Julia's lead until she was forced to crawl across the floor and sit beside the foot of his chair. Ignoring her, he addressed Lady Fredeswide firmly, 'Order your servants to bring us food and drink, dame. My men are tired and hungry. And,' his low voice warned, 'do not think to tamper with the fare as your daughter shall taste every morsel first.'

Julia's mother bowed and hurried away to do his bidding, accompanied by Ulric and Alfred and young Edwin, now released from their bonds and rubbing at their chafed wrists as their eyes darted malevolent looks. The maids continued with their interrupted task of setting up the benches and trestle tables and those Normans that could not find space sank down on the floor and fell asleep where they were.

Julia shifted uncomfortably as she knelt on the rough, cold flagstones, her arms aching and the collar about her neck chafing. She felt reduced to nothing more than a dog brought to its master's heel, except that she had never so humiliated her faithful Kenward, who now settled his great black bulk beside her and with his rough, warm tongue licked her elbow, offering commiseration and comfort. She was almost undone by his loyalty and tears stung her eyes, but determinedly she sniffed and blinked them away.

The Norman knight turned from his weary contemplation of the fire flames, his attention aroused by Julia's sniffs. He observed her flushed face and the tell-tale shimmer of brightness in her downcast eyes. Jerking the leather leash, he forced a startled moan from her lips and her eyelids to lift, revealing her rebellious gaze as it swerved to his. The movement caused a single teardrop to overflow and spill upon her cheek. He watched as it journeyed down her face and ended on her kirtle.

'Why do you cry, English?' he asked, almost casually, stretching out his legs with a sigh. 'Do you not still live? Have I not treated you with mercy?'

Julia swallowed back her tears and straightened her aching shoulders, now strangely bare and cold without the warm weight of her long hair upon them. 'My knees hurt. 'Tis all.'

'My leg hurts a fair deal more, of that thou can be sure.' He leaned one elbow on his knee and bent forward to consider her with narrowed eyes. ''Tis a pity Harold did not employ you in his company of archers, for they were a paltry few. Mayhap he would have fared better upon the battlefield.'

Julia searched his face, consumed with a burning desire to ask questions and yet fearful of his answers. By the fire's light, and with his helm removed, she could see his face more clearly.

She realised, with a small shock, that he was much younger than at first she had assumed, thinking him to be a man of her father's age, for he certainly had such a mature air of command about him. His face was tanned brown from exposure to the sun, clean-shaven but now darkly stubbled, his forehead handsomely broad, his nose Roman, his jaw a lean line beneath hollowed cheeks, his chin square and determined. She noticed too that his black hair was cut very short, shaved at the back, revealing his neck, an unnerving sight, so used was she to the long, unruly bush of hair sported by Saxon men. There was something menacing, she thought, about that naked show of male strength. He raised one fierce brow, smiling slightly at her boldly inquisitive stare.

'I can promise thee, English, I have no horns, nor a tail.'

'Nay, Norman, I see that is true. But your face—' she blushed, for his was the most handsome face she had ever seen '—is cut... and...bruised, as though you have come to blows with many men. Tell me, what has befallen England and King Harold?'

'Do you not know of the battle that was fought on Santlache Ridge and Caldbec Hill?'

'We know of nothing. No visitors or travellers have passed this way for three weeks.'

He sighed, a weary breath escaping from both body and soul, but he checked his first utterance of a devastating explanation as Lady Fredeswide approached him bearing a cup of cool elderflower wine, and a trencher of cold meat and hard yellow cheese. She was preceded by the maid Gytha, who held out a bowl of steaming water, in which the knight washed his hands, carefully wiping them dry on the linen draped over Gytha's wrist.

He thanked the two Saxon women and, as warned, he fed small morsels to Julia kneeling at his feet. She tried not to flinch from his fingers touching her lips and eyed him steadily as he watched her for some long moments, then he pressed the cup to her lips and tipped the sweet liquid into her mouth. Julia drank thirstily and with a chuckle he snatched the horn away, admonishing her sternly to leave some for him.

Mother and daughter watched him partake of the simple fare, their breath anxiously held, eyes wide and wary, until at last he swallowed the last of the food, which did little to appease the empty ache in his belly. Then, needing only the prompting of their avid stares, he began.

'Early yesterday morning, at about nine before noon,' he said, 'we marched up the old Roman road that our scouts had discovered would take us to London. We came upon Harold Godwinson suddenly as he was still marshalling his forces at the crossroads by an old hoar apple tree. He had little choice but to engage, and we had none at all, what with the sea to our backs and Harold barring our way. All day we fought. At first we did not think that the battle would go our way, for we could not penetrate Harold's shield wall. And then we realised that they had almost no cavalry and few archers. We made good use of a small trick that has worked time and again—pretending to flee and thus drawing the Saxons down from their ridge to pursue us. Then we would turn back and cut them down on the open field. Later, in the afternoon, Harold's brothers, Leofwine and Gyrth, were killed.'

Here Julia gasped and her eyes flew to young Edwin, and then quickly away as the Norman's own dark eyes followed the path of her concern.

'And then Harold...' here he hesitated, his guts still twisting and recoiling at the shameful death dealt to a noble warrior who was king '...was struck down and he lies slaughtered upon the field. Alongside hundreds—nay, thousands—of your countrymen. After that, we fought our way up the hill. It was soon all over by dusk.' He looked hard at Julia, 'And we are the victors.'

Her face had paled with shock and her voice was a whisper. 'It cannot be true!'

A shadow passed over his eyes. 'It is true, English. Never have I fought such a battle and I have spent many years fighting wars for William. The bodies of dead men and horses are piled up like…like hay in a barn. Streams ran red with blood. I would not be surprised to find my sword's tally to be over a hundred men for one day, one battle. Some say four thousand men, from both England and Normandy, have lost their lives.'

Lady Fredeswide laid a hand on her daughter's shoulder, a worried frown creasing her brow. They exchanged a glance as they both realised that their kin could now all be dead…could even have been slain by this Norman or one of the many foreigners that now usurped Foxbourne Keep.

Julia turned her attention back to the Norman knight and asked him urgently, 'I beg you, sir, release me from these bonds and allow my mother and me to go to this…this Caldbec Hill to find my father and my brother.'

'Nay!'

Julia was startled by the ferocity of his refusal and she shrank back.

''Tis no place for gentle-born womenfolk.'

'Please, sir, have I not begged? At least…' Julia thought quickly, fearful of his wrath and seeing the dark brows draw together in an angry frown '…will you allow our bailiff to go?'

Black eyes stared at her dispassionately, his mouth compressed in a tight hard line. What could this English demoiselle know of the carnage, brutality, and butchery of hand-to-hand combat? If her father and her brother had fought yesterday under Harold's banner, then they were almost certainly dead.

'Very well. But I hope he has a strong stomach, for there is little that lies upon Caldbec Hill that can be recognised as human.'

Julia blanched, but she could not allow her mind to dwell on a thought so dark as he presented to her. She turned her head and met the pained eyes of Ulric and he came at once to her silent beckoning.

'Milady?'

'Have you heard now about the battle on Caldbec Hill?'

'Aye, milady.'

'Go, then, to this place, and seek your lord.'

Ulric bowed and for a long moment unspoken thoughts and wishes passed on the wings of their glance. Behind their backs the Norman commander jerked his head in summons to his lieutenant,

Ruben D'Acre, and softly instructed that two men-at-arms accompany the Saxon bailiff.

'And,' he ordered calmly, 'should he desire not to return or yield any other mischief, slit his throat.'

D'Acre bowed in acknowledgement before turning away to select two luckless men for the journey.

'Godspeed,' whispered Julia in farewell to Ulric before slumping against the chair, by rights her father's in which sat her captor. She was already exhausted, her shoulders sagging and her face overcome with both fear and tiredness. Julia watched Ulric don his cloak and depart with the two Norman soldiers. What news, she wondered, would he bear on his return?

By now the foreign invaders were calling for drink stronger than ale and elderflower wine. Of those knights gathered around the Black Knight one now lunged at Julia, one side of his face horribly scarred, and she gave voice to a frightened cry. He shouted insistently, trying to make her comprehend his wants. He seemed to believe that the louder his voice, the greater would be her ability to understand French. Disturbed from his conversation with D'Acre, the Black Knight broke off and intervened. Julia was relieved when his booted foot planted squarely in the chest of her aggressor and pushed back the belligerent knight.

'What ails you, Gilbert?' he asked, irritably.

'She has the keys to the storeroom, where the best wines are kept. We tire of this dishwater the old crone insists on pouring.'

His commander turned to Julia and ordered briskly, 'Give him your keys.'

'How can I,' she replied tartly, 'when my hands are bound?'

He looked then to Gilbert and gave him a curt nod of permission. Gilbert de Slevin needed no second bidding as he leaned over Julia and ripped the keys, girdle, precious leather pouch and all, from her waist. He took the opportunity too, to try to fondle her breasts at the same time and Julia screeched at him.

'God rot you in hell, thief!' she cursed him, twisting away to avoid his groping hands.

Gilbert laughed and said in French to his commander, 'She's a feisty thing. Be sure to toss her my way when you have finished with her.'

His commander gave him a cold glance. 'Unless you wish to taste the steel of my sword instead of Saxon wine, desist from touching her. Leave me to counsel with Ruben and enjoy my moment of rest.'

Gilbert bowed stiffly, a wry smile touching his lips, but not his eyes, as he withdrew with a last lingering leer for Julia.

She was curious to know what words had passed between the two Norman knights, and she wished that she had learned to speak the French tongue as Father Ambrose had often suggested. That the two Normans were not in accord was obvious and that they had been discussing her was also plain, but she was frustrated to be in ignorance of their conversation.

The afternoon was drawing on and Julia feared that the Normans would eat and drink Foxbourne bare, like a plague of locusts. Once, as she sat quietly observing the crowded hall, apparently ignored, his squire came to her, knelt down at her side and offered her a drink from the cup of wine he held. She thanked him and there was a glimmer of sympathy in his pale blue eyes as he murmured something French, encouraging by its tone.

Her limbs ached painfully from being bound and crouched on the cold floor, but she did not dare move or beg for release, for fear of what may follow. She worried that the Normans would stay for the night, maybe for many nights, and when they sought their beds they would seek women too.

She glanced fearfully up at the Norman commander, still sprawled in his chair by the fire. How many times had her father so favoured that chair after a hard day's hunting and hawking, or riding over his estates? She looked at this soldier's face, so dark and so hard, and yet so starkly naked without the beard and long hair that she was used to seeing on a man's face. She noticed again how the shaved hair at his nape revealed the latent strength of that strong column. His shoulders were broad and powerful, his long legs bulky with muscle beneath the chainmail of his armour. Her glance fell to his hands, dangling loose-fingered from the armrests of his chair. His fingers were brown, smooth-skinned and surprisingly unblemished. They looked lean and strong, used to hard work.

The thoughts that now plagued her, causing her brows to crease in a troubled frown, were centred on what it would be like if he should choose to force her to his bed. She could only wonder about that unknown act she had heard whispered about amongst the serving girls. Why, thought Julia with alarm, my bones would be crushed beneath his great weight! She was sure that... The Norman knight turned his head then, as though sensing her perusal and Julia blushed hotly to think that her thoughts were written plainly upon her face. Their eyes met, and his glance moved leisurely over her face, pausing to rest upon her lips, with a speculative gleam.

Her blush deepened when she realised that her fears were very few, if this man should choose to lay his hands upon her, and she was ashamed at the little flicker of excitement that burned in every part of her that was woman. It should not be so, she admonished herself; but it was so, and she could not deny that she was attracted to his dark masculinity, his aura of strength and, yes, even his honour. This was not a cruel or vicious man, not a man like Randal, she was sure. Greatly daring, she lifted her chin and asked, 'How is that you speak my language so well?'

A slight frown marred his brows, and he answered brusquely, 'My mother was Saxon.'

'Indeed.' Julia was eager for the conversation, to learn more about him. 'Where was her family home?'

'Dover.'

It was then Kenward lifted his head from his paws and gave a loud, deep bark that rolled like thunder around the hall and startled everyone into sudden silence.

The Norman commander stirred in his chair and he glanced at Kenward with suspicious eyes. Before he could enquire of Julia what ailed the dog, his squire came running down from the tower, excited and breathless as he called out, ''Tis our Duke! He approaches from the east with a party of some one hundred men!'

Her captor rose at once and snapped out orders in readiness to meet their liege. The ground trembled as horses galloped across the meadow, surging to a halt before the doors of Foxbourne. There was a great commotion, shouts and a rising swell of cheering as a large group of knights, a mix of high-ranking nobles, army commanders and body-guards, all led by the striding figure of William, now marched into the hall.

He was squarely built and red-haired, this Nor-man Duke, a proud and skilled warrior who had the love of the men he commanded. He came now into their midst and with some humility accepted their jubilant and noisy fanfare.

From where she sat crouched on her heels, Julia looked up at the forest of legs clad in leather and steel. Swords clanked in their scabbards, a back-ground chorus to the deep melody of male voices, their words unintelligible to her, but the jubilant note of victory as plainly obvious as the nose on her face.

The Norman she had dubbed the Black Knight, her captor, called for a toast. The assembled com-pany of men raised their assorted goblets, drinking horns and tumblers to toast William, Duke of Normandy and now Conqueror of England, and they gave a great shout of 'Huzzah!' that rang to the rafters.

William turned to his knight and thanked him for the honour of his toast, for his loyal service upon the battlefield. He clasped his arms about him in the French fashion, offering his cheek, but in the middle of this action William jumped back and exclaimed, 'In the name of God! What creature is it that hangs from your belt?'

The Black Knight laughed, a baritone, little-used sound, and he lifted the long hank of Julia's hair. ''Tis no creature, sire. Upon my arrival at this keep I was fired at by an archer and slightly wounded. The archer, sire, was an English lady, the daughter of this keep's lord, who surely now lies dead upon Caldbec Hill. To punish her I cut off her hair, for she is young and unwed and I could not in good conscience punish her in any other way.'

'I see.' Duke William scanned the gathered throng thoughtfully. 'And where is this English wench now? I trust no harm has befallen her. You know well my feelings on undisciplined behaviour amongst my knights.'

'Sire, I know well indeed, and though there are some who would have me rape and hang her, I assure you that no such thing has occurred, nor to any woman in this keep.'

'Good. Bring her here. I would see this brave heart that would dare aim an arrow at one of my knights. I see she is red-haired. I can avow that is a mark of either great courage or vile temper. In my case, both!' William ruffled his own rather dirty, sweat-lank ginger locks to a chorus of polite laughter.

The crowd of men parted and Julia was revealed, still kneeling on the floor. Her captor had fastened the leash to his vacant chair and now he came forwards and lifted her by her elbows off the floor, untying the leash with a snap.

'Sire, may I present my Lady Archer?'

There was a round of laughter, but William was not best pleased. 'For pity's sake remove that contraption about her neck. It looks all too much like a noose and I for one have had a gutful of death and violence this day past.'

With his dagger the Black Knight swiftly cut the leather circled around Julia's neck and, although she gasped, he left not a scratch upon her. But her wrists he did not touch and these remained bound behind her back.

'She is not mad or dangerous?' enquired William.

The men, Duke and knights and nobles, considered Julia's slender form. The top of her head barely reached to the shoulder of the man who held her leash, and she looked too small and fragile and feminine to be either mad or dangerous.

'Perhaps, sire, we should consider all Saxons to be dangerous, until they have sworn fealty to you.'

'Indeed? Then she shall swear.'

'I think she will not do so.'

'What makes you so sure, my good knight?'

'Her arrow in my leg makes me so sure, your Grace.'

Laughter echoed thinly and Julia frowned, annoyed that she could not understand them. William noticed her brows drawn together in puzzlement.

'Does she speak French?'

'Nay, sire.'

'Not one word?'

'Not one word, sire.'

'Then, by God, she shall learn! And so shall all of England! Norman and Saxon will live side by side, and together we will become one race. A strong race, a proud race. On this very day shall begin a new age and it starts here and now with this girl.' He checked for a moment, considering, his agile mind quickly reaching a decision. 'I shall give her in marriage to one of my knights and they shall join honourably in holy union and bear new life. That will, pray God, in some small measure, atone for the great loss of life when I did do battle with Harold for this kingdom, a fact that burdens me sorely with its tragedy.' William paused, taking breath upon his enthusiastic speech, casting his eye about his men and considering which one of them was still unwed and best suited to his purpose.

Hugh de Monceux was young and fit, but he was of noble and wealthy family; he had greater plans for Hugh, as did his family, who would not be best pleased to find their son wed to a Saxon wench of doubtful rank and privilege.

Perhaps, then, Ruben D'Acre, a capable knight and an amenable fellow but, alas, William seemed to remember there was recently a betrothal, unfortunately a love match, to the youngest daughter of the Count of Arromanche.

His gaze then fell on Gilbert de Slevin, but instantly dismissed him. William had need of his ruthless wiles at court; besides which, Gilbert had a reputation for beating his women and he would not care to see this pretty, spirited thing broken and battered.

As the men shifted restlessly, coughed here and there, murmured surreptitiously and sipped their wine as they awaited William's verdict, the Duke noticed the tension in one particular knight's face, and he considered this man thoughtfully.

Falk de Arques was twenty-eight years old and he had fought for William these ten years past. It occurred to him that de Arques had never married since the betrayal of his betrothed, Vernice something-or-other, several years ago. Although there were always lemans to ease a man's desires, de Arques, as far as he knew, did not even keep a mistress.

Aye, indeed, it was high time the younger man settled to marriage, thought William. Like him, Falk was also a bastard son of a wealthy Norman

count, but unlike him Falk had not been acknowledged by his father and given no lands and no
fortune in Normandy. William's gaze fell on Julia,
and then on his knight and he thought, by God,
what a race this pair would breed! Brave, beautiful
and bold!

'Falk de Arques, you shall take this Saxon lady
to wife and lay claim to this keep and all land,
chattels, rents, dowers and livestock belonging to
it.' William turned about impatiently and demanded, 'Is there a priest? Come, brother, you
shall do the honours in French while these Saxons
fetch their priest—' Odo, the Bishop of Bayeux
and William's half-brother, now came forwards, a
little frown of surprise on his mild face '—for it
is my will that I would see these two properly wed
and we ride for Hastings before sunset.'

Falk de Arques considered William with a look
of shock that he tried valiantly to hide. He had no
desire to marry, nor to settle in England, but he
knew better than to argue with his overlord, especially one such as William. He turned then to
Lady Fredeswide and said, 'Madam, your daughter
is about to be wed.'

'Wed?' exclaimed she, stammering in confusion. 'But, but…t-to wh-whom?'

The Black Knight bowed and replied with a sar-
donic and resigned tone, 'To me.'

Chapter Three

The chapel at Foxbourne had been built on the western wing and late afternoon light now flooded in through a single arched window behind the simple wooden altar, bathing the gathering of people in a golden glow. It was a small room and only those most important to the ceremony were allowed to be present.

The vows of Lady Julia of Foxbourne and Falk de Arques were to be conducted in both French and English by the Norman Bishop Odo and by a very nervous Saxon, Friar Ambrose.

Almost from the beginning the ceremony came to a halt and threatened not to proceed at all as a major stumbling block presented itself, an impediment that William in his regal arrogance had not considered—the bride was unwilling.

Julia masked her fear by lifting her chin and squaring her shoulders, staring boldly into the Duke of Normandy's face and declaring, 'By what right do you give me in marriage to this man? You are neither my father nor my king!'

Her words were obligingly, though with wary softness, translated by her prospective bridegroom and as soon as their meaning became clear William exploded with a volatile mixture of anger and amusement. He surveyed the slender Julia, so boldly defiant amidst the battle-seasoned foreign knights that towered head and shoulders over her. William bowed to her, a mocking smile touching the corners of his mouth.

'Tell the demoiselle this—I applaud your courage, milady. But, like all of England, you *shall* submit to my authority and, like all of England, you shall be taken by force, if necessary, and conquered. If you choose rape rather than submission to your husband, then that is your own choice and your own folly. For I am certain that your future husband is a man who would treat you honourably, as Normandy would treat England, with honour. But resistance can only bring violence and pain. Now, enough of this nonsense, I have no time to tarry over a nervous virgin. Get on with the marriage ceremony!'

William's command was quickly obeyed and the two appointed men of God prepared to make them husband and wife.

However, Julia clenched her teeth and refused to speak, despite the insistent glower of William, who then exclaimed, 'Where is the dame who claims to be this vixen's mother? Bring her forth and she shall speak on her daughter's behalf.'

There were a few gasps, mutters from Bishop Odo, but in the past twenty-four hours all manner of normal daily life had been swept aside, and anything was possible for a man who had, by the force and power of his own skill, taken into his possession an entire country. Lady Fredeswide had not Julia's brave stubbornness and she complied with this autocratic request, her voice no more than a trembling whisper but sufficient to declare the marriage vows.

When it came time to exchange rings Julia's mother removed her own plain wedding band and gave it to the Norman knight, who held her daughter's hand in the palm of his. Julia glowered resentfully and tried to pull away as he slid the ring down the fourth finger of her left hand, but his grip tightened on her wrist and his eyes stared hard with dark warning. Pursing her lips, she tossed her head back as though she cared not at all about this ridiculous farce, but the effect was somewhat spoiled by the fact that she no longer had a glorious mane of hair to toss.

At the end, William proclaimed, 'Now, take your bride to a chamber, consummate this marriage and bring me the evidence. Before we ride I would know that this is a true alliance and, God willing, mayhap, in nine months from now she shall bear a babe, the first of our new generation.'

Falk de Arques hesitated, his glance falling on Julia's calm and unknowing profile as she stared resolutely ahead at the golden-tinged glass panes of the window.

'What is this?' demanded William. 'One of my bravest knights, whom yesterday I did see fight a battle against thousands of warriors, now turns coward before a skinny Saxon wench!'

Falk stiffened, stung by this insult, 'I am no coward, sire.'

'Then do as your liege commands.'

He bowed and turned to politely take Julia's arm and lead her away. At once, knowing she was now wed to him, giving him rights over her that he would now seek to claim, Julia pulled her arm free, stepping back, and her eyes darted wildly about the room, seeking an escape.

Lady Fredeswide spoke softly for her daughter to be calm. Several Norman knights called out their advice. Falk accepted one suggestion as he quickly sidestepped and caught Julia with two large hands upon her narrow waist. He swiftly lifted her up and threw her no-great weight over his broad shoulder, securing her there with one arm clamped tight to the vulnerable crook behind her knees and the other clutching at her bottom. Winded, Julia could do no more than beat upon his chainmailed back with both of her fists, to no avail.

He carried her from the chapel, followed closely by his squire, down the spiral flight of steps, taking care to avoid banging his bride's head upon the stone walls. Marching along the corridor below, he opened the solid oak door at the far end. He guessed this to be the lord's chamber, dominated by a great tester bed, the floor adorned with bear-skin rugs and furnished with a table, two carved chairs and several tall, beeswax candles mounted on wrought-iron sconces.

He was forced to lower Julia to the ground, in order to unbuckle his sword belt and remove the heavy, restrictive weight of his hauberk. As soon as her feet touched the floorboards, Julia wasted no time in running for the door and wrenching it open.

Two Norman knights, grinning broadly, greeted her cheerfully in French as Julia made to dart past them. They caught her easily by the wrists and dragged her back into the room.

'Shall we hold her down for you, Falk?'

'Nay, Gilbert, let her go and get out!'

The man who was now her husband had freed himself of his armour. Julia glared at the one knight who had spoken, who held her wrist in a painfully tight grip, the one called Gilbert. She vowed silently that she would not easily forget him, as he had been the one to steal her keys and her pouch from her waist and he had a distinctive scar puckering one side of his cheek. In the heat of her fear and anger, she spat at him. With a vile oath he raised his fist to strike her back in retaliation.

But the blow did not fall. Falk caught the upraised arm in a brutal grip and forced it down, his black eyes blazing a fierce warning to Gilbert de Slevin.

'That is my wife you raise your hand to!'

'Pah! She's naught but a Saxon bitch and you cannot call her wife until you have bedded her.'

'We have been wed by holy vows and royal decree. If that is not good enough for you, de Slevin, then take your case to the Duke. Now, get out, before you and I come to blows! All of you, get out!'

'Very well, but you would be wise to teach her who is master if you are not to end with her dagger between your ribs.'

Gilbert bowed stiffly, insolently to Julia, and the Normans departed. Julia clenched her hands together as the door banged shut behind his squire, taking with him a weighty armful of Norman armour and Julia's last hope of salvation. She raised her eyes, alone now, to the man towering over her, her bosom heaving in a panic.

Silently, carefully, he stepped towards her, one hand making a placatory, inviting movement. Instinctively Julia backed away. She looked around for a weapon, an escape, but there was neither. Desperately, she held out her hand to ward him off.

'Don't touch me!' she cried, darting nimbly away.

'Come now,' he said softly, 'I will be…gentle.'

This, however, did not encourage Julia and she shouted at him, 'Nay, Norman! I will never submit to you. Murderer! Thief!'

Her words ended on a scream as suddenly he dived and grabbed her around the hips, lifting her easily and flinging her again over his shoulder. He turned and strode towards the bed. Her head was pounding as she hung upside down and, raising herself awkwardly up, Julia glimpsed the threatening expanse of her parents' bed.

To one side she saw the table still spread with parchment, ink and quills that she had been working at the night before, amazed it was so short a span of time ago. Then her vision blurred as his shoulders swayed with the movements of his hand throwing open the covers, until the somewhat creased and well-worn, but nevertheless pristine, sheet was laid bare. The breath was knocked from her lungs as he, this man, this dark stranger, flung her down upon the mattress.

The length of his big body quickly followed, pinning her down with his weight before she had a chance to escape or strike at him. His shoulders were terrifyingly wide and all but blocked out the room from her sight. Upon her breasts and ribs the hard, flat expanse of his chest pressed her painfully down, and his muscular legs captured her flighty knees in an iron grip. The strong odour of his sweat and dirt, his maleness, stung her nose. She was surrounded by him. Julia knew there could be no escape. Their eyes met.

Lightning blue clashed with midnight black.

Her breath fluttered from between her parted lips and collided with his. As he made a movement to lower his head down to her she tried to scratch his face, but he was too quick. With one large hand he circled her wrists and held them tightly above her head, out of harm's way.

Looking down at her, his bride, Falk was almost bemused, his wits scattered, for he had never seen anything so lovely, so clean, so pure as Julia. The women he had known had all been whores, even the highborn so-called *ladies* of the court; even the one he had loved and lost.

As Julia struggled, her sweet breath blowing on his face while she panted like a terror-stricken and trapped animal, he considered what to do.

Gilbert de Slevin would have struck her senseless and ripped her clothing to shreds by now. Falk had seen him do it often enough, secretly ashamed that he was powerless to stop such brutality. But a man did not interfere in another man's relations with a whore.

His glance fell upon her tender lips. His senses were acutely aware of her soft body, small and slender beneath the heavy muscle and hard bone of his bigger, more powerful male body. He had never raped or abused a woman in his life, for ladies liked his handsome face, and his easy manner with them had been entirely due to the fact that he had been raised and nurtured by a loving mother until the age of twelve. On her death his father, the Comte de Arques, had belatedly taken responsibility for his eldest son, even though a bastard, and had sent him to be fostered by Duke William. Thus the boy, and now the man, had always held women in tender regard.

He had never before baulked at any task given to him by the Duke, no matter how difficult or dangerous. Deflowering his bride was neither, but at this moment he was, to his dismay, reluctant to accomplish the chore he had been set. He knew her to be innocent, but he was not. Indeed, he was well versed in the art of bedsport, but this experience did not include virgins.

Admonishing himself for a fool to hesitate, and reminding himself that he was a warrior come to conqueror these peasant Saxons, and also fearing imminent intrusion by the impatient Duke, he sought to conclude the matter swiftly. With his free hand he loosened the drawstring of his chausses and pulled down the flap, where bulged his eager manhood, before reaching for the hem of Julia's skirts and lifting them up into a bunch about her waist, exposing her pale limbs.

He prised apart her tight clenched legs, and shifting his weight he held them open with his knee. Along the soft white length of her inner thigh his palm slid. He did not look at her now, but down at his darkly tanned hand moving up her pale, untouched flesh and his breath became harsh with forced restraint.

Julia felt her head spin as her senses reeled. But not for the reasons she should have felt, not anger or outrage; the truth was, she felt faint because never had she felt such a gentle touch.

Then he came upon a sight that caused his breath to catch in his throat and stilled the advance of his exploring fingertips. His eyes fell upon a cluster of bruises that stained her hips and buttocks, some faded and yellow, some darkly purple and fresh.

'What is this?' he asked, glancing up at her face, turned aside, her eyes tight shut.

''Tis naught,' she whispered.

'Tell me.' When she did not reply he shook her wrists insistently. 'Tell me, English. 'Tis no fall from a horse that bruises your backside, and I would know now if you have taken a tumble from a two-legged beast, for I assure you I will not give my name to another man's bastard!'

At that Julia opened her eyes and stared at him, her glance growing hot with a blush that crept up her neck and cheeks at his implication. 'I have never lain with a man, Norman! I carry no child! If you must know…'twas my brother. He is a foul-tempered, lazy, drunken sod!'

'Your brother! I thought he fought with Harold.'

'I have two brothers. One has remained at home because of a broken leg.'

'I see. Which one was he?'

'He was not present when you…arrived. I believe he ruts in the barn with some poor maid, although my bailiff would pretend to me otherwise.'

'And he beats you?'

'Aye.'

'With his fists? His boots?'

She glared at him defiantly then. 'Aye, Norman, aye. Say what you think. I am damaged goods and you will not have me.'

Falk was thoughtful for a moment. 'Your bruises will heal, there is no lasting damage.' He was reluctant to admit too soon his feelings for her, and earn her scorn for his weakness, for his tenderness to women had oft been the weakest link in his armour, which he would never again allow any woman to exploit. 'If you tell the truth, then I look forward to teaching my brother-in-law a lesson in manners, but if you lie…'twill take me but a moment to find out if you are virgin or not.'

Julia swallowed, her lips pursed together, and with a resigned sigh she looked away from his dark male eyes. 'If I could stop you and wish you to hell, then I would, but, as you see, Norman, your grip is stronger than mine and all men are the same. Are they not?'

'Nay, English, not all men are the same, but in truth I will not be wed to a woman who is another man's leavings.'

His hand resumed its journey. To her shame tears sprang from her eyes and she could scarce contain the little sobs bursting from her tense-held ribs. After all these years, when she had longed for love and a husband and to learn the secrets of the marriage bed, now it was to be in this loveless fashion.

'Hush,' he whispered, his face hovering close above her own, 'hold fast, my lady English, for I would not hurt you. Not even for William would I rape my own wife.'

With some reluctance and an effort of self-control, for the feel of her slender body lying beneath him had excited his, he pulled down her skirts.

Falk reached for the dagger concealed at his waist and he released her wrists from above her head. Before she knew what he planned to do, he held out his own hand and cut his thumb a small jot. Julia gasped, shocked and confused, staring while he vigorously shook the drops of blood that spurted forth down upon the centre of the linen sheet.

Looking up, his task deceitfully accomplished, he saw that a few drops had spattered on her chin and he reached out to brush them away.

Julia cried out and flinched at his outstretched hand, still holding the dagger.

'There is—' Falk cleared his husky throat '—there is blood upon your chin. I would but wipe it away.'

Slowly, he tried again, this time sheathing his dagger before reaching out. With his thumb he gently cleaned her chin. Their eyes met and held for a long moment. He cupped her face between thumb and forefinger, examining this wife that he had so suddenly acquired. Silently cursing himself, Falk was unable to resist the vulnerable pink sweetness so temptingly close to him. He leaned down and pressed his mouth upon her trembling lips, gently persuading them apart, and slid the tip of his tongue between them before encountering the barrier of her clenched teeth.

Julia met his dark, knowing gaze, stunned, for a man had never kissed her in such a manner before. The feel of his mouth moving on hers was strange, and yet far from unpleasant. She felt a sudden warmth flood her veins and weaken her already paralysed limbs further.

With a throaty groan, as her lips softened, his kiss deepened and he gained entrance for his tongue. He slid into the warmth and moistness of her mouth, thrusting and tasting with hot, eager maleness. A small, surprised moan escaped from her throat and Julia felt a fierce warmth creep through her limbs. All thought fled from her mind and there was only sensation. His hand slid down from her waist to curve over her hip, pressing her closer to his lean body, while his mouth moved insistently, drinking her in. She was hardly aware of her own hands moving to his shoulders, partly, instinctively, holding him back, partly reaching out and touching him, feeling the bulk of his shoulders beneath her palms. As she trembled at his ardour, his mouth eased, his lips softly kissing her cheeks, her neck, her lips again, until at last he forced himself to stop and lift his head away from her.

When he spoke his voice was husky, his accent thick, his black eyes penetrating in their forceful gaze. 'When I take you, English, you will not tremble and cry with fear. I find no pleasure in a maiden's terror and our union *will* be one of pleasure, such sweet pleasure as you have never known. And I pray that as surely as William desires our marriage to absolve him of the slaughter of your nation's manhood, so too will I be cleansed of the blood that stains my hands.' His gaze swept over her face, memorising each feature. 'But I give you fair warning, wife. If you are not virgin when I return to claim you, then I shall kill you. And also the man who would dare take what is only mine for the taking. Do I make myself clear?'

Julia stared at him, managing to nod her head in dazed acknowledgement. His weight lifted and she only had a moment in which to draw breath before he raised her up, tossed her over his shoulder again in one fluid movement, and ripped the bloodstained sheet from the bed.

Bearing his trophies, he marched downstairs to the great hall, where the household of Foxbourne waited nervously—the Normans with rowdy and raucous expectancy. Some of the knights now laughed and applauded Falk, slapping his arm and shoulder as he passed through the noisy throng, congratulating him on Julia's scream and the speed with which he had done his duty.

Ignoring them all, he silently presented the sheet to William and then he delivered Julia into the care of her mother. He set her down carefully on her feet and exchanged one last, deep glance with his virgin bride before turning away to his squire to be re-armoured and to latch on his sword.

William gathered the leaders of his army, his nobles and knights, his bodyguards, and departed, leaving a half dozen men-at-arms as garrison and a promise to Julia that he would soon grant leave to her new husband to return to Foxbourne.

Chapter Four

They rode hard from Foxbourne and arrived at the wooden castle being built upon the high cliffs of Hastings just after nightfall. A fresh breeze blew in from the sea and the Norman commanders dismounted wearily. But the Duke kept his men at his side for many more hours as they discussed the greatest battle any of them had ever fought, and planned their strategy for future days.

William planned to march on Dover, take and secure it, before moving on to Canterbury, the religious heart of England. From there he would march across country to gain the capital, London. He would strike hard and fast, swiftly building wooden castles at every strategic point and using the terror of a formidable reputation as an unseen weapon to aid his army in forcing Saxon England to yield on bended knee.

It was well after midnight when at last Falk de Arques sought his rest in one of the many tents. He sat by a fire and ate the food and drank the wine that his squire had procured, without even noticing what it was he placed in his mouth. His thoughts dwelled on the trembling and bruised body of his red-haired wife, and he wondered, with a spark of anger, what manner of a man it was that did that to his own sister. He chafed at the fact that he had not been able to meet this sibling face to face and wondered how his wife, at this very moment, fared. His fist clenched. She was his now and there would be bloodletting for anyone who inflicted damage to her. With this thought in mind he summoned his squire, despite the late hour, and insisted that a message be relayed to his captain of the guard at Foxbourne.

'Tell him,' instructed Falk to a sleepy-eyed scribe, 'that my wife has a brother, Randal by name, who is at large somewhere in the area. He is not to be allowed within spitting distance of my wife and if he is captured he is to be brought to me bound hand and foot. Or, if I am not yet returned, he is to be held in the dungeon.'

Sander, his squire, looked up quickly from where he polished his master's boots. 'I do not think these English halls have dungeons, my lord.'

'Mmm.' Falk rasped a thumb over the stubble of his jaw and pondered on this unusual fact. 'Well, then, he is to be kept prisoner far from my wife. I leave it to Hervi to decide exactly where.'

The scribe left then to despatch his message, and Falk fell once again into a state of numb lethargy. From one of his saddlebags tossed upon the floor spilled the skein of Julia's hair. He thought to rise and pick it up, stroke its soft silk, but he was too exhausted. He had never seen hair that colour before on a woman, all red and gold streaked together.

He wondered what her breasts would be like and why he had not availed himself of them, small as they were. So close, it would have taken him but a moment to rip open her kirtle and taste the pink buds that had pressed tight and hard against his chest…but no… He sighed and drank the last dregs of wine.

How many men had he killed in battle…only a week ago? Fifty? A hundred? What difference would it make to have taken one Saxon female, who was, after all, his legal wife? But her cry of fear had pierced him to his soul as no arrow or sword slash could. Now he dreaded to close his eyes in sleep, lest he hear again the cries of dying men butchered upon Caldbec Hill, and the anguished cry of his virgin wife seemed louder than all the rest. He did not know which one was the more repugnant, for they were threaded together in a tight knot he could not even begin to unravel.

Realising that he was too tired to think clearly, Falk let the goblet slip from his fingers and fell asleep in his chair, fully clothed.

A few weeks later he received a reply to his urgent message regarding Randal, late of Foxbourne, and the news caused him some moments of grim reflection. As William advanced on London it was noted that Falk de Arques fought like a man possessed by demons, but none were so keen as he to make an end to war and receive William's leave to return home. Home? With chagrin he realised that his heart had already decided home was where his wife lived!

'My poor lamb!' Lady Fredeswide folded her daughter into her arms and smothered her with a hug, 'Do not fear, dearest, for the pain will soon go away and 'twill not be so bad next time.'

Julia glared resentfully at her mother as she was clasped to that woman's ample bosom. She did not dare tell her parent that she was still virgin and, truthfully, she wished that she was not, for now she still had that ordeal to face, the fear of which could only grow tenfold with each passing day. Exasperated, Julia struggled from her mother's arms and declared, 'God willing there will be no next time! Mayhap I will soon be a widow, as my dear husband is at the forefront of William's army and slaying Saxons is a dangerous occupation!'

Running from the great hall and out into the walled gardens at the back of the keep, Julia found a secluded and shady spot amongst her herbs to weep away all the fears and hurts and shocks of the day.

Two days after the departure of the Normans from Foxbourne Ulric returned. His visage was so grey and gaunt that Julia at once sprang from her place beside the fire in the hall, where she and Lady Fredeswide attended to the sewing of winter garments, and ran to him with hands outstretched.

'Oh, Ulric, tell me some good news!' Seeing how cold and stiff he was, Julia clapped her hands and ordered a servant to bring mulled wine and food, before leading Ulric to the comfort of a chair by the fire. She knelt at his feet, her tender face raised expectantly to him.

'Milady, 'twas a sight so terrible I think it will haunt my dreams for the rest of my days. I would not burden your young heart with details, suffice to say that Lord Osbert and your brother Wynstan, and all our knights, are dead. Along with most of the finest of England's noble warriors.' Ulric's voice broke then and this man, who all her life had been Julia's rock, crumbled and wept with the weight of his sorrow.

Julia whispered soothingly, patting his back and allowing him to sob upon her shoulder. She was not surprised by his news, but ventured, 'Could you not, dear Ulric, bring them home for burial?'

'Nay.' He could not begin to describe to her the tragic sight of broken bodies, of men young and old, that lay littered upon the fields of battle.

'But…how can we be sure they are indeed… dead? How can we put their souls to rest without a Christian burial?'

'Be sure!' Ulric exclaimed angrily, weary, defeated as he stared around at the faces gathered about him. 'They are dead, all of them! Butchered by that bastard from Normandy! What would you have me do, mistress? If I could find a head to identify my lord, I could not be sure that the arm and the leg that lay nearby be his, or that of another. Why, even our poor, brave king was so brutally slain that his mistress, Edith Swanhaels, has been called in to identify the marks upon a torso they *think* may be that of Harold!'

Julia held up her hand to stay him, shocked, and unwilling to hear more. She rose then and turned to her mother in confusion. Despite her efforts to stop herself, Julia began to weep. She retreated into her mother's embrace, pressing her face into a plump shoulder as she hid from the truth that lay before them as cold and stark as death itself.

'Oh, what is to become of us?' asked Lady Fredeswide fearfully, patting Julia's shoulder, her own cheeks shining with tears.

'We do as Englishmen have always done,' admonished Ulric, taking a deep draught of the mulled wine Hilda had brought him. 'Make the best of it and survive. No doubt 'twill only be a matter of time before William seeks to reward his noblemen and his army with the rich pickings that is England!' He could not disguise the bitterness that filled his voice. 'There will be many demesnes such as Foxbourne who no longer have a lord. My Lord Osbert's title and lands will be given to whomever it pleases William to reward. Along with his wife and daughter.'

Lady Fredeswide and Julia exchanged a knowing glance. Hanging her head and staring down at her feet, Julia left it to her mother to break the shameful news.

'You are wise indeed, Ulric, to predict events so accurately. The very day you left for Caldbec Hill, William of Normandy arrived and before he departed our Julia was wed to one of his knights. So, already we have a new lord.'

'Nay, mistress, you jest!' Ulric looked at them both with wide-eyed disbelief.

'I would not jest over such a matter, Ulric. Did I not hear my daughter's cry when the knave did bed her? Did I not see with my own eyes the bloodstained sheet he presented to William? 'Tis no joke. Lady Julia is now the wife of a Norman knight who goes by the name of…of…' Lady Fredeswide paused for a moment, searching her memory and turning to Julia with a frown.

Julia snorted. 'A foul, heathen name—Falk de Arques. I shall not call him so!'

As Ulric and her mother both turned to survey the subject of their tragedy, Julia had the grace to blush. Lady Fredeswide explained the circumstances of the impromptu wedding and William's command the marriage be consummated immediately.

''Tis surely not legal!' exclaimed Ulric.

'We can only hope that it is, for think what shame it would bring if Lady Julia were to bear a bastard.'

Julia wriggled uncomfortably from her mother's arms, declaring with a defiant sparkle in her eyes, 'Well, I can tell you, here and now, if the Norman cur is foolish enough to return alive from his war, then it shall be more than my arrow he feels in his leg!'

'You are wed to the one you wounded with your bow?' asked Ulric, scarcely believing his own ears at this tale that grew ever more incredible, 'The very one who cut off your hair?'

'Aye, Ulric. One and the same.' She touched her shorn tresses defensively. 'And if he ever dares to claim me again, then 'tis my dagger in his heart!'

'Fighting talk and fighting spirit, milady, but utter foolishness! A bed of roses is far more comfortable than one of thorns. And…' here Ulric lowered his voice and glanced over his shoulder at the Norman soldiers left to hold Foxbourne, lounging at the trestle tables as though they owned the place '…I hear tell that William is ruthless in his campaign and hangs anyone who will not swear fealty. The country has fallen to him like a pack of cards. The old order is gone and we are all under the Norman yoke.'

'What say you, Ulric?' protested Julia, 'Should I give myself gladly to a murdering foreigner, a beggarly knight who is little more than a paid soldier? The slayer of our own kin and king?'

''Tis not murder upon a battlefield, milady. But methinks you will find life most unpleasant if you do not accept your position as his legally wed wife. No one is asking you to display fine or tender feelings for him. In time, you may even be able to use your position to benefit Foxbourne.'

Julia remained silent, her mouth set in a somewhat mulish pout. To soothe their discord and settle her own self, Lady Fredeswide sat down at her harp and began to play. There was little the woman truly excelled at, but she knew her fingers had been blessed with a rare gift when set to pluck the harp strings. Soft, clear notes echoed about the hall like the ripple of a waterfall, only sweeter, moving the mind and the soul to joy.

Kneeling at her feet, Julia laid her head against her mother's knee and let the melody soothe and comfort her. One by one the household servants crept into the hall to listen and it was Ulric that invited Father Ambrose to come forwards and say prayers for the departed souls of their lord and his son.

Afterwards, Ulric detained Julia and discreetly ushered her to a quiet corner in the kitchen, where he whispered, 'I have news of Randal.'

Julia gasped and looked around to be sure that no Norman ears hovered close by. For days now they had wondered about Randal's whereabouts. As the Norman soldiers had ensconced themselves at Foxbourne, so too had an orderly sense of peace, instigated by Randal's absence. Julia even had hopes of her bruises finally fading for good and the effect on her mother had been nothing short of miraculous, as her nervous system, so long plagued by the threat of violence, began to settle.

'I heard a rumour that he is running with a band of Saxons who oppose William, led by a handful of survivors from the battle. Some say they even have their camp in the Ringwald.'

Hardly able to believe that anyone would dare sleep in the haunted and holy grounds of the Ringwald, Julia asked after one of the serfs, 'And Wulfnoth? What news of him?'

'He too is with them.'

'But…what can they do, Ulric? They are but a few against thousands.'

Ulric shrugged and shook his head. ''Twill all end in stretched necks, mark my words.'

The dark days of winter were soon upon them. The Normans made it plain they would control the day-to-day running of the keep, making frequent reports to Falk de Arques by messenger, and receiving each time a reply. Not a grain of wheat or barley was left unaccounted for, most of the horses were sent to the advancing army, along with all the cows and pigs and half the sheep, to be slaughtered to fill the bellies of Norman soldiers.

Instructions were sent to improve the defences of Foxbourne and work began on a moat—an arduous task that drew idle gawpers. The serfs watched with sour glances as the Normans tore up the green meadow, leaving a dark, muddy scar that had to be abandoned when the ground froze too hard to be broken by a shovel.

They settled back into a dull routine and Julia could scarce believe that any of the events of October had really occurred. The ring that had been placed on her finger Julia returned to its rightful owner. Despite her mother's protests that she no longer had need of it, Julia refused to wear the ring with which her mother had been wed to her father. It was not easy to forget that somewhere out there in the realm rode a man who was by name her husband, but forget she tried.

Each day she feared his return. He had sent no message to her personally and she suspected that his arrival would be unheralded. Sometimes she climbed to the top of the tower and stared out over the battlements at the wintry landscape. The trees were now stark against the pale sky and a chill wind bit into her body, even wrapped in a thick fur-lined cloak and with Kenward always at her side, pressing his warm black bulk to her thigh. There was, however, nothing to see, except that which she had seen every day of her life—the meadow, now crudely disfigured, the woods, the crows cawing noisily and the far distant hills. Once she thought she heard the pounding of horses' hooves, but looking all around and straining her eyes, she could see nothing.

Brooding over the events of her wedding day, as she bent her head to the mundane task of sewing, Julia recalled that deep and disturbing kiss. She had not expected to feel such…warmth. After all, the man was a stranger. What did she know of him? Yet there had been such a flair of passion between them, so unexpected, that she knew she could not honestly call him a stranger any more. He had reached inside of her and claimed something that no one had ever claimed, or even asked for, before. It was not love…surely? That gay and giddy emotion of ballads and romantic tales, love? No! Lust, more like! Suddenly Julia wondered why her husband had chosen not to… Here her cheeks flamed and she glanced furtively across the hearth to her mother, to see if she had been observed. But Lady Fredeswide's face was bowed in concentration, placidly and contentedly placing stitch after stitch in the shirt she mended.

Julia's fingers stole up to trace the outline of her profile and she wondered, again, if it was her form and figure that had put him off. Mayhap she was hideously ugly, for she had never seen her own reflection. Just then her mother looked up and her brows knitted in question.

'Mother, how do I appear to you?'

Lady Fredeswide bit off the end of her thread, 'What do you mean by that, child?'

'My face, Mother,' Julia demanded impatiently, irritated by her parent's apparent dimness. 'Is it…comely? Or not?'

Her mother smiled then, her gaze resting on Julia's flushed, oval, creamy-skinned face. 'Why, my child, you are the prettiest maid I have ever seen.'

'But I am not so very young.'

'No, but you are not so very old either. And I am sure your husband thinks you are pretty too.'

Julia snorted. 'Who cares what he thinks?'

But she was pleased to know that she was not ugly. Exactly why she should be pleased, though, eluded her for the moment.

In December preparations were made to celebrate the feast of Christmas, but they were subdued as so many of the men that had been there to take part in the festivities in years past were now gone, and their empty places left a great sorrow.

Ulric brought in the Yule log on Christmas Eve, with much grunting and groans from him and Edwin and Alfred. They managed to lever the massive log into the fire's hearth in the great hall, where hopefully it would burn for the next twelve days and nights, bringing much-needed warmth and cheer.

Julia and her mother helped the maids to decorate the hall with garlands of holly and mistletoe. Each bunch had to have twelve pieces of holly, and twelve red ribbons were festooned in bows about the hall. The Normans, unwelcome and unwanted, made themselves useful with their strong backs and arms, volunteering to go out into the forest to cut logs for the kitchen and solar fires and to hunt for meat. On their return, bearing gifts of one deer and five rabbits, they teased the maids with their French songs and charm.

''Tis shameful!' complained Julia bitterly as they sat before the fire with their embroidery and keeping a stern eye on preparations for the evening meal. 'Do you see how Hilda and Gytha flirt with the Normans? I have a good mind to box their ears!'

Lady Fredeswide smiled indulgently, scarcely bothering to raise her eyes from her needlework. 'They are men far from home, and we are women with no men.'

'Mother, pray do not tell me you find this behaviour in the least tolerable?'

'You have much to learn, child. God made man and he made woman, and he made woman to love man.'

'Oh, stuff and nonsense! God made man to fight and…and…force themselves on women, not to love them!'

Her mother knew better than to argue with Julia, but she cast her a curious glance. 'You seem out of sorts this evening, daughter. Are you… mayhap—?'

'What?'

'With child?'

Julia laughed and then realised her mistake as her mother eyed her with some confusion. 'Nay, Mother, I am not with child.'

'A babe can be a great comfort. Mayhap, when your husband returns…' Lady Fredeswide noticed how uncomfortable Julia always looked at such talk. Nay, more than that, she seemed quite distressed.

The marriage having been so sudden Lady Fredeswide feared that she had failed in her duty to prepare Julia for the marriage bed, and she sought now to make amends.

'I do not think that this Falk de Arques is a cruel or dishonest man. It was not well done that you should have had to lie with him in such haste, but I am sure, given time, he would be an honourable husband and—' her voice fell to a whisper '—there is great pleasure to be had in coupling with one's husband.'

'Please, Mother, I do not wish to speak of such things.'

'In his haste he hurt you, but it need not be so again.' Her mother spoke gently, hoping to allay her daughter's all too obvious fears.

But Julia would have none of it. Setting aside her sewing and springing to her feet, she clapped her hands, demanding the attention of all those in the hall. She tossed a lute to Edwin, a drum to Alfred and, picking up a pair of bells, led them into a merry tune. It was not long before the maids were clapping their hands and singing, and sliding inviting glances to the Norman soldiers behind Julia's back.

After the evening meal, which perforce was simpler than in years past, they whiled away the hours before midnight mass by singing and dancing and playing games. Julia's favourite was Hoodman's Bluff, and she chased about the hall to find her quarry with hands outstretched and gasping with laughter.

Kenward cavorted with clumsy glee at her feet, ever hopeful of being the one to be grasped within his mistress's seeking hands, and butting out of the way potential rivals, until Julia tired of falling over him and the many grumbled complaints urging for Kenward's removal could not be ignored. He was banished to the kitchen. He padded off at Julia's sharp command, with a sulky droop to his head, to sit in the doorway of the kitchen and watch the proceedings with a protective eye and lolling tongue.

Julia did not hear the pounding on the outer door, nor see the cloaked figures that came in from the cold, stamping snow-crusted feet. But she felt the sudden draught and sensed the stillness of those around her as the music came to an abrupt end.

'What is amiss?' she called out. She tried to remove her hood, but someone had tied the knot too tight. Sudden fright caused her to panic and call out, 'Edwin, untie me at once!'

There was a hush upon the previously noisy gathering and Julia heard footsteps and the clank of steel. She caught her breath and stood like a startled wild creature as she sensed a large figure loom over her. She felt his warmth only a moment after her senses remembered his male scent. The bulk of his arms brushed either side of her head and she heard the rip of cloth as he cut the ties of her hood, accompanied by Kenward's growl, swiftly followed by Edwin's rebuke that quietened the dog. For a moment she held her eyes tight shut, and then she opened them and looked up into the dark face of Falk de Arques.

He smiled down at her, 'Greetings, wife.' He sheathed his dagger and then pulled her roughly into his arms, head and shoulders stooping for a kiss.

His lips were cold. Julia gasped at the touch of them. He quickly took advantage of her gasp to open her mouth wider and the heat of his tongue was like a firebrand. He held her full weight as shock weakened Julia's legs and she felt little more than a rag doll as her arms hung limply at her sides, her upper body crushed against his chest.

Julia noticed that he did not wear armour and he seemed taller and broader than she remembered. Unpractised in the art of kissing, she did not know how to breathe through her nose while her mouth was occupied by his tongue, and now she struggled and shook her head, pushing her hands flat against his iron-hard midriff. Realising her predicament, he lifted his head, laughing softly while his hands still clutched her waist and held her tight against him. In her ear he whispered, 'Later I will teach you how to kiss without suffocating.'

Julia glared up at him. His eyes searched her face and found a lovelier likeness than the one stored in his memory. 'Have you no greeting for your husband? I have ridden hard for three days to be with you this Christmas Eve.'

She snatched herself free from his grasp and stood back, glaring furiously up at him. 'Aye, Norman! Go to—'

'Forgive my daughter, sir—' Lady Fredeswide, seeing there was trouble on the brew, stepped quickly forwards to be the broker of peace '—for we are so quiet here at Foxbourne that I have not trained her well in the greeting of visitors. Come, we bid you welcome. Julia, take his cloak!'

Surprised by her mother's sharp tone, she looked at her parent with hurt eyes.

'Julia,' said Falk de Arques.

She turned her head enquiringly, and looked up into his black eyes.

'I had almost forgotten your name, wife.'

She curtsied mockingly. ''Tis fitting, milord. For you know me not at all and never shall!'

Her mother elbowed Julia aside, with a sidelong frown of warning, and exclaimed loudly, 'You are limping, milord. Are you wounded?'

''Tis nothing,' he replied as he walked slowly, his left leg not quite keeping time as he reached a chair by the hearth and sank down with a weary grunt. He looked up and caught Julia in the trap of his hard stare. 'Is that to be the way of it?'

Pretending that no one heard him Lady Fredeswide clapped her hands and loudly called for the maids to bring hot water and the bathing tub to the lord's chamber, then instructed Julia to fetch her unguents from the storeroom.

'But, Mother—'

'Your husband is wounded. It would be unchristian, to say the least, to leave his hurts untended. Hurry, now, child! Edwin, bring food and mulled wine for these men.'

Falk de Arques had not arrived alone. He had six men with him and these were his squire, he of the white-blond hair, and his personal bodyguard, five Angevins as fierce as they were loyal. Fetching her small leather box containing the herbal remedies that helped to ease their ailments, Julia carried it to the fireplace and opened it up.

'Not here, child! Let him eat first and then we will take him up to the solar.' With a cluck and a sigh she hustled Julia away, fearing her daughter would cut off her nose to spite her face. 'Go you now and prepare the way. We will need hot water and linen to clean the wound and bid his squire bring up clean garments, for his are all wet and muddy.'

'Mother, I—'

'Go now!'

Falk smiled from where he sat. 'Aye, go now, wife. Wait for me in our chamber. And take that hound out into the yard, for I mislike the way he looks at me and bares his teeth.'

Julia felt a hot blush sting her cheeks. Her heart lurched fearfully and she went to Kenward, stroking and patting his black head before whispering in Alfred's ear that he should tie the dog up in the kitchen. Without a word to her husband she turned and left the hall, making her way up to the solar chamber and there set her chest down upon a table, where lay her writing paper, quills and ink. She watched silently as the maids brought in a large wooden barrel and the servants were all employed in bearing bucket after bucket of steaming hot water—first Alfred, then Edwin, Ham and Chester, and finally Ulric manfully carried two large pails.

They tipped all the water into the tub until it was halfway full.

Her mother came in then and went about putting the chamber to rights, ordering Edwin to stoke up the fire and to remove his truckle bed. As she gathered her hairbrush and rosary beads, Lady Fredeswide said, 'Edwin will sleep in the hall with the other men. 'Tis high time the boy found his place out of babyhood and I will sleep in your brothers' chamber. They certainly have no need of it. 'Tis only fitting that the new lord and his lady have the solar.'

'Oh, Mother!' Julia clenched her hands and could scarce keep a sob from escaping from the constriction of her throat.

'Tush, now! Your bed has been made, Julia. Now lie in it with good grace and bring no shame upon your father's house. It is unworthy for a wife to be bitter and hostile to her husband.'

'How can you say that to me? How can you truly expect me to give myself to him! A stranger, who has but moments ago walked in the door!'

'Bathe him, tend to his wounds, dress him. Whatever else may follow is a wife's duty. Remember, Julia, we are at his mercy and it may well be that we fare better if your husband is kept sweet of mood.'

'I will not sell myself to that…that bastard!'

'Hush, now.' Lady Fredeswide glanced nervously over her shoulder at the sound of footsteps and voices in the passage. 'He comes.'

'Do not leave me! I beg you, Mother! Please!'

With a sigh, her mother whispered, 'I will help you undress him and bathe him, but...' here her voice lowered '...he is a soldier and a man, and those two breeds are always eager for a woman. He will want to be alone with you shortly.'

In answer Julia clung to her mother's hand, while Falk entered, aided by his squire, and then Lady Fredeswide shook her off and bustled about, directing matters as Falk was led to stand before the bathing tub and the warm fire.

But the Norman knight, as always, took command. 'Leave us,' he said sharply, his eyes on Julia, 'I'm sure my wife is not such a young maid that she cannot tend to her husband alone. Is she?'

'Nay, my lord, but—'

'Go!'

Falk unlatched his sword belt and handed it to his squire, who stood uncertainly with Lady Fredeswide, the maids and Ulric. With a short laugh, Falk demanded, 'What is this? Rebellion? She and I have been wed these two months past and not yet spent a night together.' With extreme politeness he said, 'I hope no one minds if we now seek our privacy.'

There was a quick flurry of embarrassed movement and then the door banged shut and Julia was left standing alone, with him.

'Ah, that is far better. Peace. Come now, wife, help me undress.'

With difficulty Julia untwisted her fingers and moved towards him, but in her blind state of anxiety she tripped over a bucket, stumbled and fell to the floor. At once Falk came to her aid and, with two hands upon her waist, scooped her up. He held her for a moment, her back pressed against his chest, and Julia froze, her breath held in abeyance somewhere in her throat.

'You do me little credit, wife, to tremble in such a manner. I will not toss you upon the bed and take you all muddy and stinking as I am.'

He let her go and silently Julia set about unlacing, unstrapping and removing his garments, until he stood almost naked. She tried not to look at his body, but at her fingers as they worked, and she was aware only of a blur of skin the colour of creamed honey, and the bulk of his heavily muscled torso. Here and there were cuts, bruises, and upon his left leg two deep gashes that she had difficulty separating from the leather of his chausses. Out of the corner of her eye she saw how he grimaced and flinched when she peeled the fabric away, feeling beneath her palm coarse dark hairs as she pressed back his skin to gain a better leverage.

'You may…remove your loin cloth and get into the bathtub.' Julia turned her back and carried away the malodorous pile of clothes, dumping them by the closed door to be washed on the morrow. She did not return until she heard a splash and knew him to be safely ensconced in the water, sitting upon the stool therein.

He gasped and shivered, 'God! This water is hot.'

'Shall I bring cold?'

'Nay. Wash me. And my hair, 'tis crawling.'

Julia picked up a bar of precious lavender soap and moved to stand behind him, rolling up her sleeves and leaning forwards to scoop handfuls of water over his head. Goosebumps rose on the skin of his shoulders, so broad and powerful in their width and Julia watched, fascinated. Slowly, silently she washed his hair, the only sounds in the room being the soft rasp of her fingers on his soapy locks and the crackle of the fire.

Falk released a long sigh and relaxed deeper in the water. 'I would say this is as near to heaven as a man could get. These many weeks past we have lived in tents with wind and rain and mud, and the foul stink of men and horses unwashed and wounded.' His eyes travelled to the bed, standing four-poster square and inviting across the room.

'This night will I sleep for the first time in a bed since leaving Normandy.'

Julia's fingers tightened and she felt the urge to give a vicious tug. But those shoulders and the bulging biceps of his muscular arms, and the memory of how painful a man's fists could be, urged her to proceed with caution. She reached for a square of linen, damped it in the water and then rubbed soap on it, using this to wash his back, down his arms, the dark thatch underneath, his neck and across his chest. Everything that was female in her and long starved for the touch and sight of a man now greedily luxuriated in the feel of his muscled flesh, the sight of his handsome profile and undoubtedly beautiful body, despite the cautious warnings of her mind.

Her eyes noted the sprinkle of hair upon his chest, which converged into a narrow line on his midriff, running down to his navel and from there... Julia did not dare to look below the surface of the water. Her hand moved in circular motions, scrubbing at his firm flesh and she wondered about washing him below his waist. But as her hand moved past his navel he suddenly sat up straight and caught her narrow wrist between his fingers.

'Not there.' He could not begin to tell her how her nearness affected him. He wanted this night, which he had lain awake thinking about on many occasions, to be unhurried, each moment of pleasure to be savoured and lingered over slowly. He knew that if he gave in now to the wild urges of his body he would throw her down on the floor and take her before the water had even dried on his back.

Julia dropped the cloth into the tub and moved away to search for a fine-toothed comb. Finding it, she returned and carefully, thoroughly, combed his soapy hair over and over until it was clean. Then she picked up a bucket of cold water to rinse his hair. Without warning, or mercy, she tipped the contents over his head and he swore out loud, glaring at her. She quickly stepped away and handed him a linen to dry with, before moving to her box on the table to fetch a jar of comfrey cream.

'Sit you in that chair,' she said as he stepped out of the tub with a surge and splosh of water, 'and I will dress your wounds.'

Through lowered lashes Julia watched as he dried himself and wrapped the linen about his waist before sitting down. She was amazed at how big he was, how much space he seemed to take up and how small she felt standing next to him. At least, once he was seated, she had the advantage of him. Opening the jar of cream, she scooped a little on to her middle finger and dabbed it on a small cut on his shoulder, moving to his back, where there were three and a large bruise, and down his right arm to tend a gash to his elbow.

Then Julia steeled herself and knelt between his knees, pushing up the damp linen and exposing one of the two more serious wounds on his left leg. Gytha had set a kettle of water and witchhazel to boil on the fire and Julia now reached for this and carefully poured some boiling water on to a clean cloth.

'This will hurt,' she warned, and pressed the steaming linen to the scab on his outer thigh.

He drew a deep breath and stiffened. 'Cease, woman!'

'How brave thou art, Norman knight,' chided Julia mockingly.

He growled and relaxed in his chair as she drew away the infected matter, disposed of it and spread the soothing, healing comfrey ointment over his wound. Only to have the whole performance repeated as Julia gave the same treatment to a deep cut on his calf, just above the ankle.

'There,' she said at last, rising to her feet with a twitch of her nose, 'I suppose you'll live.'

'Not so quickly, little wife.' He caught her about the waist and pulled her down upon his lap. 'There is one more need that only you can tend to.'

Julia blushed, her eyes lowered and not meeting his. Then she felt his hand slide around her neck and cup the back of her head, drawing her close as he lowered his face down to her. She stiffened and remained still as his mouth found hers and he kissed her. She closed her eyes for a moment and let his lips move as they would, but when she felt the hot, wet tip of his tongue she pushed him back and tore her mouth free.

'Nay! I cannot!'

'You know as well as I do this night can have only one outcome,' he said, with some gentleness. 'You can no more stop the sea from breaking on the shore, than stop me from making you my wife.'

'I am not your wife!' Julia tried to leap up, but he gripped her firmly about the hips and forced her to remain balanced upon his hard thighs. 'Do you think a poxy French bishop has any legal right to wed me? I think not! Why, I did not even speak, nor say I do.'

'We were legally wed in a Christian marriage ceremony and by the royal decree of William, King of England.'

'Pah! William is no king!'

'Tomorrow, on Christmas Day, he will be crowned king in Westminster Abbey.'

Julia gasped, staring at him, her heart beating fast in agitation, 'Well…I-I…I do not love you! I despise you! I hate you! I will not submit to you, Norman, never!'

'I do not ask for your love, English, for 'twould be a prickly thing indeed.'

'Oh!' Outraged, she lifted her hand and smacked it hard against his cheek.

He took the blow, without a curse, and then he smiled and told her, 'I admire the passion of your hatred.'

And with that he slid his hand deeper into her hair and pulled her close against him. His mouth found hers and kissed her in such a way that Julia had no doubt that he had had much practise. She felt dizzy and weak, her traitorous lips supine and greatly interested in the gentle assault of the male lips now moving thoroughly over hers. With a guilty start Julia felt obliged to struggle in protest. She dropped the jar of comfrey cream upon the floor and used both hands to push at his chest. Her lips throbbed against her teeth and she felt much the same as when she had sampled her first goblet of wine. Almost without her knowing it, Julia raised one hand from his chest and touched the side of his jaw, enthralled by his movements as he worked on her mouth, feeling beneath her soft fingertips the rough stubble of his masculine face.

Falk's fingers tugged loose the lacings of her kirtle and she made a small, startled sound as she felt cool air upon her breasts, followed by the heat of his intruding hand. She tried to drag it away, but he was strong and resisted the pull of her two-handed grip about his wrist. His fingers found her nipple and fondled it for a while, until he lifted his head, freeing her bruised lips, and told her in a gentle, husky voice, 'Take off your clothes.'

Blushing painfully, she met his dark eyes. She thought to refuse, to challenge him, but she knew, instantly, upon meeting his gaze that such resistance would be futile. 'Let me rise and I will do so.'

He let her go and Julia rose unsteadily to her feet. She thought to move away to find a dark corner in which to disrobe, but, clutching hold of her gown, he checked her.

'Here, milady. I am in no mood to be chasing you about the room.'

Stalling for time, she wobbled awkwardly as first she slid off her hose and shoes, refusing to balance herself with one hand on his nearby knee. Standing barefoot between his spread legs, Julia pulled her gown off her shoulders and over her hips, shrugging it down past her knees. She felt vulnerable enough clothed only in her shift before his male eyes and her trembling hand hesitated, at her shoulder, unable to relinquish the protection of fine linen that shrouded her nakedness.

'Come here.' Seeing her distress, his hands fastened on her waist and drew her nearer. He reached up and slid the straps from her pale shoulders, down her arms, along the way revealing her small, pale breasts tipped with tiny pink nipples. His gaze devoured her milk-white skin, warmed by the golden glow of the fire flames, as inch by inch he revealed her naked body until, finally, her shift fell in a pile about her ankles.

Looking down, she saw the linen about his waist join her discarded clothes and felt the heat of his body burn her. A fierce blush swept up from her toes to her scalp as his hands guided her back to her place on his lap. She felt beneath her buttocks the rough hair of his legs, one side of her body surrounded by the hard planes of his muscled chest and stomach, and pressed against her thigh the thickness of his shaft. Julia swallowed, trembling like a leaf. She started as his hand found her breast, her knees clenched warily. For a while he amused himself caressing her breasts, and then he bent his head and Julia gasped at the feel of his mouth. His tongue found her nipple, sliding softly and slowly around the tender peak, his teeth nibbling, until with a groan he murmured, 'Your skin is pale like snow, yet your hair is bright as a flame. You are fire and ice. Melt for me, little wife.'

He growled at the feel of her slender body. The smooth velvet heat of his shaft reared up against his belly, hot and throbbing. He parted her knees, murmuring reassuringly as his hand slid between the slim softness of her thighs, seeking her hidden delights, enjoying the almost-forgotten pleasure of a woman's soft, pliant body.

Falk stood up, taking Julia with him. She cried out, as the ground seemed far below, and clutched at the column of his neck with both hands. He carried her to the bed and laid her down. It felt cold beneath her back, but only for a moment, as the heat of his body covered her like a blanket. She recovered her own senses and reined them in so tight she felt sweat dew her brow.

When he lowered his head and tried to kiss her she struck him hard in the mouth. This time, though, taken by surprise at her sudden change from docile maid, he tapped her back, upon the cheek with his open palm and little force, but still it stung and Julia gasped with shock.

'You hit me!'

'Well, you have hit me twice now.'

'You are a man, 'tis your lot in life to come to blows!'

'And you are a woman, 'tis your lot in life to be bedded by your husband. Now, stop this nonsense, for I have no wish to hurt you. I swear in the name of God that my wife shall not be virgin come morning!'

For an answer Julia glared mutinously at him and for a moment they fought a silent battle of wills, their weapons the exchange of furious looks.

'For the love of God, English, yield to me! For I would not have your first time be one of pain and fear.'

'I fear nothing you could do to me!' But her legs trembled as the bulk of his thigh slid between them. 'But I will not yield to you.'

'Then you leave me no choice but to take what I want.'

'A Norman trait, I believe.'

For long moments he looked down upon her, noting her bitter tone. Then his knee nudged her legs wider, and she closed her eyes, refusing to look upon his handsome face and his dark eyes, for one look would melt her resolve and she would yield like any silly maid. She fought with her own self-discipline not to move her hips as he pulled her closer against his lean, hard body, determined that he would not make of her a fool.

Falk wondered whether to caress his wife a little longer, more intimately, and prepare her for what was about to happen, but gazing at her stony profile and holding her body in his arms, he realised it would be to no avail. Best to put them both out of their agony now. With a groan, closing his own eyes as goosebumps of pleasure rippled over his skin, Falk moved swiftly.

He whispered an apology for hurting her, and Julia gritted her teeth, determined that she would not cry out, no matter how bad the pain. She breathed in his scent as her nose was pressed against the base of his neck. If she moved her head a fraction her lips could kiss the firm, salty skin…no! No! She tried not to notice what he was doing, how her body reacted…and then she could not help but give a small yelp, quickly smothered against his throat, as a searing pain ripped through her, quickly followed by a feeling of fullness, of possession. In that moment she knew that she would always belong to this man; just as their bodies were entwined, so were their lives.

She closed her eyes and surrendered to the inevitable. He felt her body sigh and relax beneath his, and his dark eyes swept over her face, noting her closed eyelids, her mouth soft and rosy from his kisses. Slowly, he began to move.

His fingers slid one between each of hers, in an intimate, possessive grip, and she felt the damp gleam of sweat upon his skin. The bed creaked and shook as his rhythm grew faster, and more furious. At last he gave a deep, loud groan of satisfaction and fell upon her breast, his breath harsh and quick beside her ear. Then he levered himself up on to his elbows and looked down upon her face. When she did not look at him in return he released himself carefully from their union and glanced discreetly at the bed as she rolled away, searching for the signs of fidelity, yet already convinced her maiden's fortress had not been breached by another. They were there, several rusty spots upon the pale linen. Satisfied, he lay upon his back with one forearm covering his eyes. He felt weak with the heady pleasure her body had given him. He was aware of her furtive movements as she curled on to her side, knees drawn up, but completely ignorant of the tumult of stunned emotion that had her heart pounding. Then he too turned over on to his side, and fell asleep.

Chapter Five

In the distance Julia heard the muffled ringing of bells and remembered that it was Christmas Eve. She lay still for a long time, assessing the breathing of the man who lay stretched out in the bed behind her, the man who was in every sense of the word her husband. His breathing was deep and even and she realised he was asleep. Well, she thought, a little annoyed, so much for that! The greatest event of her life was obviously of little import to him.

She sat up and swung her legs off the bed. For a moment her vision blurred as a wave of dizzy nausea swept over her. Glancing over her shoulder, she checked that her husband was still asleep and his snores confirmed that he was.

Slowly, wincing, Julia made her way to the fireplace and picked up her clothes from the floor. Then she realised that she could not, would not, go to the house of God with the stain of his taking upon her. Furtively, looking quickly and often to the bed, she washed and then dressed.

She had no candle and stumbled in the dark to find her way along the short passage and down the narrow spiral of stairs to the chapel. When she entered, most of the household were there gathered, and they all turned to stare at her.

Lady Fredeswide noticed at once the over-bright of her daughter's eyes, her crimson cheeks and chafed neck, her hair all tangled. Wordlessly, she offered her arm and Julia sank gratefully against the warm bulk of her mother's stalwart body.

All through the mass, as Father Ambrose's voice droned on in Latin, Julia stared about her as though she had never seen this, her world, before. Nothing could ever be the same! All was changed, especially she!

She looked at her mother, at the maids Hilda and Gytha, at Ham and Chester, young men they often flirted with, and she was appalled and amazed that any woman could want to do… *that*…with a man. Even now she still throbbed between her legs, her breasts felt swollen and her lips crushed. Where was the pleasure in this coupling?

At the end of mass, when everyone had left, Lady Fredeswide stayed with Julia and knelt with her before the altar, ostensibly in devout prayer for this Christmas Eve spent for the first time without their lord. But as soon as they were alone, her mother took Julia into her arms and held her tight as she wept a storm of tears.

'What ails you, child?' asked Lady Fredeswide, stroking back Julia's hair and her tears. 'Anyone would think...' and then suddenly it dawned on her '...why, Julia, you were virgin still this eve!'

'Aye, Mother,' sobbed Julia, ''twas a ruse, the bloodied sheet. He cut his thumb and said that he would not rape his own wife.'

'Oh, Julia!' Lady Fredeswide folded her daughter more tightly into her embrace, smiling to herself. ''Tis fortunate you are that he showed such tender care. There are few men who would not have done so and scarce given a thought for the misdeed.'

'But he has done so! Why did you not tell me how terrible it would be?'

Her mother blinked, unable to answer for a moment, but then told Julia gently and firmly, ''Tis the way of the world, my child. He is your husband, and you are his wife, did you think he would leave you a virgin forever?'

'Nay.'

'Did you fight him?'

'Nay, I cannot say that I was unwilling and he—he tried not to—to hurt me...but still, he did! He spoke of pleasure but I could find none.'

'Nor will you if your body is rigid with fear and anger. Next time…' here her mother's voice sank to a low whisper '…do not fight him, but lie soft and still. 'Twill be easier.'

'Nay! I will never lie with him again! Never!' Looking up then, Julia implored, 'Let me sleep with you in Wynstan's chamber, please, Mother.'

'Nay,' said Lady Fredeswide firmly. 'You will only incur his wrath and we know not yet what manner of a man he is.'

They exchanged a knowing glance, each remembering beatings undeserved and unprovoked, meted out only on the merits of a foul male temper. Her mother persuaded Julia to go back to her chamber, to get a good night's sleep, for she was tired and all would seem much better in the morning. Reluctantly Julia crept away, and let herself back into the lord's chamber.

The fire had died down and Julia placed several more logs upon it, before sitting down to slowly remove her shoes, slide off her hose, and wriggle out of her kirtle. She folded it neatly over the chair, but resolved that this night she would keep on the armour of her shift. Then she tiptoed across the room and slid into the high bed that she had slept in for so many nights of her life, and was now largely occupied by the broad expanse of a long, muscular body that was both male and Norman.

For a long while she lay awake, lying rigidly upon her back and listening to his soft snores. Then her eyes closed, and slowly, at last, she fell asleep.

Julia woke once during the night. She sat up with a start and a frightened cry upon her lips. Instantly, his soldier's instincts well honed, Falk turned to her in the dark and muttered roughly a question of enquiry.

''Tis naught,' she replied, lying back down, 'a nightmare only.'

He listened to her uneven breathing, and felt the vibration of her shudders. The fire had died down to embers, leaving the room cold, and he seemed to have most of the covers on his side of the bed.

'Come here.'

Julia turned her head suspiciously. 'Why?'

He sighed. 'I would warm you and comfort away your nightmare. 'Tis what husbands do.'

'Indeed?' There was no disguising the bitterness of her voice. 'You surprise me, Norman.'

'Do I, English?' He rolled towards her and pulled her across the width of the bed. Julia collided with his towering bulk and gasped. He lay on his side and lifted one arm to tuck it beneath her neck, drawing her close against the heat of his body. Slowly, she lowered her head and settled it upon the hot, fleshy bulk of his bicep, his chest a wall before her face. Heat emanated from him and flooded into her own chilled body. She had to own that it was not unpleasant. His foot dragged her chilled toes to his calf and held them there, which was most definitely not unpleasant.

They lay silently for a long while, the only sound their ragged breathing, for each was struggling to control their emotions. Julia held herself tensely, and when his hand found her hip her start was violent.

He murmured soothingly, and let his palm slide slowly up her back until it rested between her shoulder blades. He felt the material of her shift and wondered when she had donned it, remembering that she had been naked beneath him, and remembering too that he had hurt her. But that could not be helped and he liked to think that he had been as gentle and careful as any man could be with a delicate virgin bride. Was she so very young, then, that she did not understand what happened between a man and a woman? He did not think so, for she seemed sensible and mature, but then...she was slight of build, her breasts soft and small. How old was she?

'Tell me, wife, what is your age?'

'What?' Julia moved her head to look up at him, in the faint moonlight. 'My age? I am...two and twenty.'

It was his turn to exclaim, with surprise, and relief, and confusion. 'You are certainly no young maid. More than old enough to understand what a man wants from a woman.'

'Indeed?' Julia pursed her lips, somewhat chagrined at her obvious failure to have acquired this elusive knowledge. 'And pray tell, husband, where would I have learned this understanding?'

'What?' He glanced at her, surprised that she should question him. He expected meekness, acquiescence…not defiance.

'It sounds to me,' continued Julia in a tart tone of voice, 'that a wife is expected to be chaste and innocent right up until the wedding night. Then she is expected to know all the tricks of the most experienced whore. Is there a particular manuscript I might read that contains this information? Perhaps the monks keep it in a special section. Under the letter ''F''?'

He saw the laughter in her eyes and the dimple in her cheek, and bristled defensively. 'What nonsense is this? And I do not care for my wife to speak coarsely.'

'I have not done so, my lord.'

'F, for—'

'Fornication, sir, what else?' She looked at him with innocent eyes.

'Oh.' He cleared his throat. 'I do not expect you to have such knowledge. I merely express my con-

cern and I am sorry…if I hurt you. I have never
taken a virgin before, but doubt whether you
would have felt any less pain if ours had been a
marriage of true love. 'Tis your ignorance of passion that causes you pain.' He paused then,
thoughtful, and smoothed his fingertips over the
velvet skin of her shoulder. She smelled sweet and
womanly, and she felt so slender and soft lying
against the hardness of his warrior's body that desire stirred in him. But he did not want tears, and
he preferred her cries to be those of pleasure. Lowering his voice a notch, he murmured, 'There is a
secret that you must learn, little wife, for we will
be a long time married, God willing. And if we
are not to spend that time in misery 'twill be better
for us both.'

He tried then to explain to her how a woman
reached her climax, and Julia blushed hotly in the
dark. But when he slid his hand over her belly and
touched the vulnerable, V-shaped mound at the
juncture of her thighs, she struck his hand away
with a sharp blow.

'Do not touch me!'

'I would but show you what I mean.'

'Nay!'

'I swear I will not…take you…with my own
body…but touch you with just my finger.'

'Nay, Norman! 'Tis still sore. Do not.'

Julia clenched her legs tight shut and dragged at his wrist with both hands. In some confusion, he withdrew and rested his hand upon his thigh, away from her. Never before had a woman said him nay, for ladies seemed always eager to join their bodies with his. But then, they had always been willing and she, his wife, was not. Did this make a difference? he wondered. Would she not be able to feel desire and passion if he forced her to yield?

He did not know, and he was too tired to find out. He felt her ribs tremble and heard her sniff as she wiped surreptitiously at her face.

'Hush, now. I am not such a heartless beast that I would use you again this night, for 'tis obvious that you are…shocked. I have seen it so in young knights after their first battle, 'tis weeping and vomiting because they could not stomach the shock of blood and guts spilled in combat. Mayhap a virgin maid feels thus, the first time, for 'tis also a violence upon your body and blood spilled. Despite your not-so-tender age you have much to learn.'

With that he turned over and presented her with his back, before his snores announced his return to sleep. Julia stared for a long while at the dark outline of his broad shoulders, moving slightly with the rise and fall of his breathing, not at all sure whether his words were a comfort or an insult.

* * *

It was tradition at Foxbourne to exchange gifts after the first mass and before the midday meal. When Julia descended to the hall, she wore her best kirtle of green velvet and a cream-damask girdle embroidered with gold thread, her hair brushed and shining and her body smelling cleanly of lavender soap. She carried in her arms the gifts she had worked on all year, except those that had been intended for her father and her brothers and these now lay, hidden, in her dower chest.

Falk stood with a goblet of wine and watched her as she made a fine show of bestowing her gifts upon her mother, young Edwin, Ulric; even each of the house serfs received some small item. That there was nothing for him, her husband, was obvious.

He, on the other hand, had brought gifts for his wife and mother-in-law, did not favour the servants, but had brought supplies from London that boosted the ravaged pantry and promised a skinful of Burgundy wine for all. Etheldred and the maids scurried about in a sweat of excitement and hard work as they prepared a feast like Foxbourne had never seen before.

Amidst the activity Falk came to Julia and bestowed upon her a small leather pouch, leaning down to kiss her on both cheeks and say, in a low voice, 'Happy Christmas, sweet wife.'

Julia winced and squirmed at the intimacy of his voice, at the knowing looks thrown her way by maids and knights all alike. She stood staring at the pouch as though she suspected a viper would leap forth and bite her. Lady Fredeswide spoke, to fill the void that Julia's silence had opened, 'I am sorry that we have no gift for you, my lord, but I am sure Julia will make amends.'

Falk smiled politely, bowed, and looked down upon the still, silent figure of his wife. Reluctantly, at the behest of her mother's sharp finger-poke in her spine, Julia opened the pouch and tipped the contents into her palm. There were two items of jewellery, one a ring of gold—a marriage band— and the other a delicate silver and amber necklet.

Before she could decide what to do with them Falk's brown, scarred fingers descended into her palm and picked out, first, the ring. Turning her left hand over, he slid it down upon the slender, pale length of her fourth finger. Then he reached for the necklet and fastened this about Julia's throat, his fingertips lingering, deliberately glancing over the sensitive skin at the nape of her neck. She flushed, a flare of red-hot heat that burned her body from the soles of her feet to her scalp: he had set his seal upon her, for all the world to see.

When they sat down to eat their Christmas Day meal Julia watched Falk carefully, seeking to find fault and point out his uncultured Norman manners. But he shared his trencher with her diligently and offered her first choice of sliced ham and goose, cutting the best portions with his own silver-filigreed knife and deft ease. He neither spat nor dribbled nor gobbled, did not belch or pick his teeth or talk with his mouth full. Perhaps the only fault that she could find was that he ate a great deal, but his appetite was applauded by her mother and Etheldred, whereas her own miserable picking was condemned as a fault.

Falk, seated between Lady Fredeswide and Julia, used the opportunity to obtain information, his conversation this morning with Julia, as they had risen from the bed and dressed, having proved monosyllabic and fruitless. He asked many questions about Foxbourne: how many serfs were retained and their skills, the lands entailed and the crops they yielded, as well as the numbers and nature of livestock. He asked about their neighbours and the nearest towns, about their priest, Father Ambrose and, finally, he asked about Julia.

'I am curious to know,' enquired Falk as he addressed himself to deboning a roasted capon and dividing the meat between himself and Julia, 'why your daughter has reached the age of two and twenty without being wed.'

'My husband,' replied Lady Fredeswide after a long, thoughtful moment of silence and avoiding the baleful glare of their subject, 'was a difficult man. He was not inspired to provide a dowry that attracted any suitable offers. And, well, Julia is a headstrong girl and her colouring is neither fashionable nor well liked.'

Falk paused to cast a critical eye over his wife, perusing her as he would a horse, before replying, 'Her colouring is unusual, but not unattractive, and though she may be on the thin side, no doubt a babe or two will fill her out more amply.'

Here Julia set her goblet down with a thump and she opened her mouth to make a caustic retort. But beneath the table her mother kicked her ankle and she bit back her words; after all, it was Christmas Day, and she should make an effort to keep the peace. It was not going to be easy to learn how to be a wife, and she must be careful not to cause offence, thus bringing the Norman's wrath down upon her household.

The day passed quietly, with music and dancing and story-telling for entertainment. There was plenty to eat and most were glad just to sit about with a full belly and a warm fire for company. As they made their way to bed that night, Julia had thought her fear would make of her a knock-kneed simpleton, but it was a tiny flicker of excitement that made her fingers tremble as she undressed. Modestly she climbed into bed still wearing her shift, but Falk made no comment. She wondered if he would want her again, and she lay there tensely, her palms folded upon her breast like a marble effigy, awaiting her fate.

Falk undressed and glanced at Julia, hiding the smile that tugged at the corners of his mouth. He thought it would not be wise to make any comments about martyrs and what cold bedfellows they made, but slid beneath the covers and lay on his side, gazing at her profile in silence, until at last she turned her head and raised her brows in question. Silently he crooked his finger at her, several times, until at last she obeyed and shifted over to lie close against him. Then he bent his head and kissed her gently on the lips before whispering, 'Goodnight, sweet wife.'

Rolling over, he fell promptly asleep and Julia suppressed a sigh. This was more familiar to her, the selfish, uncaring attitude of men.

'Goodnight, husband,' she responded sharply, and then presented him with her own back before falling into a deep, dreamless sleep.

They were jolted out of their uneasy truce at dinner the next day, their meal rudely interrupted by a commotion at the door. Several Norman soldiers dragged two hand-tied men into the hall, amidst a mêlée of barking dogs and angry shouts from both parties.

A spew of foul language blasted into the air and flew across the hall. Julia stared wide-eyed and horrified as her brother Randal was dragged forwards by two Angevin guards, followed closely by the long-absent Wulfnoth.

A pair of malevolent eyes, surrounded by a mass of unkempt and filthy red hair, fastened on Julia, and Randal shouted, 'Look at her! The Norman whore eating from the hand of a Norman bastard!'

Falk did not look up as he calmly speared himself an apple and began to peel it with concentration. He asked quietly, again without raising his glance, 'Who is this?'

Julia's voice sank to a nervous whisper, ''Tis my…my brother.'

Falk frowned and leaned closer, unable to catch her soft answer and bending his head so that his ear would be nearer to her face. 'Who?'

Again Julia stammered her reply, aware of her knees shuddering together beneath the table. Her fear was not of Randal, but of what would now happen to him.

A muscle tightened in Falk's jaw, but he merely chewed, swallowed a slice of apple, and then announced to the captain of his guard, 'Hang him.'

'Nay!' Julia's hand shot out to clutch at Falk's arm, 'You cannot hang a man who has done no wrong. A man you know naught of and have not even looked upon!'

'Done no wrong?' asked Falk, turning his head and looking now directly into her eyes. 'Then you confess to a great love for this brother? I will spare him if it is so, even though he is a rebel who has harassed the countryside in these parts for some months now and has proved to be a thorn in my side.'

'He is my kin.'

'And he is loved as you love, say, your mother?' Falk sat back in his chair and contemplated her pale face, flagged on both cheeks by a bright flush.

'I do not need her to plead for me, Norman!' shouted Randal, thus sealing his fate. 'I would rather hang than be saved by a filthy slut who has opened her legs for swine like you!'

Falk leapt so quickly to his feet and vaulted over the width of the table that the astonished congregation scarce saw the fluid movement. The point of his blade found its mark on Randal's throat, despite the matted thatch of stinking beard.

'You brag loudly, Saxon, for a coward who was too well occupied abusing his womenfolk to attend his king upon the battlefield.' Falk towered over his belligerent brother-in-law, yet did not touch him apart from the tip of his dagger, as Randal was held back by both arms by the Angevins, Hervi and Piers. 'You would do well to mend your manners, for I am no skinny wench to be knocked down by one blow.'

Randal raised his head to glare a look of such vile hatred at his sister that Falk stepped back, and commanded his captain, 'Hang him! Hang them both.'

'Nay!' Julia leapt to her feet, shaking off the hand of her mother snaking in apprehension about her elbow. 'If you do this, Norman, I...I...will not...be wife to you! I shall seek an annulment!'

Falk smiled grimly and looked down upon Randal. 'My wife pleads for mercy. But I have no inclination in that direction. William rules with an iron fist, and so shall I in my own demesne. Take them away and keep them under close guard. I will attend the hanging personally.' He turned his back on Randal, who was dragged away shouting vile abuse and all but frothing at the mouth with fury and fear, while Falk strode to his chair.

But he did not sit. He grasped Julia about the upper arm and pulled her with him almost as roughly as her brother had been escorted from the hall, leading her up the dark, narrow spiral of stairs to their chamber.

Julia felt her heart lurch and she stumbled on the steps. With a curse, Falk reached back and hauled her up, swinging her into his arms with an impatient growl. He carried her into their chamber and slammed the door shut with one swift kick, before dropping Julia none too gently upon her feet. She flinched, prepared for the blow that his fury must be eager to deliver.

'Look at me!'

Carefully, Julia squinted open one eye.

'I will not beat you, English, for I am not such a man. But—' here his voice was cold and hard as steel '—never, and I mean never, say nay to me in my own hall!'

He took a step closer to her and Julia took two backwards.

'Do you understand?'

'Aye, my lord. I will remember only to tell you nay when we are in the meadow.'

He stared at her, for a moment, and then laughter burst deep and rich from his throat. Quickly closing the space between them, he seized Julia about the waist and pulled her against his body. 'By God, wife, I find you to my liking! But you speak foolishly of an annulment. 'Tis far too late.'

His voice was low and husky, as he bent his head. She turned her cheek away, to evade his mouth, but he caught her chin between thumb and forefinger and tipped up her face, his lips finding hers. His kiss was hard and demanding.

Julia heard his groan, felt the heat and maleness of his body, and felt too her feet leave the ground as he lifted her with two hands upon her hips and propelled her swiftly backwards to lay her down upon the bed. At once Julia realised his intention.

'Nay!' She hammered her small fists upon his chest, and shook her head, twisting away from his mouth as it sought hers.

'Why?' he asked, hoarsely, watching the hot colour flood into her soft lips.

'Because you are Norman! And you have sent my brother to be hanged!'

'And for that you should thank me.' Grasping her jaw between his fingers he kissed her again.

'I hate you!' Julia said, when the kiss stopped.

He smiled mockingly, his eyes upon her lips, 'I could have sworn otherwise.'

His hands moved, one from behind her head and the other from her waist, and moved to the neck of her kirtle, which he now tugged from her shoulders, revealing her shift, and this he pulled down to her waist in one swift movement, baring her breasts. With a furious curse Julia landed a half-dozen blows upon his broad shoulders with clenched fists, blows that glanced off as easily as rain.

'Take me then, Norman. Do as you will, for 'tis only my body that you force me to surrender. It has naught to do with my mind, where dwells my heart and my soul. That you shall never take from me!'

He stared at her with some surprise, for he had never before considered that a woman might possess a heart and a soul. A woman was only a body, to be pleasured and enjoyed and this was a concept he had always lived with. But this woman...nay, she was not *just* a woman. He did not yet understand the way she made him feel, and, indeed, it was true that he could take her, wanted to take her, now, urgently. But when he thought what his next move must be, to hold her down, and force himself inside her, he could not do it.

With a sigh of frustration mingled with annoyance, he levered himself off the bed and bowed to her before striding to the door, announcing, 'Your pardon, my lady, if I do not linger to play the tender bridegroom. I have a hanging to attend to.'

Julia sat up quickly, snatching up her shift to hide her vulnerable nakedness and calling out, 'My lord!'

He checked with one hand on the door handle.

'I beseech thee, do not do this terrible thing. Last night, you spoke of your hopes of a long and happy marriage. That would be impossible if you were to murder my brother.'

He turned slowly, to survey her lying dishevelled and flushed on the bed, her clothes clutched like a shield to her bosom. A dark glint hardened his eyes. 'I am King William's man, and I am honour bound to set down the rule of law as he dictates. I hang your Randal because he is opposed to my king, not because he is your brother.'

He turned then and left the room. Outside the door he found the dog Kenward waiting. The black animal rose from his haunches and thrust forward to find his mistress, looking up hopefully as he encountered again the closed door. Falk paused, and surveyed Kenward, stretching out a hand to his dark head. After the first wary cringe Kenward sniffed at the warm hand fondling his ears, found his mistress's scent and wagged his tail. Falk chuckled. Kenward raised his huge paw and scratched at the door panel.

'Nay, you shall come with me. Let us inspect this brother who has her loyalty when he deserves none. Come, let us see what is to be done with him.'

Foxbourne had no dungeon and the prisoners were kept in the hayloft of the nearest barn, just behind the walled enclosure of Julia's herb garden. Falk entered with two of his Angevins and began his interrogation first of Wulfnoth.

The serf was a miserable sight, filthy, thin from hunger and cowed into dull-eyed silence by weeks of Randal's heavy-fisted and futile leadership. Falk studied him for a moment, before indicating to his captain, Hervi, that the Saxon serf should be hauled to his feet to face him. With arms folded over his broad chest, Falk considered thoughtfully.

'You are Wulfnoth?' he asked, in the English tongue.

A nod, a glare, a glance sliding away to the floor.

'How long have you belonged to Foxbourne?'

'All my life. I was born here. I am falconer.'

'And now you run wild in the forest with a pack of animals?'

''Twas no idea of mine.'

'If you had a choice, would it be Lord Randal or Lady Julia you serve?'

Wulfnoth looked up quickly. 'I'd lay down my life for Lady Julia.' He glanced over his shoulder where skulked Randal in a dark corner, and spat.

Falk smiled and rasped a hand over the beard stubble of his chin, before replying, 'I have need of a good falconer. Do you solemnly swear to serve King William, and the Lady Julia, who is now my wife, and thus you would serve me?'

It did not take Wulfnoth long to evaluate his options. With a clenched fist thumped to his heart he declared, 'I swear.'

Falk gave the order for Wulfnoth to be released, for his hair to be shorn and his stinking self scrubbed as well as fed. The serf went off feeling he had made the best bargain of his life.

With a sharp jerk of his head Falk indicated that the remaining prisoner be brought forwards, and here his expression hardened into a less benevolent mask. He eyed the red-haired Saxon with distaste, noting that his colouring was much darker than Julia's and his disposition certainly more vicious. His glance fell to the clenched fists held tensely at his side and the thought of those fists touching Julia, bruising her pale skin… He fought to control the white-hot fury that almost made him reach for his sword and slice that creature's head from its neck. But Falk controlled himself, drew a silent, calming breath and asked, 'What of you, brother? Do you swear fealty to William, and promise to abide peaceably in my household?'

Randal swore a vile oath, and spat a slimy gob aimed at Falk's boots. 'You are no brother of mine!'

'Are you not sibling to the Lady Julia?'

'Aye, I am!'

'Then, as I am her husband, that would, unfortunately, make you my brother. In law at least.'

'A pox on you, Norman! When England is again under the rule of Saxons, 'tis your balls I'll have on a platter!'

Falk laughed out loud. 'Despite the pretty pleadings of your sister I can find no reason to show you mercy. Although only God knows why she would want to save a brother who has shown to her none.'

Randal glared resentfully. ''Tis no business of yours.'

'Ah, there you are indeed mistaken. Julia is very much my business, as is Foxbourne. 'Tis now mine, from the tower top to the meadow stream and everything in between.'

A snarl and several vile oaths exploded from Randal. 'Hang me, Norman, for I would not live in my own hall under your thumb.'

Falk shrugged. 'Very well.'

He turned to stride away and in that instant Randal lunged, smashed his knuckles into Hervi's face, wrenched a sword from Pier's scabbard and swung with more violence than accuracy. Amidst shouts of warning Falk turned and drew his own sword, confident that Randal had met his match. But in the confines of the hayloft it was difficult to swing his blade, to be ever wary of the low-beamed rafters and the trapdoor at his heels.

Steel clanged on steel. Falk never took his eyes off Randal, side-stepping neatly and luring the maddened Saxon towards the square hole yawning open and dangerous. Below, Kenward barked, quickly joined by the other dogs as they sensed the thrill of a fight. Falk lunged, and cut Randal on his forearm. He squealed but gave no surcease.

'To the death, Norman,' he snarled through clenched teeth. 'To the death.'

With a salute of his head Falk pressed forward in his attack, swung round and angled Randal into a swift back-stepping parry. With a shout, Randal realised that his foot had found nothing but thin air, and he toppled down through the open trapdoor, landing with a thump and a groan in the barn below.

Quickly, Falk clambered down the ladder and reached the bottom just as Randal had found himself a horse and prepared to mount.

'Fleeing already, Saxon?' asked Falk with a sneer, his sword held at the ready, panting hard as sweat beaded on his forehead.

Randal swung round. For a moment he seemed uncertain whether to flee, or continue the fight. By now he had a vague inkling that the better swordsman was not he, and Falk was considerably taller and more powerfully built. But still, cleverness had never ranked as one of his traits and now the thirst for vengeance was unquenchable. He lunged and again clashed swords with Falk, engaging in a furious assault that gained him little ground.

The dogs, excited and sensing an opportunity for revenge against the one that had so often punched and kicked them, joined in the mêlée, hampering both combatants. Randal swore at the dogs, lashing out with his feet as they jostled about him, barking with a furious and deafening clamour.

'Kenward!' shouted Falk. 'Get out! Out!'

But Kenward, brave protector, now made a grab with his bared fangs at Randal's sword arm, yelped as he was thrown off, but returned again and again in his determined defence of the one whose scent belonged to his mistress. A lifetime of hatred erupted from Kenward as he launched himself at Randal. The cold silver light of a sword flashed through the gloom. Kenward howled, was thrown backwards, and lay still.

Falk yelled his war cry with fierce, unstoppable rage, his arm pumping mightily as he fought to break Randal's grip upon his sword hilt. Randal stumbled beneath this onslaught, fell to his knees and Falk thrust his sword into the Saxon's soft belly. Blood gushed, Randal gave a surprised groan, toppled down and lay half-dead upon the straw and dirt and dung of the barn. With one quick slash to the throat Falk finished him off. Turning his back and striding swiftly to find the still, black form of Kenward, Falk knelt down to see how the dog fared. With one hand on the barrel of his ribs Falk sought to find any sign of life. At first he feared the worst, and then he felt the faint flutter of a heartbeat.

The other dogs had limped away with tucked tails and furtive grins, silent, shivering, crowding about a figure that stood silhouetted in the door-way. Looking up, Falk encountered Julia standing there, with her mouth open upon a silent scream and her face white with shock.

Chapter Six

'What have you done?' Julia forced her legs to carry her forwards, her glance flinching between the bloodied, prostrate forms of Kenward and her brother.

Falk eyed her stricken face, rising slowly to his feet. Deliberately, he cleaned his sword upon a clump of straw and sheathed it before making his explanation.

'I offered him sanctuary, but he would have none of it. Then he attacked my men and tried to escape.' Even to his own ears the words sounded too flimsy to bear the weight of a man's death.

'So you...slaughtered him? Just like that?'

'Nay, 'twas not so. He wanted the fight—'

'And Kenward? Was it not enough to cut down a helpless prisoner, that you must kill a defenceless hound too? *My* hound!'

'I did not kill Kenward!' protested Falk, coming to stand closer to Julia and stooping to look into her eyes that already glittered silver with unshed tears, jerking his head at the slumped body of Randal. 'It was him. But he is not dead.'

Julia stared at Falk, and then at her slain brother, aghast at so obvious a lie.

'The dog…' Falk gestured '…I think he still lives.'

With a small cry, tears now crowding in her throat, desperately clamouring for an escape, Julia ran and knelt beside Kenward's still-warm body. Her hand stroked his soft black fur, and with a sob she hugged him tight, caring not for the blood that stained her gown. He whimpered and trembled.

'Come.' Falk laid his hand on her shoulder. 'Let us take him into the hall.'

Julia shook him off. 'Leave me alone.'

A shadow fell over them and she looked up to find Ulric, and several of the other serfs, crowding about the doorway.

'My lady?'

She rose slowly, stiffly. 'Fetch Father Ambrose. Take my brother up to the chapel, for now, and bring Kenward to the hall.' She turned to glare brightly at Falk. 'We do not need assistance, my lord.'

Picking her way over the muddy yard, holding up her skirts and escorted by a phalanx of slinking dogs, Julia met her mother in the kitchen doorway.

''Tis Randal, Mother. And…' here her voice broke '…Kenward is grievously injured.'

Lady Fredeswide put her arm comfortingly around Julia's shoulders and together they went inside. Her mother went up to the chapel to hold the vigil over her lost son, while Julia fetched her box of ointments and hurried back to the hall to care for Kenward. The light was quickly fading and it was with a sense of haste that the household gathered in the yard; first, Randal's body was brought out, shrouded in linen sheets, then Kenward's unconscious form, and both were carried indoors.

Awakened from his nap, Father Ambrose appeared red-cheeked and rumpled, a little confused, as now before the doors of the chapel he was presented with a corpse. He peered into the gloom, where Falk loomed, large and menacing, upon the stairwell. But it was not his sword he held out to the shrinking priest, but a small leather pouch of silver coins.

'For the church, Father,' Falk persuaded in his rough, deep voice, his eyes hard, unyielding and brimful of dire warning that no questions be asked.

Lady Fredeswide had already lit as many candles as she could find and they sputtered and smoked in the cold evening air. The chapel smelled of incense and damp stone, of holly and cobwebs, the floor hard and uncomfortable beneath her knees as she knelt before the altar and fingered her rosary beads, head bowed.

In the hall Julia supervised the laying of fur rugs before the fire, making a comfortable bed for Kenward as he was placed carefully down. His tail thumped gratefully when he felt his mistress's gentle hand upon his neck, and heard the soothing murmur of her voice. Julia bathed the blood from the deep cut to his shoulder and feared that Kenward would be lucky if he survived, with only a limp to show for his ordeal and bravery. Once it was cleaned she stitched the wound neatly and covered it with a foul-smelling unguent that would promote healing. Only when she was satisfied that he rested comfortably did she rise to her feet and ascend to the chapel to join her mother.

Randal's body was laid to rest upon the altar. She knelt beside her mother and Father Ambrose, rosary beads slipping through her fingers as she prayed for her brother's soul. Glancing sideways, she spied Falk standing in the passage outside. Her eyes were sharp as sapphires. Unforgiving. Falk turned away and she heard his feet thump down the steps to the hall.

All the household serfs crowded in to the chapel. They seemed eager to join in the task of praying for the dead, somehow almost pleased to have a body over which to grieve whereas before there had been none. Julia eyed them one by one, as their lips moved in fervent prayer, hands twisted together. She realised then, with a shock, that now all who had carried her father's name were really gone. She alone remained, she who must bear the name of a Norman.

Falk decided to spend the rest of the evening drinking, sitting before the hearth with his knights, playing dice and exchanging battle stories. About him he had the five Angevins and his squire, the young Sander, whose mother was Danish. Hervi, bearded and older than Falk by ten years, was captain of the guard, while the others were also knights in their own right but had chosen to give their allegiance to Falk, confident that one day his reward would be theirs too.

Looking at them, as they sat shoulder to shoulder, throwing dice and drinking from a keg of Burgundy's finest wine, Falk realised that they had seen many battles together, more than he could number on his two hands. He would as lief be down a dark alley or face his foe across the field of honour with these men than any others.

Alun, dark and quick tempered, well skilled with a broadsword as well as a lance; Thierry, stocky and pugnacious, and a good man with his fists; blue-eyed peacemaker Luc, whose skill as a warrior belied his slender appearance, and the youngest, most handsome of them all, golden Piers, who had yet to prove himself unreliable.

They fed themselves off the pickings of the mid-day feast, abandoned hours ago upon the tables still set up. As they filled their trenchers with cold venison, pigeon pie and plum cake, Hervi made a comment about the absence of Saxon faces. ''Tis surely the best boon of the day.'

'Aye.' Thierry laughed. 'I like not these miserable Saxons.'

'They're a stubborn lot,' agreed Falk, staring into his wine goblet and seeing there the imagined reflection of a pale face, framed by wavy red-blonde hair. 'No matter how much William desires to make us one race, methinks a thousand years from now they will still hate us.'

As though in agreement Kenward thumped his tail and heaved a deep sigh as he dozed in his comfortable nest of furs.

As the evening waxed the serfs crept away, until all in the chapel were Julia, her mother and Father Ambrose. Lady Fredeswide, fearing a marital confrontation, tried to persuade Julia to depart.

'Come now, child, 'tis time you went to bed.'

'Nay, Mother, I will not leave him alone this night.'

'I will stay.'

'So too shall I.'

'Your husband will be angered.'

'I think he is not a man moved easily to anger. Besides, I care not what he thinks! I'll not be his whore this night. Or ever again!'

'Julia!'

'Do not look so shocked, Mother. Is that not what I am?'

'Nay, nay! A thousand times nay! You are his lawful wedded wife.'

Julia shrugged off her mother's arm and stared with hard eyes and a set mouth at the wooden crucifix hanging over the altar. Though she ached to her bones with exhaustion and every part of her body screamed for the ease of a soft mattress, she forced herself to sit upright upon her knees and keep her eyes open. The household grew silent as evening expired into the dead of night; the candles gutted and etched thin plumes of smoke into the air, until there were so few still lit they could scarce see a thing.

'I will go to the storeroom and fetch some more,' said Julia, rising to her feet with a jingle as her keys chinked upon her girdle.

Taking one small taper she lit her way down the narrow stairs, treading softly and carefully in the midnight dark. As she passed through the hall she looked upon the bodies huddled in their bedrolls about the glowing embers of the hearth fire. Snores of men and the snuffles of dogs filled the air and

Julia picked her way cautiously lest she fall over an unsuspecting sleeper.

In the kitchen she inched her way more by memory than by sight to the locked door of her storeroom, fumbling with the heavy key and her icy cold fingers. At last she opened the door and went in to the narrow room, aromatic with the smell of dried herbs, spices, casks of wine, soap and beeswax candles. Her fingers closed over four large candles and she cradled them in her arms as she turned to retrace her path.

A shadow detached itself from the gloom, startling Julia, and a large, callused palm pressed to her mouth, silencing her scream.

''Tis only I, wife,' whispered Falk, his voice and his face hovering far above her own, the massive bulk of his shoulders stooped over her.

Julia gasped for breath as his hand lifted. 'For the love of God, Norman, you scared me half to death!'

He chuckled. 'Did you think 'twas the Devil himself?'

'Mayhap. What are you doing creeping about in the middle of the night?'

'I could ask you the same.'

'I am lady of this house. I do not need to explain myself.'

'Aye, 'tis true. You need explain yourself to no one, except the lord and master of your household.

And that, sweet little wife, is me. Now, what are you about?'

Julia eyed him warily in the flickering yellow light of her taper, her arms growing weary as she shifted the weight of the candles she carried, lifting them up for his gaze in silent explanation.

'I will carry those for you.'

'Nay. I do not need your help!'

But he took them anyway and she knew there was little point in making it a contest of strength. Taking advantage of his willingness to play servant, she paused in the kitchen, suspecting that her mother must surely be as hungry as her own stomach-rumbling self. She tore off a hunk of bread and cut a wedge of hard yellow cheese, placing these on a wooden platter together with a mug of elderflower wine.

In the chapel Falk set the candles in place of those that had burned away, lit them and then leaned against the doorframe as he watched Julia kneel down beside her mother. After a few moments, Lady Fredeswide glanced at him nervously, and then pressed close to Julia to whisper in her ear, 'He waits for you.'

'Then he will wait long.' Julia stared straight ahead at the altar, ignoring now the platter of food that she had placed close at hand, reluctant to eat before his unwavering gaze and fervently wishing he would go. Long moments ebbed and flowed, until Julia turned her head in Falk's direction and asked coolly, 'My lord wishes to pray with us?'

He cleared his throat and then eased himself away from the doorframe. 'Nay. I do not dabble where I have no skill and little practice.'

'Then mayhap my lord will be more comfortable in his own chamber.'

Falk smiled then, seeing down what path her mind wandered, 'I am honour bound to wait for my lady wife before seeking my own comfort.'

'I will not be lying abed this night,' replied Julia stiffly, turning her gaze back to the altar and the shrouded, lumpen shape lying upon it.

'Lady Fredeswide,' said Falk in a commanding tone that made her jump, 'The hour is late and I bid you to seek your rest. We will stay and keep the vigil.'

'But—'

One glance from his glittering ebony eyes was the only spur Lady Fredeswide needed. Although her confidence had grown in the weeks past, she was not bold enough by nature to endure a confrontation. Despite Julia's hand clutching at her gown, she departed with a final bow to the altar, crossing herself three times. In all truth she could find no reason to suffer her aching bones on this cold stone floor, in honour of a son for whom she felt almost nothing besides fear and hatred.

Falk resumed his casual lounging stance upon the doorframe, the walls being too dank and cold to support his broad shoulders comfortably. He folded his arms over his chest and contemplated Julia's profile, as her lips moved in silent prayer, and her long lashes swept shadows over her cheeks. Then, restless to find occupation for his hands, he unsheathed his dagger from its hidden scabbard about his waist, the steel sliding out with a faint hiss that alerted Julia, but she resisted the temptation to turn her head and stare. From the very corner of her eye she spied that he had now begun a meticulous cleaning of his nails.

Each time he looked up to see if she watched him, Julia quickly averted her eyes and increased the pace of her rosary. Never had fifty-three Hail Marys and six Our Fathers passed so slowly. The amber beads slid between her pale fingers, golden in the faint glow of candlelight, until at last she reached the final incantation.

'Come, wife, we go to bed.'

'I cannot leave him alone. He is between heaven and hell.'

'Father Ambrose will be keeper of souls this night.' Although Falk had little doubt in which direction Randal's would eventually go.

Julia glanced at Father Ambrose, slumped in a chair and snoring softly. He had tried valiantly to stay awake, but failed. A wave of exhaustion swept over her and she swayed a little, dizzy with fatigue.

With an impatient sigh Falk crossed the floor, leaned down, fastened his arms about her and scooped Julia up into his arms.

'Put me down, Norman!' Julia pummelled his shoulders with her fists, but did not dare to raise her voice above an urgent whisper.

'A thousand prayers will not bring him back to life. We leave him in the care of God.' Ignoring her protests, he strode from the chapel, down the stairs, and along the short passage to the solar chamber.

Julia had a strange feeling they had lived this scene before. Suddenly she was reminded of the day they had been married, and he had carried her from the chapel to her parents' bed. Glancing up at his grim face, as they entered the chamber and he kicked shut the door, she wondered if he too remembered. He set her down on the edge of the high bed and then turned away to disrobe.

In silence, sitting stiffly, Julia listened to the thump of boots dropping upon the floor, the snap of leather unfastened, the slither of a tunic shrugged off. Then the mattress dipped and sagged behind her as he climbed between the covers. She could smell his musky male odour but did not turn to look at him, until his voice startled her out of her frozen state.

'This candle will gut shortly.'

Still she remained silent and fully dressed.

'Perhaps you are so weary that you are in need of assistance?'

At once Julia pointed her chin over one shoulder and shot him a fierce glance. 'I will not lie down with the man who is stained with my brother's blood.'

'Ah, I see. Now we get to the crux of it, in truly a tortuous fashion, which only a woman can deliver.'

She drew in a sharp breath. 'You are bold for a knave who has behaved so despicably!'

Falk laughed, turning to lie upon his back and release a deep, rolling encore to that laugh.

'How dare you!' Julia now spun and faced him, kneeling on hands and knees, glaring at him, 'How dare you laugh at my loss and my grief!'

Suddenly his hand snaked out and grabbed at her wrist, pulling her off balance until she collapsed upon the bed. With two hands hooked under her armpits he hauled her nearer to sprawl across his chest. He caught her defiant chin between his fingers and held her still.

'I have this day but done my duty to my king. I have naught upon my mind that will keep me awake, save for the hunger of my body that yearns to taste again your sweetness. All night I have looked upon your lovely lips and ached to kiss them.'

Julia struggled, 'You must be drunk!'

''Tis a fine answer to a husband's compliment.'

'Go to hell, Norman!'

'Undoubtedly I shall, English. Now, let us undress you and see what other parts of your soft body I ache for. Put aside your foolish notions, for you feel no more loss over Randal than I do. Do not act the hypocrite. Act the wife, and let me teach you the secrets of being a woman.'

With one supple movement he rolled over her and Julia was trapped beneath his weight, his shoulders filling her vision, his hard thighs clamped about her legs. His fingers moved swiftly to unlace her kirtle and his head descended to cover Julia's mouth with his own.

As he kissed her, deeply, searching and tasting, Julia fought her own self. She wanted this, she wanted to feel his arms about her, the weight of his body pressing against her, she wanted his possession. Even though she had not yet experienced the 'secrets of being a woman' she felt alive when he made love to her, when he filled her with his body and groaned with pleasure. And yet she was so consumed with guilt because this man was Norman, and he had her brother's blood upon his hands, that she had not allowed herself to feel the same pleasure.

Falk nuzzled her neck, persuading her with every touch and the erotic murmur of his voice against her cheek. She closed her eyes in surrender and let him do as he would. The fact that he touched her so gently, so slowly, only made her more eager and she had to bite her teeth together to hide from him her excitement. Her resistance was only token and they both knew it. He parted her thighs and covered her body with his own. If she did not learn the lesson he wanted to teach her, at least she did not fight him.

Two days later the funeral procession wound its way down to the burial ground beneath the great oak on the leeward side of Foxbourne. From the tower top Falk watched, picking out even from a distance the small, dark-cloaked figure of his wife, her shoulders slightly bowed and her face hidden by the hood of her cloak.

Randal's body had been placed on a wicker hurdle and this was carried by the four male serfs, Ulric, Ham, Chester and Alfred, with Edwin trying to squeeze in on a corner and puffing out his little chest with the desperate need to prove himself a man.

The grave had been burrowed from the frozen ground by half a dozen Norman knights, and it had been no easy task. Now they stood about watching as the Saxons buried their dead, and Julia eyed them as she despatched Randal to his eternal rest. She glimpsed Falk standing bare-headed and un-cloaked upon the tower ramparts, arms akimbo, and she remembered how they had spent the dark hours of the night.

It seemed animal lust was as uncontrolled in fe-males as it was in males, and that knowledge chilled Julia with a bleakness well matched by this bitter winter's day and the ceremony they were about. Finally, it was done, Father Ambrose made the sign of the cross and they departed, thankfully, for the warmth of the hall and hot mulled wine.

In her chamber Julia set aside her rosary beads and her cloak, brushed out her hair and warmed her fingers by the fire. The door opened and Falk came in. Their eyes met across the width of the room. She blushed and dropped her gaze, and he refrained from a triumphant smile, knowing full well that he might have conquered her body, but he had not, as she had once told him, won her mind, where dwelled her heart and her soul.

Chapter Seven

Having subdued England as far as the northern borders, William decided to return to Normandy, taking with him the spoils of war in gold, trophies and hostages. To secure England's peace behind his back he left his most trusted vassals to govern in his absence—Bishop Odo, his half-brother and now Earl of Kent, was given the privilege of reigning over the south, while William FitzOsbern, newly made Earl of Hereford, took responsibility for the wild northern lands.

His hostages, bound for Normandy, were many, amongst them Prince Edgar and the former Earls of Mercia and Northumbria, Edwin and Morcar, as well as Stigand, formerly the Bishop of Canterbury.

The royal caravan stretched for several miles as it snaked its way from London to the south coast and the harbour of Hastings, where waited the king's ships, clothed in the white sails of victory. The noblemen rode on horseback, with many ladies, servants, provisions and baggage confined to the slow rumbling of covered wagons.

Along the way William diverted from his path and called upon Foxbourne. He paused only long enough to sup his midday meal and order his army commander to rejoin him; a king who had won his crown by force and submission could not be too cautious and William was eager to have his finest warriors close to hand.

Foxbourne was plunged into a maelstrom of activity as Falk hurried to give orders to those of his men he would leave behind to hold Foxbourne in his absence, taking with him only his squire and the five Angevins.

William was not a man to wait for anyone and he was soon preparing to mount up and ride on to Hastings. Swinging up into the saddle of his destrier, a flutter of red-blonde hair caught his attention and he spied Julia standing upon the steps leading to the great hall. He turned then, amidst the noise of shouting knights and stamping, snorting horses, armour chinking and swords clanking, and sought out Falk, who was already fully armoured and mounted upon his black destrier, Drago.

'What is this, de Arques?' demanded William, gesturing with one gauntleted hand at Julia.

'Sire?'

'Your wife, man! Is she to walk to Normandy?'

Falk avoided looking at his king and concentrated on sorting out the reins of his champing horse. Only the slight narrowing of his eyes betrayed his displeasure. 'My wife has refused to go with me, sire.'

'Indeed! Why is that? Is she with child?'

'Nay, sire.'

'Then pray, tell! By what reason can you justify leaving a young bride alone?'

Falk sighed heavily, admitting with a wry smile, 'She is stubborn and wilful and I tire of quarrelling with her, sire. My absence may sweeten her mood.'

'Ho!' William laughed heartily. 'I do not think so, man! I think you will more likely find that these Saxons are wont to plot, if left alone and given half the chance. Nay, I think your plan is vastly flawed. Mayhap a honeymoon in Normandy may be the thing to sweeten her temper. Bring her!'

And with that William spurred his horse into a canter and rode away, amidst a flurry of courtiers, banners and royal bodyguards.

Falk sat in his saddle and gazed across the crowded courtyard at Julia. Only an hour ago he had told her to pack and be ready to ride with him, but she had refused, claiming that she could not leave her mother alone. Her brightly defiant eyes had confirmed this lie and revealed the real reason, the one source of conflict between them—the fact that he was Norman and she had vowed never to surrender to the race that had vanquished her own.

Watching her as she stood on the steps, waiting for him to make his farewell, he judged what her reaction would be if he were to ask her again to come with him. Naturally she would refuse, and into the bargain would lash him with a few choice remarks honed on the knife-edge of her tongue. Then, if he insisted and raised his voice in harsh command, she would turn and flee. Having considered the likely outcome of the next few moments, Falk looked at the height and the width of the entrance door behind Julia and then touched his heels to Drago's flanks and carefully picked his way across the yard. Drago sensed his tension and pranced, tossing his head, his long black mane rippling, snorting as he felt the familiar battle-ready nerves of the fingers playing on his reins.

Upon the steps Julia tensed as Falk rode towards her, harness jangling and leather creaking as the great war horse high-stepped the path he had been set upon. His massive shadow fell over her and she looked up, squinting into the weak midday sun and saying, with evident hope in her voice, ''Tis farewell, my lord.'

'Nay, milady. The king has bid me to bring my wife to Normandy.'

Julia gave a snort of contempt, ignoring the sly glances and muffled mirth of those around as they anticipated the spectacle of their quarrel.

'William can suck eggs for all I care!'

''Tis treason to talk so of your king.'

'*My* king lies dead on Santlache Ridge!'

Falk sighed, and leaned his forearms on the pommel, sitting easily in the saddle as Drago fidgeted from one leg to the other.

'I tell you but once, wife. Pack your belongings and bring your palfrey, for we ride to Hastings this day, and from there to Normandy.'

Julia stared at him open mouthed. 'You tell me but once? Is it that my lord *orders* me?'

'Aye.' His voice was curt, taught as a bowstring, his eyes unwavering and flint-hard upon hers.

'But I am not a servant for you to order!' Emboldened by these months past when Falk seemed satisfied with their nightly trysts and acquiesced to her every whim without a murmur, Julia now folded her arms across her waist and stared up at him with mocking amusement, waiting for his reply. When it came, she did not like it very much.

'A wife is subject to her husband inasmuch as a servant is to his master. The king has ordered me to bring my wife to Normandy, and bring her I shall.'

Julia took an uncertain step backwards, her arms unfolding, fists clenched at her sides. 'Nay, Norman, I shall not go!'

'Come. Now!'

'Nay!'

Noting the lowering of his dark brows, and the grim look on his face that struck a frisson of fear down her spine, Julia gathered up her skirts in one hand and spun on her heel, fleeing indoors to gain the safety of her keep.

Falk spurred Drago forwards. With a shout of encouragement he urged his horse up the steps and through the open doors of the hall.

Julia shrieked as she heard the clattering of hooves behind her and felt the hot snort of Drago's breath upon her back. All around others screamed and shouted and ran to get out of the way as the massive beast thundered in. Julia ran, but she did not get far. Falk swooped with practised ease and with one arm around her waist he lifted Julia off her feet and flung her face down across the bow of his saddle. Then swiftly he wheeled Drago on his hind legs and clattered outside.

The breath was instantly knocked from Julia's lungs by the force of this manoeuvre and she felt dizzy as the ground swept past at frightening speed. She could do nothing as Falk carefully guided Drago back down the steps, to the fanfare of a great cheer and clapping as his men congratulated him on this daring exploit, but Falk disregarded their acclaim. He paused only to speak to one of his Angevins, choosing Alun, and to Sander, whom he detailed to collect Julia's belongings and her horse and to follow them as quickly as possible.

The four Angevins remaining, mounted on their warhorses, streamed swiftly to his side and with Julia slung across his saddlebow like a sack of grain, Falk de Arques galloped out of Foxbourne.

They had not ridden far when Falk paused to lift Julia up and to settle her pillion across the pommel. As soon as her world tilted up the right way and she could draw breath, she vented a piercing scream of fury and slapped Falk hard in the face.

'How dare you!' she raged. 'How dare you do this to me! Take me back at once!'

Falk remained silent. He showed no sign of emotion and kept his eyes firmly on the horizon. Drago, upset by her screams and her attack on his master, now swung his head around and tried to nip Julia on the ankle with his great yellow teeth. She shrieked and instinct made her leap closer to Falk's broad chest, clutching with her arms at the column of his neck, being the only bastion of safety available to her. She lifted accusing eyes to her husband's, pointing with one finger at Drago's twitching ears. 'That creature tried to bite me!'

Falk replied solemnly, 'He is trained to kick and bite anything he considers to be my enemy.'

'But you cannot let him bite me!'

'Can I not?' He stifled a betraying smile of amusement.

'Nay, indeed!'

'Well, then, behave and sit quietly.'

'Have I any choice?' she asked, craning her neck to look over his shoulder at the receding view of Foxbourne's tower.

Glancing down at her, Falk transferred his reins to one hand so that he could put his arm around her waist, settle her more firmly and comfortably for them both, informing her in a pragmatic voice that only enraged her further, 'Nay, English, you have none.'

It was difficult riding with Julia pillion, and Falk paused several times to wait for Alun and Sander, but they did not appear and Falk cursed his absent knights soundly.

'Your language is most foul, sir,' reprimanded Julia primly, clucking her tongue in disapproval.

He shot her one quelling look and turned the prancing Drago back on to the path, urging him to a bone-shaking canter as they approached the van-guard of William's entourage.

'I could find a wagon for you to ride in,' suggested Falk.

Julia eyed the slow-moving wagons and the agonised grimaces of the ladies who rode in them. Alarm sprang to her mind at the thought of being abandoned amongst strangers. She realised, with a shock that was by no means small, that she had been set adrift in a world where she knew no one, except for this man, her husband and her most hated and sworn enemy.

Her eyes lowered to her jolting lap, Julia murmured stiffly, 'I prefer to stay with you.'

He said nothing, but did not press the issue and rode on swiftly past the wagons.

As the day wore on, Julia complained bitterly about her tender rump and her parched throat, but the pace was relentlessly set by William and there was no pause for rest. In the open country between Pevensey and Hastings they feared ambush, although only madmen would dare to attack so large a force, and one headed by a skilled soldier such as William himself. At Pevensey half of the travelling party split from the main higher-ranking vanguard, to be accommodated there for the night, as Hastings Castle could not provide shelter for all. There were ships here too, ready to take them to Normandy on the morrow, if the tides and wind were favourable.

'My arms are weary,' moaned Julia, as they slid from around Falk's waist. 'I cannot hold on to you any longer.'

'Cease your whining, English.' His admonishment was gruff-voiced, but once again he transferred both reins into his left hand and held Julia with the other as she drooped wearily against his chest. Truth to tell, he would have ridden to Jerusalem and back if it meant that she would be transformed from Boadicea into this creature that now rested like a wilted flower in his arms. Soft strands of her hair tickled his chin and he breathed in her scent—a subtle aroma of lavender and herbs and young woman.

The sun lowered in the grey sky and the chill wind now bit more fiercely with teeth of ice. Julia huddled closer to Falk and the folds of his cloak. It seemed her world had been reduced to nothing but this bumping, jangling, endless ride and she did not want to think, for the future was too terrifying to contemplate. She had never been further than Pevensey in her whole life and now they were almost at Hastings. Leaning against Falk's uncomfortably hard but warm chest, sheltered from the wind by his bulk, she could have wept as needles of fear pierced her anxiety and drove like stakes into her mind.

A fine, soft rain began to fall, each drop stinging her eyes and cheeks, soaking her hair into wet rattails, despite the shelter she sought beneath his chin. She shivered, bone-cold and exhausted.

It was dusk when, at last, the distant sweep of the stony-blue sea was sighted and the silhouette of the Norman castle reared skywards upon the craggy outline of cliff, jutting starkly here and there as workmen scurried about to complete the building works. Seagulls swooped and wheeled overhead, their cries loud and mournful and Julia's eyes followed them, envying the birds their freedom.

Falk and his Angevins clattered into the castle yard through the North Gate, riding carefully amidst the crowd of William's entourage. Hervi sprang from the saddle before his horse had even come to a halt, and he ran to hold Drago's reins as Falk endeavoured to dismount. But with Julia's limp weight in his arms this was clearly impossible.

'Take her!' Falk ordered, delivering Julia as carefully into the arms of Thierry as he would a babe to its mother.

Then he vaulted down and gave swift orders for the care of the horses and his demand to see Alun and Sander as soon as they arrived. Taking Julia back into his arms, he swept into the castle great hall and carried her to the warmth of the fireside.

It was chaotic inside, to say the least, and there was a great hub-bub of noisy feasting, dogs snarling and yapping, children screaming and running about, but even this mêlée was not enough to rouse Julia from the torpor of her misery.

'Sit there and do not move,' commanded Falk, placing her down in a small gap upon a settle already crowded with a matron and her two daughters. For a brief, worried moment, he glanced at her pale face, framed by limp, wet hair, her expression lifeless, before setting off in search of much-needed food and drink.

Slowly, Julia raised her head and looked around her. She had never seen so many people all in one place, at one time. Their voices rose and fell in a rolling wave of sound, for they talked mainly in French, punctuated here and there by Saxon English, from those who were William's hostages, or newly sworn subjects. She frowned, confused, hating the fact that she could not understand the conversations ebbing and flowing all around her.

Through the crowd she saw a face she recognised. A Norman knight, the one called…she pondered for a moment…he had been the one to rip the girdle from her waist…yes, she remembered now…Gilbert! He smiled at her through the shifting figures and his eyes roved so boldly from her face and downwards that a blush flared across her cheeks. Gilbert raised his goblet in salute and bowed. But Julia did not care for the design of his smile and turned away to stare at the fire flames, too late to see her husband pause by Gilbert de Slevin and exchange sharp words with him. He too had seen the glance that had swept over his wife, but he was far from innocent and knew lust when he saw it.

'Have a care,' warned Falk softly, 'for I am a jealous man.'

Gilbert bowed again, this time with marked deference to Falk. 'Have no fear, for I would not be foolish enough to tamper with anything that had your seal upon it.'

'Fear I do not feel, de Slevin, but I would protect her from the devious games of men.'

'Then I commend you for your chivalry. However, I trust that does not extend to your own bedchamber. I hear William waits anxiously for news of your offspring. Or is she such a child that she spurns your advances?'

'That is no business of yours,' growled Falk, hiding his alarm at the accuracy of Gilbert's barb.

'Nay, indeed. I apologise.' Gilbert's voice was as smooth as silk, yet his eyes feral and cunning like a fox. 'But I would lay a wager that Mathilda drops a sprog long before your virgin bride.' He clapped Falk on the shoulder in a seemingly friendly gesture. 'If the task of getting her with child proves too difficult, let me know. I would gladly take her off your hands.'

Falk clenched his fist, but managed to restrain himself from smashing it into Gilbert's face. He had a vague, uneasy feeling about their conversation and he watched as de Slevin melted away into the crowd, no doubt in search of easier game.

Julia felt a measure of relief as Falk returned, bearing a wooden platter piled with wedges of bread, cheese and sliced cold meat, and in his other hand a pitcher of cool, thirst-quenching mead. She ate delicately, too tired and despondent to be hungry, while Falk stood at her shoulder and tore ravenously into the food, his eyes narrowed with thoughtful speculation as they roamed over the gathering. Rarely were so many powerful men gathered under one roof, an impressive mix of noblemen, clergy and army commanders.

Often his gaze strayed to the main entrance door as he waited for Sander and Alun to arrive and when at last the latter did, soaked to the bone with rain and spattered with mud, Falk demanded savagely, 'And where in hell's teeth have you been?'

At once his knight dropped to one knee, head bowed and fist clenched to his heart in abject apology. Alun did not rise until Falk barked his leave, and then he explained, 'It took some time to persuade Lady Fredeswide to gather my lady's belongings, and then even longer to convince her that she could not join us on the journey. When at last we were under way, we were set upon by thieves.'

Falk stood up straight, flung aside the chunk of bread in his hand, and demanded, 'Where is Sander?'

Alun hung his head. 'My lord, he fought well, and bravely, and even though we could not save most of my lady's belongings, we still have her horse. Sander was sorely wounded. He is in the infirmary, where I have asked the monks to tend his hurts.'

Falk swore. He turned to Julia and explained to her in English what had happened, adding, 'Sit you there and do not wander. I'll be back in a moment.'

Falk strode swiftly away, followed in his wake by the five Angevins, alerted by his exclamation, their departure attracting some attention.

Julia stared, bewildered, as several hounds fought over the scraps Falk had tossed amongst the rushes on the floor. The matron sitting next to her stretched out one plump leg and gave an accurate kick that scattered the dogs with a yelp, and they slunk away to forage beneath the trestle tables. The woman turned to Julia and spoke to her in French, then, realising that she did not understand, in thickly accented English. 'Your husband… leaves?'

'Nay. One of his men has been wounded and he merely goes to see how he fares.' Julia's eyes wandered in the direction Falk had taken, suddenly aware that she had been left all alone.

She remembered that Sander had once been kind to her and she was anxious as to his welfare. Tentatively, she tugged at the matron's sleeve, asking her, 'Do you know where the infirmary is?'

The matron frowned, then she nodded and gestured to the young girl seated next to her. 'My daughter, Alys, will show you.'

With some trepidation Julia followed the Norman maid, thankful that her guide was a tall girl as well built as her mother, who shouldered her way through the crowd growing more noisy and boisterous as drink and high spirits flowed freely. At first Julia was relieved to leave the hall and took solace in the dark quiet shadows of a long corridor, but then, inexplicably, she felt uneasy and hurried to keep pace with Alys. Some moments later, Julia barged into Alys as she came to a sudden halt.

Craning around her broad back, Julia saw that a knight, who was vaguely familiar, blocked their path. He spoke to Alys in French and with a start of alarm Julia recognised his voice and realised that it was Gilbert de Slevin. Clearly he endeavoured to dismiss Alys, and with a shrug and a curious glance at Julia, she hurried away.

Julia glanced past Gilbert, and over one shoulder at the passage behind her, noting at once that they were alone and that she had little idea in which direction to go to gain the relative safety of either the hall or the infirmary. Where was Falk? she wondered. Instinctively, she clenched her fingers together, holding them as a shield to her breast as she raised wary eyes to Gilbert.

He smiled, and spoke to her in French, then with one quick glance over his shoulder he grabbed her elbow and pulled her behind a tapestry-screened alcove.

'What are you doing?' demanded Julia, her heart suddenly slamming painfully hard in her chest. For a wild moment she thought he would try to kiss her...but no, surely he would not dare!

Gilbert clamped his sweaty palm over her mouth, silencing her protest, and thrust her up against the wall. His other hand sought frantically to pull up her skirts, his knee forcing apart her legs. He spoke again, his voice soft yet savage in its threatening tone. Even though she could not understand a single word his meaning was clear enough.

For a brief moment Julia sagged, dizzy with shock, frightened, and then, as she felt his male body press hotly against her hips and his breath came in excited pants on her cheek, she realised that if she did not act quickly, he would do far more than kiss her. In that moment she could not think of how vile his rape would be, but only how Falk would react if he found out.

Terror leant her strength and Julia sank her teeth into the palm that had slackened over her mouth as Gilbert fumbled with the lacings of his chausses. Instantly, he grunted with pain and shot away from its source, giving Julia just a moment in which to duck past him, and run. Her heels pounded on the wooden floors as she flew pell-mell down several corridors, until at last she burst into the light and noise of the great hall.

She chose an unfortunate moment to make her entrance, as a brawl had just erupted between several drunken knights, and barking, snapping dogs only added to the frenzy. She gasped and stumbled as a flying elbow caught her on the side of the head, knocking her backwards, and she would have fallen and been trampled underfoot had not an arm latched about her waist and pulled her clear.

'Where have you been?' asked Falk, sternly, looking down into her flushed face and wide eyes.

Julia felt relief wash over her. Never had she thought to feel so at the sight of him, but now she did not struggle as he half-carried, half-dragged her to a window embrasure and set her steady upon her feet.

'I—I was worried, about Sander, and came to look for you.'

Falk grunted, his glance suspicious, but then he let the matter drop and said, 'Let us find our bed for the night. Tomorrow will be another long day and a hard journey.' Glancing about with a wry smile, he added, 'And the company grows rough now that William has departed for his chamber.'

Demurely, Julia acquiesced and fell into step at his side. 'Is Sander well, my lord?'

'Well enough.' He paused to accept a lighted tallow candle from a servant, but his face was set in a grim mask that discouraged further discussion.

Julia held her tongue, almost running to keep up with his long stride as he led her up stairs and along narrow passages poorly lit by wall sconces.

The castle was so overcrowded that there was scarce enough accommodation for everyone. Most of the knights were billeted in the armoury and stables, while the keep itself did its best to house the unexpected noble numbers. A dormitory, normally for the use of the monks of this new monastery, had been set aside for married couples of lesser rank and it was to this chamber that Falk led Julia.

The shadows were pitch black around the dim light of their tallow candle, but Julia could see that the room was long and narrow, with a row of ten wooden-framed cots on each side. Many were already taken but Falk found one, with their baggage set down atop the mattress by the castle steward, in the farthest corner. She studied the lumpen mattress and felt suddenly sick with such a longing to be safe home at Foxbourne. She stared glumly at her feet, aware of Falk as he set about removing his boots and unbuckling his sword belt. The sword itself he laid beneath the mattress. From his saddle bags he took a blanket and flung it upon the bed, and then himself beneath it, without undressing further.

'Come,' he invited Julia, patting the narrow space still vacant at his side, 'Lie down and sleep.'

Hesitantly, Julia turned and looked at him. There was little space for her slender length and she remarked, ''Tis fortunate for you that I am not overly plump.'

He smiled, white teeth gleaming in the dark. 'Nay, English, 'tis fortunate for *you*. Come now, for I too am weary and will only rest when I know that you lie safely at my side.'

Remembering Gilbert, Julia shivered, sat down, removed her boots and swung her feet up off the floor, lying with her back to him. Falk blew out the light and shrugged under the blanket, apparently soon able to settle down to sleep, while she swallowed hard and blinked back the hot sting in her eyes. For a moment she wondered if she should tell Falk about the assault upon her, and then instantly dismissed the idea; there would be blood spilled and she could not have that upon her conscience. Even now she could scarce believe that the incident had happened at all. It had been so quick, so unexpected. And in all truth and fairness, nothing had been done to her person that could not be easily forgotten.

She stared at the long room full of beds and strangers and listened to the murmur of unfamiliar voices; here and there a laugh, a cough, a sharp tone, a querulous complaint. It was cold too, and smelled rankly of tallow and stale rushes, damp wool and unwashed bodies. She sniffed and rubbed her eyes with her sleeve.

The weight of Falk's arm as he laid it about her waist caused Julia to start, but she did not struggle, nor pull away. With his hand flat against her quivering ribs he drew her close against the heat of his body. She could feel his heart beating against her left shoulder, a strong, steady beat, and his male smell was familiar and of some small comfort.

But still, sleep did not come and she lay awake for a long time. Falk dozed fitfully, alert to her wakefulness. Julia sighed and closed her eyes yet again, willing her brain to fall into sleep's oblivion, but still it refused her bidding. Then a furtive movement caught her eye, and instantly she froze. She heard a moan and noticed the humped-back movements that rocked the timber frame of the bed next to them, only two feet away. With a gasp she realised that the occupants were coupling before her very eyes!

Instinctively, Julia wriggled and rolled over until she faced the broad wall of Falk's chest. Her movements woke him and he opened his eyes, at once noticing about their neighbours the same as Julia. Their movements were now obvious, accompanied by some bodily noises, and Julia raised her hands to cover her ears.

Falk drew the blanket closer about them, his arm shielding her face until she was buried in a protective cocoon. Feeling how she trembled, he leaned down and touched a kiss to her temple, seeking only to offer her comfort, but Julia stiffened and her eyes flew to his face in a hot fury.

'Do not even think to use me so in this hellhole!' she hissed.

'Be calm,' he murmured, 'for I certainly think no such thing. I have no desire to show my rump to those I must dine with or lead into battle and, charming as your charms are, English, I will not avail myself of them in public.' His voice was low and urgent against her ear. 'Now, for the love of God, go to sleep!'

Mollified by his words, Julia settled her head down again. She wriggled and shifted, trying to get comfortable on this most uncomfortable of beds.

'Can you not shift over?' she demanded, 'I scarce have room to breathe.'

'I am on the edge as it is. Come closer, put your head on my shoulder and straighten your legs.'

Following his instructions Julia rearranged her body until she was as comfortable as could be. She could smell his sweat, mingled with the tang of leather and horses and the fresh scent of rain. Her legs were stretched out against the hard bulk of his, leaning on him instead of bent defensively at the knee. She feared that her closeness would arouse him to ardour, but after a while she discerned his heavy breathing and the hint of a snore as he slept deeply, head thrown slightly back.

A man's body is a most curious thing, thought Julia. Every inch of her was aware of his great muscle-sculpted form—the shoulders that towered over her and the large hand on her waist, his long legs. But what aroused her curiosity the most was the area below his hips, now bulging soft and warm against her belly. When he made love to her his manhood was hard against her soft flesh, but now she felt its cylindrical length lying dormant in his groin, soft as her own breasts. She was intrigued to find that his manhood stirred when she nudged her belly against it, moving and growing.

'Wife?'

Julia started at the husky whisper of his voice above her head, and gasped a guilty reply, 'Aye?'

'Are you asking me to lift your skirts?'

'Nay!'

'Then do not press against my shaft in such a fashion, for you will not like the consequences.'

Blushing hotly in the dark Julia stammered to explain, 'I am sorry. I...I was merely curious.'

Falk grunted, amused, exhausted, and frustrated. He inserted an inch of space between them, stifling the wave of desire that his swollen shaft ached to ease within the silk-soft warmth of her body. He forced himself not to think about her, her skin, her scent, the gentle curve of hip and breasts, and fell back into the black depths of sleep.

'Julia?'

She groaned and shrugged off the annoying hand shaking her shoulder.

'Wake up. 'Tis dawn and time to rise.'

Julia moaned again and turned her head into the warm, comfortable pillow of his shoulder, drugged with the heaviness of bone-weary tiredness and too little sleep. Suddenly she was dashed into wakefulness as her pouting lips were captured by a pair of firm male lips, rough stubble scratching her chin. Her eyes flew open and stared into Falk's gleaming black gaze. In retaliation she clenched her teeth and refused his questing tongue entrance, at which impasse he lifted his head and smiled.

'I see now I have your attention.'

She glared at him and grumbled, ''Tis a fine way to greet me good morning.'

'Fine indeed.' He chuckled, and slapped her rump. 'Now, lift your arse and put on your boots, for there is much work to be done if we are to shift this menagerie from England's shores to Normandy.'

Julia sat up slowly, rubbing her eyes and stretching cramped limbs. All around them others were waking and dressing. She was careful to keep her back turned to their adjacent neighbours, for she did not think she could face them in the broad light of day. Looking up, she encountered Falk's eye and he could not hide his grin as he observed her blush and guessed her thoughts.

Hastily, Julia bent to retrieve her boots from the floor and tug them on. Then she tidied her hair with her fingers and plaited the mass into a single neat braid. It was not a long rope of hair; it would still be many months before her hair regained its former glory well below her hips. Glancing resentfully at Falk as he leaned one forearm against the wall and stared broodingly out of the narrow wall slit at the ships bobbing in the harbour below the cliff, she wondered if he still possessed the severed length of her hair.

At the moment, however, this was the least of her worries. She felt the pressing need of her bladder to be relieved and her eyes wandered desperately about the crowded chamber.

Seeing her expression Falk asked, 'What is it?'

''Tis…naught.'

'Tell me.' He came then and knelt on one knee at her feet, looking up into her bowed face. ''Tis time you trusted me, Julia, for I am your husband and 'tis my duty to care for you. No one else will.'

'That fact had not escaped me.' Julia sighed. 'If you must know, I have need of the garderobe.'

'Is that all?' He offered her his hand. 'Come, I too have a need. We shall find it together.'

They left the dormitory and went out into the passage. Julia had to admit to herself that she was glad of his tall presence at her side, her fingers ensconced within the safety of his large, strong hand. He led her down gloomy corridors and narrow spirals of stairs and, remembering the fearsome quarrels of the knights on the evening before, and the lurking presence of Gilbert, Julia did not complain at the possession of his grip.

Squires, ladies' maids and castle serfs ran hither and thither in attendance to the many lords and ladies seeking to make their ablutions and don their finery. Julia did not hold out much hope of finding a bowl of water and a cloth for herself, but miraculously Falk obtained both and she was glad to wash her face and hands and arms; the rest would have to wait until such time as there was more privacy. As it was they stood in a dark alcove near the reeking garderobe and conditions were surprisingly spartan, Julia considered wryly, for a king's castle. Somehow she had always imagined great luxury and comfort at the court of a king.

Downstairs in the great hall Falk found them a place at one of the crowded trestle tables and they sat down to break their fast on spartan fare much the same as the night before—bread, cheese and ale. Julia thought longingly of Foxbourne and curd cheese tarts, bacon and hot milk.

Falk still chewed when one of William's courtiers leaned over his shoulder and whispered in his ear. Wiping his mouth with the back of his hand he rose from the bench and said to Julia, 'I will see you later. Stay in the hall until 'tis time to leave for the harbour.'

She looked up quickly, her eyes wide and making no pretence to hide her anxious concern. 'Where are you going?'

He smiled slightly. 'To work.' After hesitating a brief moment, he bent his head and kissed her on the lips, entirely pleased with the novelty of her subdued uncertainty.

Julia watched her husband walk away through the crowd. She noticed that he was certainly a head taller than most men, and quite the most broad shouldered. She did not like the way several ladies twisted their heads or glanced covertly sidelong, and she realised that she was not the only female to notice how very handsome was her husband. This stirred an emotion within her she did not like, which was entirely new to her, and she angled a severe glance at several ladies.

Falk's progress was hampered by the many people who stopped him with a greeting, a question, or just a clap on the shoulder. Apparently her husband was both well liked and highly trusted. This knowledge only served to remind Julia how alone she was, the Saxon wife who spoke no French, gifted to Falk de Arques in wedlock as easily as she had given the servants their Christmas gewgaws.

Had she but known, she was not alone, for Falk had stopped to speak to his Angevin, Piers, and detailed him to be Julia's bodyguard in his absence. Piers leaned discreetly against a pillar at her back, idly picking his fingernails with the lethal point of his dagger, but his eyes ever sharp and watchful of her slim form and bright hair.

Crumbling a crust of bread, Julia longed to escape from the dark, stuffy hall, the incomprehensible chatter, but Falk had bade her stay. Rising from her place, Julia walked slowly to an arrow slit and squinted out at the bright gleam of the sun on a silver sea. She watched seagulls arc and wheel in the blue sky, for it was a clear day, even if the wind did blow and chop at the lapping waters of the Narrow Sea.

Such a yearning for freedom came over Julia that it throbbed and ached within the confines of her chest. If only she could just wander out of the door and walk away. She imagined herself walking down the hill and how her legs would gather speed and she would run…run…run home to Foxbourne.

No one seemed to pay her the slightest attention. Her glance slid to the imposing arch of the open entrance door. She glimpsed the courtyard beyond, horses, the sky, and the castle walls…freedom beckoned as tempting and tantalising as a shiny apple upon the Forbidden Tree. And then her eyes met with a pair of eyes as blue as her own, and she recognised the Angevin, Piers by name, who straightened up from his lounging stance and sheathed his dagger. His glance was as binding as a gaoler's ball and chain.

Hope was crushed. The dream burst like a soap bubble and she knew that there could be no escape. A moment later a shadow fell over her, blotting out the light of day, and Julia looked up into the sombre face of Falk. She had no doubt that he had seen written upon her own face, as plain as any parchment map, the route she so desperately desired to follow.

Falk looked upon the tension etched in every taut line of Julia's lips and jaw, the obvious glint of defiance shadowed by uncertainty that darkened her eyes. His hand clasped her shoulders and pulled her none too gently towards him in the parody of an embrace. Lowering his mouth to her ear he murmured, 'You would be wise to remember, English, that whatever your feelings for our marriage, there is much beyond the safety of my arms that would seek to harm you.'

Julia had no opportunity to answer, as a commanding voice rang out, 'Come now, my good knight, time enough later to fondle with your bride!'

William swept past them, borne on the gust of his ceaseless energy and the mob of people ever at his side, clapping Falk on the shoulder in passing and breaking apart their apparent embrace. Amidst a chorus of laughter Falk and Julia were swept from the hall and out into the bright, windblown day.

Chapter Eight

Julia stood at the port side of the ship and wrapped Falk's cloak more tightly about her as the chill March wind cut into her body. She watched England's shoreline fade into a smudge of lavender blue on the receding horizon and her eyes swept all around, her vision filled with the cloud-strewn sky and grey sea and the white sails of the fleet of ships that ploughed valiantly through the scudding waves.

She was thankful that she was at least dry, for Falk had carried her aboard with great care and easy strength, whilst some of the other, plumper, ladies had been less fortunate and dropped in the soaking surf as their bearers had staggered beneath the weight of their burdens.

On the wind she heard the snort and shriek of horses transported in several of the following ships; she thought that a particularly angry, piercing snort might be that of Drago and could well imagine that proud beast experiencing the same discomfort as she did. Looking over her shoulder, she spied her husband engaged in deep conversation with several Norman knights, and had no doubt they were discussing their favourite topic—war. She had come to the conclusion that these Normans were fearsome men who enjoyed a life of fighting and conquering far more than her own amiable, hearth-bound Saxon folk.

It was with an aching sense of sadness that Julia realised that her family and her homeland were now both far away and there was no place in the future when she could imagine seeing either again. Resentment at this enforced separation bit hard into her heart and she could not contain the glower in her eyes as she stared at the man she was now bound to for her lifetime, and his. She must go where he went, and live where he lived, and dance to his tune when he clapped his hands…well…we shall see, thought Julia, determined that she would have a marriage far different from her parents.

The weather deteriorated rapidly and she sought shelter beneath the awnings at the rear of the ship. The pitch of the deck moved with an alarming tilt and Julia began to feel a most peculiar sensation float up from her belly, a strange dizziness, and a sweat of panic soaked her palms and beaded her forehead.

Falk came to her side with a napkin of food and a flagon of wine, offering it to her in silence. The smell stung her nostrils. Suddenly her stomach heaved and she stumbled to find some place to empty its contents, barging into Falk in her haste.

'What ails you, English?' he demanded, wiping a splash of wine from his tunic.

'I am ill!' A great wave of nausea assaulted her senses and she cried out with alarm, 'I am dying!'

Falk laughed, earning himself a furious glare, and helped her to the ship's side, holding her head over as she vomited into the churning sea, ''Tis naught but seasickness. For a moment I thought—'

'Thought what?' Julia wiped her mouth on the cloak's hem and stared up at him, with huge eyes and a pale face.

His glance slid away, embarrassed, but when she persisted he answered, 'That mayhap you were with child.'

Her mouth formed a circle of surprise.

'Does the thought of a babe so revolt you?' he asked, noting her expression.

'Nay, Norman, for I am fond of children. 'Tis only the thought of my babe being born in Normandy that so revolts me.'

His sharp intake of breath was enough to tell her she had well and truly stung him with her barb, as she never had before. For a moment, seeing the black look upon his face, she feared that he would strike her and she shrank back from his anger. Without a further word he turned on his heel and strode away, leaving her slumped and retching against the ship's high wooden side.

Truly, Julia felt no joy in that moment and she wished she could take the unkind words back. But such a feat was as impossible as plucking a star from the sky and could not be done. Her mind was fractured and set apart with a bitterness that was as sour as the taste in her mouth. She thought to go to him and make apology but, watching him, with his comrades, laughing, ignoring her, she had not the courage and stayed where she was. Instead, she slid slowly to the deck and lay there in a crumpled heap, looking up at the cloudy sky and praying to God, to Jesus, to Mother Mary and all the angels and saints that this journey would soon be over. Now and then she staggered to her feet to retch, but her stomach was empty and there was little relief.

It was late in the afternoon when the coast of Normandy was spotted and William's fleet of ships sailed into the harbour of St Valery-sur-Somme. The Normans exclaimed with joy and eagerness, the Saxons watched and waited in wary silence. Julia hung back, merging into the shadows of the covered deck, whilst the others made ready to disembark. She was reluctant to leave this ship now, for it seemed to be her only link with invisible England. But leave it she must, and when the ship was beached on the sandy shoals Falk appeared to take her ashore.

Without demur, for indeed she felt weak from a full day of illness, and contrite for her cruel words, she let Piers pick her up and hand her over the side of the ship into the waiting arms of her husband. They handled her as though she were nought but a feather and Julia had no moment to fear the exchange, for quickly she passed from deck to Piers to Falk and he splashed through the wavelets that soaked his boots and leather chausses.

Julia linked her arms around his neck and looked at his face, so close to her own. His eyes were very black, fringed with dark lashes. His nose was perfectly straight, nostrils slightly flared in a way that reminded her of Drago, his lean jaw stubbled darkly as he had not shaved for these two days past, and his mouth…

'What do you stare at?' he asked harshly, looking straight ahead.

Julia blushed and bit back her retort. Enough had been said by her quick tongue for one day and now she held on to it.

'Silence, eh?' He shot her a fierce glance, and wondered what thoughts, what devious schemes, lay behind her pretty blue eyes.

Striding out of the fetters of the low sea biting at his ankles, Falk dropped her quickly upon her feet and Julia grabbed at his tunic to steady herself as her knees buckled weakly. He caught her elbows and set her more firmly, puzzled by the bruised look that she lifted to his frowning gaze. Then, without a word spoken between them, he turned away and went to assist with the unloading of other ladies, armour, baggage and, finally, the horses.

Julia sat for hours upon the beach. Falk paused only once, for a brief moment, to tell her they would pitch tents and make camp, as the day had vanished and there was no more light to continue their journey. A mile inland they found a sheltered field with a running freshwater stream. The knights were seasoned campaigners and lived much of their lives under canvas, on the trail from one battle, siege or royal tournament to another. Some of them had their own women to tend to the mundane chores of cooking, cleaning, sewing torn garments, but not the Angevins, as Falk did not permit them to keep women, although he frequently turned a blind eye to the procured services of camp followers.

Watching the flurry of activity, Julia realised that she was completely helpless and of little use; she had never been required to cook a meal, and had certainly never carried buckets of water from a stream, nor scrubbed out three-legged iron pots.

The Angevins put up tents, with a few grunts and much silent, efficient elbow grease. Sander gestured to her as he held back the pale cream canvas flap of one tent, smaller than the other two, and threw down a pile of furs and sheepskins upon the groundsheet. Laying his hands palm to palm against his cheek, he indicated that this was where she would sleep. Julia rose with an effort from the rock she sat upon and all but floated on weightless legs to the tent, ducking beneath the portal of the low opening and gratefully sinking on to the comfortable pile of furs.

She lay down and watched through exhausted, half-closed eyes as Piers and Luc found wood and built a fire in the midst of the three tents, such that it would both light and warm each one, a welcome comfort despite the acrid stink of smoke and the flutter of ashes. By the time Falk returned with the other three Angevins and all their own horses, a pottage of rabbit, worts, and onions bubbled away in a gravy of thick red wine. The smell of it made her feel sick and, spotting Falk approaching with an indignantly snorting Drago, she crept deeper into the gloom of the tent.

Julia dozed for a short while, still fully dressed and wrapped in the comfort of her borrowed cloak. Darkness had fallen when she woke and she stirred, propping her cheek on one hand to stare through the loose flap of the tent opening at the fragmented shapes of the men passing to and fro.

Sander came and offered to her a chunk of bread hollowed out and filled with rabbit stew, but with a grimace she refused and waved him away, accepting only a hornful of wine. He returned to the campfire, leaning down to show Falk that the meal had been rejected. Falk glanced over his shoulder at her, shrugged and calmly proceeded to eat the food himself. Throughout the evening he did not come himself and speak to her. Julia could hear the deep voices of the seven men gathered about the crackling fire, their occasional laughter interspersed with the masculine habits of coughing and spitting. In the background were the sounds of similar campfire gatherings; the distant, reedy music of a lute and thump-thump of a drum, as some still found the energy to dance, and the horses tethered on a long line of rope added their own chorus of snorting, whickering and stamping.

Julia lay back and closed her eyes. Even in the dark and at a distance she could pick out the deep timbre of Falk's voice, but she could not understand a word as he spoke in French.

Again, that aching sense of loneliness and anguished longing to be safe home at Foxbourne came over Julia, and she knew with dreadful certainty that such a feeling would be with her forever, like an incurable ailment. As the hot tears trickled from her eyes, she stuffed her knuckles into her mouth, turned her face into the muffling pile of a sheepskin and sobbed until her head ached.

The fire was banked up to ward off the chill of night and Hervi had procured a cask of strong apple brandy from a merchant of the Seine-Maritime district. They made extravagant toasts to celebrate their homecoming, and loudly proclaimed their pride, with exaggerated tales of bravery and skill, to be amongst the men who were both survivors and victors of a great battle that would forever be known as the Battle of Hastings.

It was late when Falk stumbled into their tent and noisily unbuckled his sword belt, dropping both sword and dagger with a thud upon the floor that woke Julia from her uneasy sleep. He sat down and pulled off his boots before his tunic and shirt, and then he struggled with undignified clumsiness and rude curses to remove his chausses.

Julia sat up and stared at him accusingly in the fire-lit gloom, exclaiming, 'You're drunk!'

He glanced at her for a moment, before replying sharply, 'Pray do not preach, for I have little patience for any more of your moaning.' He sat down with a thump. 'Besides, I am not drunk. I have been drinking, aye, but I am far from drunk. What is wrong with that, anyway? Do English men not enjoy the pleasures of the vine? Or are English men much the same as English women, and care not at all for anything that gives the body pleasure?'

She gasped at his words, knowing full well his meaning. She had resisted all his attempts at courtship, and she always pretended that his lovemaking was endured, not enjoyed. What did this man want from her? she thought angrily, observing his clumsy attempts to undress, which belied his denial of intoxication. With a grunt Falk wrestled with his chausses in an effort to free his legs from their company, his feet ever catching and causing him to slide sideways. Julia folded her lips on a smile and swallowed back a giggle, for truly he did look ridiculous.

'If you are not drunk, my lord, then it must be exhaustion that makes you struggle like a babe to undress,' she could not resist commenting drily, her head propped on one palm as she watched him.

'Well, do not just sit there, wife, help me!'

With a sigh Julia knelt forwards and gingerly tugged at the fabric, then, at his harsh, impatient criticism of her feeble efforts, she gave several sharp tugs of the offending garment that quickly freed his legs.

Her fingertips touched him and she felt the solid weight of his calf muscle and the hairs covering his skin. Her fingers seemed to burn at the contact and quickly she snatched them away, looking warily up at him. He was staring at her as though she were an apparition risen from a misty lake, and Julia glanced nervously over her shoulder.

'What?' she asked. 'See you something, my lord?'

He rubbed one hand over his eyes, for to look at her all soft and rumpled from sleep sorely tested his self-discipline. ''Tis naught. Lie down and go back to sleep.'

Julia shuffled back to her makeshift bed and lay down, but sleep would not come. She stared at the black giant shadows dancing on canvas, at the faint glimmer of the campfire, round which still sat Hervi and Piers, talking softly and seriously to each other. The wind rose then and even they sought their beds, kicking out the fire into a smoky mound of ashes and leaving Julia in the dark—a terrible, frightening, lonely dark.

Behind her she heard Falk grunt as he relaxed into sleep, and then his faint snores. She shivered as the hollow howl of the wind found its way through even the tiniest gap and the ground's insidious chill crept up to seep into the warmth of the sheepskins upon which she lay.

After a while she could bear it no longer and she sat up to search for more covers, convinced that Falk had taken more than his fair share. In the dark her fingers spread tentatively in their quest.

She encountered Falk's sword, propped against his saddlebags, knocking it sideways with a clang on to his shield.

At once Falk woke. His bulk reared up in the dark, his hand reaching instinctively for his weapons and found instead Julia's unsteady wrist. 'What is it?'

'I...I merely seek more covers.'

'Are you cold?' His voice was sleep-rough, almost angry.

'Aye. I am not a soldier used to sleeping in fields.'

'Come. 'Tis warm enough where I lie.'

Julia hesitated, tempted by the inviting warmth of his body, yet equally cautious of his nakedness.

'Fear not,' he murmured coldly, 'I seek no payment for the warm bed I offer.'

In the dark Julia felt the rawness of her blush stain both neck and cheeks. Yet her cold hands and feet reminded her that it would be a long and uncomfortable night if she did not accept. On her knees she crawled over and crept into the warm nest of furs that he held open and lay down beside him, only to jerk upright as he snorted his displeasure.

'Take off your garments! You cannot sleep in clothes that are damp. 'Tis no wonder you are cold. Spread them out so they may dry by morning.'

Awkwardly, resentfully, Julia struggled out of her kirtle, but kept on her shift.

'God's teeth, English! You surely do not intend to sleep with your boots on?'

'Aye,' she answered stubbornly, 'they will help to keep my feet warm.'

'Take them off! And your hose, for I mislike their scratchy feel.'

Again, Julia sat up and reached down to unlace her boots and pull them off, tossing them aside with a clunk, her lower lip jutting in rebellion at his arrogance. She hesitated a moment too long to remove her hose and his sharp voice made her jump as he commanded, 'Make haste! Half the night is already gone and tomorrow will be a long hard journey too soon begun with too little sleep.'

'Well, 'twas not I who stayed up drinking,' grumbled Julia under her breath, rolling down her hose and digging her toes with a delicious delight into the soft, spongy wool of the sheepskins.

'What say you?' He pulled the covers over their shoulders.

'I say nothing, Norman.'

'Then there must be three of us in this tent, for I swear I heard a voice.'

'I will not parley with a drunkard.'

He growled, a low warning sound of displeasure, and Julia bit down hard on her tongue as Falk muttered something about vixens and the taming thereof. He found he was now fully awake and aware of her, of the feel of her silky limbs and soft bosom, the swirl of her hair. They lay close, side by side, but not in each other's arms. Her hands were clasped as though in prayer and held close to her heart, whilst he lay with one hand under his neck and the other tucked against his chest, careful that no part of her touched him.

It was the accidental brush of her nipple against the corded muscle of his forearm that stirred him, the tiny bud so soft and delicate against his male strength. He felt a rush of heat to his loins and her gasp informed him that he was betrayed, yet he spoke without stirring or opening his eyes.

'Rest easy, English. You will learn that it takes little to awaken a man's shaft.'

With a grunt and a groan Falk turned over, away from temptation, and forced himself to sink back into the oblivion of sleep.

The moaning of the wind rose to a keen pitch, and there came the flash of lightning and the distant rumble of thunder. Julia lay tensely, listening. As the storm approached and a clap of thunder burst from the sky above them she could not subdue her fright and turned to clutch at Falk. Her fingers fastened on the bulging biceps of his upper arm, the broad wall of his back towering above her. As she lay pressed against him his words came to mind—*I seek no payment for the warm bed I offer.*

An insidious thought slithered into the garden of her mind. More than anything she wanted to go home, to England, to Foxbourne. What stood between her and that dream was this man. Would he not be more willing to give her whatever she wanted if he was a man well pleased, and what would please him the most? She need ponder only for a moment to reach that answer, for it seemed that men were oft led about not by the nose but by their loins. It seemed to her that caution and logic could be overturned in a moment if it interfered with a man's lust, and Julia suspected that lust was indeed man's most powerful emotion.

She knew he desired her, and took pleasure in her body. If that was all he wanted from her, thought Julia with a small shock at her own ruthlessness, what harm could there be in giving it to him? Had not Ulric often told her that more flies could be caught with honey than with vinegar?

Julia slowly, so slowly, unclenched her hands and laid them flat against the hot, taut skin of his back. She waited, her breath anxiously held, but nothing happened. She wriggled closer, until her breasts touched him and she tucked her knees into the back of his thighs, the soft sole of her foot stroking the length of his calf, the sprinkle of hairs tickling her.

Falk woke. He opened his eyes carefully, aware of the small hand that had slid around him and pressed against the flat, hard planes of his chest.

'God's teeth, English, sleeping with you is like sleeping with a sackful of stoats. Lie still, now!'

He removed her hand, pushed back her knees with his elbow and swallowed a groan as he felt his shaft awaken. He moved away from her, and then stilled as she followed. Again her hand crept so lightly over his ribs and laid itself against the heavy, bunched muscle of his midriff. He drew a sharp, steadying breath, confused, and almost flinched as he felt the touch of her lips between his shoulder blades.

'What mischief is this?' he demanded harshly.

Julia froze, and could find no words of explanation.

'I may be foolish enough to think that you wish to perform a wifely duty.'

She struggled to find her voice, but managed to whisper, 'You are no fool, my lord, and as I am your wife, I know…my duty.'

'Indeed?' He laughed, but it was not a pleasant sound. 'You astound me, English.'

Falk turned over then and Julia steeled herself, resisting the strong temptation to clutch at the flimsy protection of her shift. In the dark his hands reached out and found her waist, jerking her roughly to him.

'I know not what game you play, but for the moment I like it!'

He bent over her and found her lips, his kiss fierce and hungry. With one hand he reached down and found the hem of her shift, pushing it up her legs.

'Take this thing off!' he ordered, his voice husky and a little breathless as he felt a heady rush of desire flood him. He took a deep breath, steadying himself while Julia shrugged off her shift and he tossed it to one side. The feel of her naked body made him gasp with pleasure, his fingertips exploring her velvet skin, pressing into the soft flesh of her hips, the slender curve of her ribs, before encountering the swell of her small but delightful breasts. Eagerly he bent his head and caressed one nipple with his tongue. She gave a small cry and he felt her body stiffen beneath him, the heels of her palms digging into his chest as she tried to force him back. He remembered then that she was ignorant of the pleasures of bedsport and he vowed this time to teach her. His mouth softened and caressed more gently, while Falk made an effort not to hurt or frighten her with his haste.

He slid his hand over her belly and found the mound of crisp curls between her clenched thighs. Already his body felt hot and sheened with sweat, but he noted that she was cool. The fact that she would not open her thighs for him he put down to maidenly shyness, and he used his knee to persuade them apart. But his every touch was met with her rigid reluctance and he slowly came to a halt, lying still in the circle of her arms, one curved about his neck and the other around his back in a parody of embrace.

After a long moment of this stillness and silence, Julia asked, 'Is aught amiss, my lord?'

He considered his reply carefully. 'You approach me with the ardour of a courtesan, and then lie beneath me cold and stiff like a marble statue.'

Julia gasped. 'My lord is sorely mistaken.'

'Am I? And for God's sake, cease with this ''my lord''. My name is Falk.' Impatiently his fingers twisted in her hair, forcing her face towards him, wishing to God that he could see her expression in the dark. 'Do you want me, Julia?'

Again she gasped, her body pressed up against his, his sheer maleness almost overwhelming her with his size and his strength. In a whisper she replied, remembering her plans for the future, 'Aye.'

'Aye, what? Say my name, tell me you want me!'

'Aye, Falk. I want you.'

If Julia could have seen his face she would have been afraid of the thunderous frown that clouded his brows and the black, furious expression in his eyes.

'You do not lie well, my lady.' With a sigh he set her away from him. 'I will not play your devious game, whatever that might be. Come to me willingly, or not at all, for I have little desire for a wife who complains at my every touch.'

Julia remained silent. His hands slid from her hips and found her wrists, where her palms lay flat and defensive against his chest. He held them firmly, his large fingers completely encircling their slenderness.

'Mayhap you thought to tempt me with your sweet body and then...strike! A dagger between my ribs?' he asked, softly.

'Nay! I did not think along such lines.'

'Ah, then you admit that it was not an overwhelming desire for your husband that drove you to wake me?'

'You have naught to complain about, Norman. You would have had what you wanted, and for free. I would say that a wife is a convenience that would put most whores out of business.'

He laughed then, charmed by her naivety. 'There is always a market for whores, and judging by your *wifely* performance this night, I am not surprised. It has been my experience that this act that you find so repulsive is greatly enjoyed by both ladies and whores.'

Julia flounced her shoulder away from him, her mouth set in an angry pout. 'Then Godspeed, my lord.'

'Nay, sweet little wife—' he set her several inches away from him and shrugged down under the covers '—I see the error of my ways these months past. William waits impatiently for news that you are with child. When we reach Rouen we will make every effort to oblige our king. But for tonight, lest I be accused of rape in my eagerness, I shall indulge in nothing more than sleep. Goodnight, English.'

He said the latter with such finality that Julia did not dare to argue. Inexplicably, she felt ashamed of her dirty trick. She had teased him, offering herself on a platter, and he could have taken her, without thought or care. But he had not, and she knew that had not been easy for him, knowing how he enjoyed— Here she blushed scarlet in the dark and refused to remember the times when he had made love to her at Foxbourne. How hard it had been to appear cool and detached, as though it meant nothing at all, when she had felt like screaming and tearing at him as hot, elusive desire had tormented her. She stared at his broad back in the dark, and let the rhythm of his steady breathing ease her into sleep.

* * *

The sweet, pungent smell of grass and damp earth woke Julia, and the cold empty space beside her. The faint light of early morning brightened the pale canvas roof over her head, and the tentative twitters of birds greeting the dawn reached her ears and stirred her into wakefulness.

Julia sat up, felt the cool air upon her naked breasts, and remembered, with a jolt that quite took her breath away, that she had slept naked against him all night. She blushed, a rosy hue spreading over her cheeks, for there had been a moment when she had felt a spark, a moment she had wanted to abandon all resistance and yield to him and his big body covering hers. The feel of his muscles, the rub of his hair-rough thighs against hers and the hot, velvet hardness of his shaft against her hip... Julia gasped and pressed her palms to both cheeks, scolding herself for such shameful and lewd thoughts.

Quickly she reached for her clothes and donned them, hoping to find Sander and persuade him to beg, borrow or steal a bowl of warm water in which she could wash.

Lifting the tent flap she found only Piers, squatting by the fire, cleaning the blade of his sword in an enthusiastic fashion. Knowing that he could understand no word of English Julia tugged at his sleeve and mimed washing her face. His cool blue eyes swept over her, and then he grinned know-

ingly in such a way that Julia felt her palms itch
with an urge to slap him. But she held her temper
and followed the aim of his pointing finger. Seeing
her puzzled frown, he sheathed his sword and rose
to stride briskly towards the trees behind them.

Julia trotted after him, hesitating for a moment
as she glanced over one shoulder to the safety of
the sprawling camp. Piers waited, then gestured for
her to hurry. She followed him into the dark green
shade of the trees, her footfalls muffled by the
mossy ground and the sharp smell of damp oak
and elm in her nose. They came to the banks of a
stream and Julia realised, with a shock, that she
was expected to wash in the water gently rippling
over a bed of pebbles and large stones.

'Nay, I cannot wash here!' Julia protested. ''Tis
freezing cold!'

Eyeing her impassively Piers shrugged and
turned to return the way they had come.

'Wait!'

The grime collected from travelling forced her
to accept whatever primitive conditions were on
offer and, having gestured for Piers to turn his
back, she crept further up the bank and chose a
sheltered spot between a clump of bushes. She
found a handkerchief in her kirtle pocket and used
this to wash her face and arms, gasping at the
shock of winter water upon her skin. But the water

was both sweet and clear and Julia drank thirstily from her cupped hand.

Shivering, glancing furtively about, she hitched up her skirts and tucked them into her belt before removing her boots and hose and stepping gingerly into the flow of the running water. It was not deep, coming to just above her ankles, but so cold her breath was quite snatched away. Clenching her teeth, Julia crouched down and washed.

Just then a movement on the far bank caught Julia's eye and instinctively a scream burst from her mouth as she saw a man stood there staring boldly at her. Quickly she lowered her skirts, soaking the hems in her haste, and she leapt out of the water and on to the bank in one swift, agile movement. Before her feet even touched the ground Piers had arrived, crashing through the undergrowth and his sword flashing as he drew it from the scabbard at his waist. He asked her a question in French, but his meaning was clear and Julia pointed a shaking finger at the trees.

'A man! He was watching me!'

Piers scanned the far bank but could see nothing and he checked all around them before slowly sheathing his sword and urging Julia to finish putting on her hose and boots. His hand clamped around her upper arm and he escorted her back to the camp, knowing that if anything happened to this girl he had been set to guard, then Falk would surely slice his head from his shoulders.

The smoky fire crackling outside their cluster of tents was never so welcome and Julia knelt down to warm her hands, teeth chattering with both cold and fright. Piers poured her a hornful of wine and she sipped it slowly, grimacing at the strong taste before setting it aside. Her stomach grumbled with hunger and she was wondering what there was to eat when Falk and his men came thundering up on their horses.

As her eyes met her husband's across the fire Julia felt the hot stain of a flush rise up her neck. Her eyes dropped quickly from his intimate smile. Then she risked a quick, peeking glance, noting that Piers had waylaid him and she saw how his smile vanished and his face was now grim with anger. His dark eyes flashed from Julia to the tree-tops beyond the tents. She looked down at her hands, held out to the low flicker of flames in an unsteady fashion, aware that Falk strode rapidly towards her and dropped to one knee at her side.

'Good morning, wife.'

Julia murmured a reply, but did not look up, keenly aware of his hard stare as he studied her profile.

'Piers tells me that you were frightened by a man spying on you at the stream.'

She bit her lip. ''Tis naught. He did not a thing.'

'What were you doing?' he persisted. 'Bathing? Were you…naked?'

'Nay, not entirely.'

'What does that mean?'

'Oh, please, do not embarrass me so!'

Falk grabbed her chin between his thumb and forefinger and jerked her head up, forcing her to look at him. 'I will know what this is about and you will tell me! No man stares at my wife's body and gets away with it!'

''Twas but a moment—'

'No matter! Were you washing above your skirts or below?'

She shot him a bold, defiant look. 'Below.'

Falk cursed viciously. 'Would you know this man if you saw him again?'

'Aye. I have seen him before this morn. He is the one who stole my keys.'

It took only a moment for his brain to work out her meaning. 'Gilbert de Slevin! That son of a bitch!' There was a hollow ring of amazed disbelief in his voice.

'At Hastings Castle he…' Julia hesitated, surprised by the words that had just leapt from her lips, but her instincts were now beyond all caution and sought only self-preservation. 'He tried to kiss me.'

'What!' The word exploded from Falk and Julia was both relieved and frightened that she had confessed this tale, albeit watered down.

At once Falk released her and rose to his feet. In a blind rage, white-hot in its fury, he ran to Drago and vaulted upon his back, spurring him away to find the cause of his anger and his wife's shame. Hervi and Thierry followed, whilst the others closed ranks about Julia and waited watchfully, Piers filling them in on the reason for Falk's sudden departure.

It did not take him long to find his quarry, skulking near William's tent. Falk leapt down from his horse and drew back his sword arm to smash his fist into Gilbert de Slevin's face, all in one rapid move, all thought of reason and wisdom having flown on the wings of his outrage.

Standing over the fallen body of a bloody-nosed Gilbert, sprawled upon the dewy grass, Falk snarled, 'I have told you before, de Slevin, you take an unhealthy interest in my wife. See that in future you do not come within a dozen paces of her, or I will slit your carcass from end to end and rip out your balls!'

The fracas had gathered a small crowd of interested on-lookers and even William now emerged from his tent and enquired, with some annoyance,

'What goes on here? 'Tis a fine beginning to the day to find my knights brawling.'

Falk bowed to his king and said, ''Tis no brawl, sire, 'tis a matter of honour. I am told that Gilbert de Slevin has spied upon my wife as she bathed.'

'I see. 'Tis a serious accusation. What say you, de Slevin?'

Gilbert was now rising to his knees and he wiped the dribble of blood from his nose with the back of his hand. 'He's lying, sire! I was nowhere near his wife!'

A malevolent look passed between the two antagonists.

'And why would Falk make such a false accusation?' asked William with narrowed eyes.

Gilbert shrugged, snatching a kerchief from his hovering squire and dabbing at his battered face. 'Mayhap his wife has been making eyes at me behind his back.'

'You bastard!' Falk leapt, his arm lifting to deliver another blow, but others restrained him on the command of William.

'Your wife,' mused William, in a quandary with this delicate situation, 'she is the red-haired vixen from Foxbourne?'

'Aye, sire, she is.'

'And you are sure of her fidelity?'

'She would not make eyes at any man for she is…timid in that direction.' Falk was loath to air in public the private difficulties of his marriage.

'Mayhap 'tis women she prefers,' muttered Gilbert, just loud enough to be heard.

Falk lunged again and was held back again, but his furious eyes betrayed how he longed to beat de Slevin to a pulp.

'Curb your tongue, de Slevin,' William commanded sharply, 'I will not have my knights squabbling over a woman, and a Saxon one at that. Henceforth let there be no more trouble between you two, for you are comrades-in-arms and I would not like to punish you both and banish you to the northern borders of England to fight the worst of my wars. But I will, if I have to. Now, be gone, for I am anxious to be in Rouen with my own vixen of a wife.'

William's smile encouraged a burst of weak laughter that broke the tension and the onlookers melted away, seeing that there would be no more drama to enjoy.

Falk shot de Slevin a look that carried a weight of warning and then he turned his back and mounted Drago. As he rode away he had a nasty feeling that made the vulnerable spot between his shoulder blades itch.

* * *

Julia sat upon a three-legged wooden stool. Gratefully she ate the dried apricots, honey and warm bread that Sander had managed to procure for her, washing it all down with milk so fresh that it still frothed; she suspected that it had been stolen from a cow munching innocently in a nearby field.

She smiled her thanks as Sander took away the mug and she brushed crumbs from her skirt, sighing and feeling almost human again. Idly she set about combing her hair with her fingers and braiding it into one single rope that hung over her shoulder. She was almost finished when Falk returned, and she paused, watching as he dismounted. But he neither spoke to her nor gave anyone explanation and Hervi cautioned them with a frown and a small shake of his head not to torment Falk with questions.

With expert and swift efficiency the camp was broken down and Julia exclaimed with pleasure when her grey palfrey, Snow, was brought to her. She stroked the mare's soft pink and white nose, remembering the many times they had ridden together along the coast of England, across the River Bourne and the meadows that led to her home. She felt comforted by the mare, a link to her mother, who had given her Snow as a birthday gift four summers ago.

Falk came and lifted her up into the saddle, his glance resting on her face for just a moment. She thought she saw a question there and opened her mouth to speak to him, but quickly he turned away and mounted Drago. Without ceremony they set off on the road to Rouen.

Julia looked about her curiously and noted that the countryside was less rugged than her own English land. Almost delicate in its pretty villages and tidy fields, it was warmer here than across the Narrow Sea and there were grape vines and trees already frothy with apple blossom. But she had little chance to take note of her surroundings, as Snow was unsettled by her recent transport by ship and unnerved by the nipping, lusty presence of Drago.

Julia tried her best to settle the mare, patting her neck, talking to her softly and taking a firm hand on the reins. But her constant jibbing and sideways prancing made Julia's arms ache and became such a trial that she exclaimed to Falk, 'Can you not take that beast elsewhere? His interest in my mare is making it impossible for me to ride her.'

'Indeed? Mayhap Drago has fallen in love with her.'

Julia snorted as loudly as her horse. 'I feel sure 'tis not love he seeks.'

'Is it not?'

She looked up quickly at his tone, at his penetrating gaze, aware that he had been most silent and brooding all the morn. In the next instant Julia was plucked from Snow's back and her rump landed on Falk's thigh and saddlebow.

'You are forever removing the ground from beneath my feet!' complained Julia bitterly, her arms perforce anchoring about his waist as she glanced down at the terrifying distance between Drago's back and the moving ground. But Falk's body felt warm on this cold April morning, sheltering her from the wind. She honeyed her sharp words with a smile, which Falk failed to see as he turned to hand Snow's reins to Alun, who led the mare away to a more calming distance from the stallion.

Julia wriggled and settled herself more comfortably, resigned to her fate and determined to make the best of it. She almost snuggled against the broad, warm width of his chest, but one glance up at his stern face restrained her. Her gaze fell upon the knuckles of his right hand, as he held Drago's reins, and she noted how red and swollen they were. She remembered, with a strange glow that was almost pride and pleasure, that he had not hesitated to defend her honour.

Clearing her throat and sitting up to gain his attention she asked softly, 'What happened this morn? Between you and Gilbert?'

'I hit him once in the face and would have liked to break his neck, but for William's interference.'

'Is it wise to make of him an enemy?'

'Fear not, little wife. I am a man full grown and more than capable of dealing with the likes of Gilbert de Slevin. Besides, I have never had any love for him.'

Julia shivered, remembering the look upon that knight's face as he spied upon her by the stream, the ruthless way he had grabbed her at Hastings Castle. Falk's arm tightened about her waist and his voice was very soft, yet iron-hard.

'Have no fear, my lady. He would not dare to look at you again, fully clothed or otherwise.'

'Well, there is no question of...of...otherwise,' Julia exclaimed, 'for I will not be dabbling in icy French streams again!'

Falk laughed, stirred by her sweet warmth and softness. He banished from his mind the accusing words of de Slevin, which he did not believe for a moment, convinced that Julia was neither a wanton nor a lover of women. The thought of her welcoming a feminine embrace almost made him laugh.

'What makes you smile so?' asked Julia.

''Tis naught for your innocent ears, English.'

Julia gave a derisive chuckle, blushing pink, her voice very low so that others riding nearby might not overhear. 'You have had your pleasure of me many times, my lord, do you not think I must be far from innocent?'

He looked down at her lovely, creamy-skinned face and wondered afresh at her naivety. The thought of de Slevin looking at her, defiling her with his lewd thoughts, made his hands tighten with anger on Drago's reins. The stallion pranced and lifted up his front legs, causing Julia to cry out and clutch at Falk with alarm. She looked up questioningly into his dark face.

'If you were not as innocent as you are, then I would surely kill you.'

At his words Julia drew back, shocked and a little afraid at his fierceness.

He smiled down at her, a charming smile that quite stunned her. 'I have given you enough cause for complaint at my lack of patience and tenderness. But in future, I will make amends.'

Julia was startled, to say the least, and strangely unsettled by her lack of resistance. A great weariness overcame her and she let her head droop against his shoulder as they rode through the countryside. It was a sight that a troubadour riding with William's court would sing about around the campfire—the dark, fearsome Norman knight and his Saxon lady, as pale and slender as a lily, asleep in his arms as he rode the great black Drago home from war.

Chapter Nine

By midday Snow had settled down enough for Julia to remount, and she understood Falk's insistence for her to do so as William quickened the pace in his eagerness to be home.

The afternoon darkened into evening and all thoughts of making camp for the night were denied. Julia realised, as pitch flares were lit, that they would ride the last few miles in the dark. A full moon glowed, but even so it made for an eerie sight as the moving river of orange-flamed horseman snaked down one hillside after another.

Julia clung to the saddle determinedly, weary and uncertain of Snow's footing in the dark. The lights of Rouen were sighted and many of the riders broke into a canter, as a flare of excitement lit and spread like wildfire from one knight to another, and she became caught up in a reckless gallop.

On the wind she shouted at Snow and tugged on the reins, her hair whipped across her face and

Snow champing at the bit in her eagerness to let loose and run free alongside the pounding destriers. She lost sight of Falk, who had ridden ahead for most of the day, out of deference to her mare, but she was aware of Piers and Luc flanking her on either side. As Snow threatened to overpower Julia, tossing her head and snorting in an overexcited manner quite unlike her, Piers leaned down and grabbed the reins, forcing the mare to slow down.

Gratefully, Julia clung with two hands to the saddle pommel and breathed a sigh of relief as the castle gates came into sight and they clattered across a long wooden drawbridge, the like of which Julia had never seen before. The high, massive walls of the inner bailey closed about them, the crenellated ramparts stretching away on all sides. Julia counted at least six towers within her sight, each of them crested by a fluttering flag bearing William's family crest.

Her legs were shaking as Luc lifted her down from the saddle and she felt quite faint with exhaustion and hunger, her throat parched from thirst and the dust of their long journey. All around her was a noisy mêlée of arriving travellers, of snorting, prancing horses and the jubilant bellows of knights welcomed home by their Norman womenfolk.

The two Angevins escorted Julia inside, leading her through the great hall and up several wide, spiralled staircases and along corridors hung with tapestries and well lit with flickering wall sconces. Tired as she was, she noted with curious interest that William's castle was much like she had imagined a royal castle to be—vast, beautifully and amply furnished, and obviously well kept judging from the gleaming cleanliness of the dark-polished oak chests, tables and chairs. The colours of the tapestries were warm reds and lush greens, amber and even some gold thread, hinting that the lady of this castle was neither poor nor idle.

At last Luc halted before a solid oak door and, after a short knock, turned the iron ring handle after Falk bade them enter. He stood in the middle of a small, adequately furnished but not luxurious chamber, stripped to his loincloth as Sander washed the dust from his body before donning his best tunic, a black garment emblazoned with dark blue.

'Welcome to Rouen,' Falk greeted Julia, wiping his face and neck with a towel and dismissing the Angevins with his thanks.

Julia took a few steps to stand before the hearth and warm her aching backside, looking about her in a somewhat bemused and helpless manner. She watched as Falk dressed and latched on his sword belt, raked his damp hair with his fingers and then glanced her way.

'Make haste, wife, for there will be a feast this night like no other. We will eat, drink and dance until dawn.'

Julia blanched, for a moment utterly shocked that he expected her to participate in a feast that, to all intents and purposes, celebrated the death of her brother, her father, her king and, indeed, her nation. By now she knew a little of Falk's character and she did not relish engaging in conflict with him; she sought to find a way out as tactfully as possible.

'My lord, the journey has left me exhausted. I beg of you that I may retire. Besides which, I have no clothes except those in which I now stand. I fear,' she added glancing down at her plain, rather grubby brown wool gown, 'that my finery has been left behind in England.'

He paused for a moment, and his eyes were hard as he stared at her across the room. She felt he saw through the thin fabric of her excuse and laid it bare. But for some reason unknown to her he did not argue.

'Very well, my lady,' he replied coolly, with a small bow, 'Sander will see to your needs.'

He left her then, and Julia felt strange, almost bereft. For some long moments she simply stood there, waiting for him to return and drag her from the room. It was what she had come to expect of Falk de Arques. But he did not return and Julia turned to Sander and with a great deal of pantomime, laughing and some frustration, eventually managed to make clear to him that she wished to have a very hot, deep bath.

He gestured for her to follow him and he led her through to another chamber, somewhat smaller. A carved four-poster bed stood solid, hung with dark blue brocade curtains and Julia tested the mattress and fluffed the pillows, drawing back the linen sheets and fur covers to inspect its cleanliness. In this chamber too a fire glowed in the hearth, flanked by a pair of carved and padded chairs, and in the far corner stood a large, rather dusty, bathing tub. Sander rolled it out and positioned it before the fire and then went off, presumably to find buckets of hot water with which to fill it.

While she waited for him to return Julia wandered back to the solar and helped herself from the platter of food left standing on a large table dominating the room. There was a sweet, sticky apple tart and half a roasted chicken, some bread, cheese, and a pitcher of wine. She ate sitting curled up in a chair before the fire, licking her fingers and enjoying the comforting taste of decent food and filling her belly with warmth, stifling a twinge of guilt that she should enjoy anything at all that was Norman.

Her eyes wandered about, noting that Falk's quarters were practical and spartan. There lay about bits of armour and leather, boots and weapons of war; there was little in the way of books, quills, writing paper, ink, no ornaments or tapestries and only one fine silver candlestick.

At last Sander returned, trailing several female serfs, their eyes downcast as they carried buckets of steaming water on yokes borne across their shoulders and emptied them into the tub. On a coffer in the bedchamber Sander laid out soap, towels, a twined bunch of bay leaves and camomile to soften and scent the water. Julia thanked him and closed the door, glorying at last in her privacy as she stripped off her kirtle, stiff and stained from the journey. Naked, she sank down into the tub of water with a sigh of pleasure.

In the great hall Falk sat down to eat, mindful of the fact that the space beside him was sadly lacking the presence of a lively tongued, red-haired young female. He concentrated on the much-missed Norman cuisine and rose to his feet to exclaim 'Huzzah!' along with hundreds of others as toast after toast was proclaimed with the strong red wine that William favoured. He listened politely, if with little interest, to several ladies who hovered at his elbow, until a small brown-haired woman swept them aside with a mere glance of her regal eyes.

'Ah, Falk de Arques. I am pleased to see you have returned to us unscathed. Many a heart would be broken if your handsome face had been scarred in battle, or, worse still, lost to us for ever.'

Falk bowed deeply to Matilda. 'I am honoured, your Grace.' Not yet crowned Queen of England, she was at the very least still Duchess of Normandy.

She laughed then, a throaty, slightly wicked sound. 'But hearts are about to be broken, nevertheless. My husband has announced the news that you have wed.' Matilda looked about her with frank curiosity. 'Where is she? I am eager to see this Saxon creature who has made a husband of our most determined bachelor.'

'Alas, your Grace, my wife was not feeling well enough to join me. She has retired for the night.'

Matilda snorted her displeasure. 'But I want to see her! William has told me much about these Saxons and their land. Pray tell she is not as dull and miserable as the rest of them?'

Falk smiled then. 'Nay, your Grace, my wife is certainly not dull.'

'Then come…' Matilda slipped her arm through his '…let us go and surprise her.'

A personal visit from the Duchess in one's own chambers was deemed an honour amongst most Normans, but Falk, with some alarm, feared that Julia would not view the matter in quite the same light. He tried to politely dissuade Matilda, promising that he would present his wife first thing on the morrow, but she would have none of it and swept him along. William joined them, and soon a dozen people were fair galloping along the corridors in their eagerness, jealousy and drunken revelry to see the famed 'Saxon Lily' of the troubadour's song.

Julia forced herself to stir, as she lay half-asleep in the delicious water. She dipped her head under the surface and then rose back up with a splutter, eager to wash her hair while the water was still hot. With a lazy hum she lathered up a bar of soap and closed her eyes, shivering with the sheer pleasure of washing her scalp and the long tresses of her hair. She rinsed off the suds and then sat back to savour and enjoy her bath, but jerked up as she heard a noisy disturbance at the door.

'Sander?'

There came the distinctive babble of many voices and with alarm Julia looked to where she had laid a towel to warm before the fire. She would have to climb out of the tub to reach it, a minor matter when she was alone, but now a major problem as in that instant several people came wandering into her bedchamber as casually as they might stroll around a garden.

'In the name of God!' exclaimed Julia, with anger and more than a little fear, her eyes searching the strangers and lighting upon Falk. 'What on earth—?'

Falk turned to a woman so small the top of her head barely reached to his heart and began to speak to her in French, waving a hand in Julia's direction. Julia's eyes narrowed, recognising William amongst the onlookers, but no one else. Her fear that Gilbert de Slevin might be with them was groundless, but still she was outraged at this intrusion.

Crossing her arms over her chest, Julia spoke loudly and clearly to Falk. 'Is this how Normans treat their wives? Like freaks in a fair? Should I demand a coin, my lord?'

Falk raised his eyebrows to the ceiling, in a helpless gesture, and then turned to Julia and offered her the towel that lay warming upon a chair before the hearth.

'Nay! I do not rise from this tub until all these people are gone! And why does that silly little woman keep staring at me?'

Falk bit hard on his tongue. On one side Julia chastised him in English, and on the other Matilda demanded in French to have a good look at *la femme Anglaise*.

William, sensing that two stubborn wills were about to clash, tactfully laid his arm about his wife's shoulder. 'Come, my sweet, you have my assurances that I have chosen a fitting bride for Falk. She is healthy, courageous and her hair is red, like mine. Why, if I did not already have such a fine wife I would mate with her myself!'

At that Matilda seemed to suddenly lose interest in Falk's Saxon wife and with a final piercing glance at Julia she allowed herself to be led away. At the door she turned to Falk and said, 'Stay, sir knight, we would not want you to be separated from your bride on your first evening home.'

Falk murmured his thanks, bowed, and cast a wary glance from the corner of his eye at Julia, fair spitting like a furious cat. He escorted their guests out into the solar and finally closed the door upon them as they went off down the corridor. He fastened a bar securely across the door and snuffed out the candles, bidding Sander goodnight as his squire lay down gratefully upon his pallet before the fire.

Closing the door of their bedchamber, Falk glanced cautiously around to see that Julia had risen from her bathtub and was wrapped in a towel, her hair a sleek wet curtain down her back. He approached her carefully, noting the pink flags of fury riding high upon her cheeks and the bright glitter in her sapphire eyes. The sight of her all rosy and gleaming from her bath stirred an ache deep within him.

He stood awkwardly, and offered, 'My apologies.'

For an answer Julia took a step forwards and slapped his cheek with one sharp blow. 'How dare you treat me like a cow at market, to be viewed and examined! And you're drunk again!'

With a curse he grabbed her flying wrist in mid-air and jerked her hard against him. 'As I told you before, my lady—' he ripped the towel from around her and threw it down upon the floor, like a gauntlet '—I have been drinking, but I am far from drunk!'

His dark eyes challenged hers, his gaze lowering to the swell of her soft pink lips, parted slightly as she struggled with her quick and uneven breath. The firelight glowed golden upon her damp body, and he felt a rush of heat to his loins, as he looked even lower still. He drew in his breath sharply, his head descending, and his mouth found hers.

Julia gasped as Falk kissed her. His mouth tasted of wine, his lips firm and needing no direction as he parted her lips and explored with his tongue. With a groan Falk slid his hands around to cup her buttocks, kneading the soft flesh and pressing her against him. Through the fine cloth of his chausses she could feel his arousal, hard and straining for release. His mouth abandoned hers, and she gasped for air, feeling it cool upon the moistness of her lips, her head thrust back, unknowingly baring her throat to the kisses he branded along its slender length.

Suddenly her knees felt weak and she reached out to clutch at his shoulders, to support herself. A tremor shook Julia. She felt his lips and his tongue upon her breast, first one and then the other. Of their own will her fingers slid into his hair, clutching at him, and she felt her body burn. Suddenly she was pulling at his tunic, eager to feel the heat and hardness of his smooth muscles against her skin.

Falk helped her and tore off his clothes, his gasps mingling with hers. There was an urgent need to reach each other as quickly as possible and it was only a matter of moments before he too was naked. Falk pressed her up against the wall, one hand supporting her slender waist and the other supporting himself. He slid his thigh between hers, the bulk of hard muscle rough with hair and so male against the delicate female smoothness of her legs. She sighed and moaned, eyes closed, pressing against him as he lowered his head and returned his lips to her nipple, taking it into his mouth and circling the tiny bud with his tongue. He slid one hand behind her knee, lifting her thigh, and Julia's eyes snapped open.

He moved his head a fraction and looked down, holding her gaze. He saw the uncertainty in her eyes, felt her back bend as he stooped his body over her. She being so small and he so tall he feared to hurt her, to crush her against the rough stone wall. He swept her up into his arms, carrying her to the bed and placing her carefully upon the mattress. Julia glanced up at him—shy, exposed, and vulnerable.

Falk lay down at her side, his hand in the small of her back turning her to curve her body against the long length of his. Catching his breath for a moment, his rigid self-discipline calming and cooling the mighty dam that threatened to burst too soon, Falk concentrated mindlessly on smoothing the long swathe of her damp hair. Then he rolled over and straddled her on elbows and knees. Looking into her anxious eyes, he paused and gently stroked her cheek, her lower lip, her chin, her breast, her flank, and then the hidden part of her that ached for his touch, at the same time kissing her deeply. Again that cry came from her throat, half-strangled, and he felt her resistance.

'Let go, little wife,' he whispered in her ear, 'let go and I will catch you.'

Julia let go. Just for this moment, just for this night. She wanted to know. She must know. She circled his broad back with her arms and drew him closer, parting her thighs, and after the first initial intrusion welcomed the hard fullness of his shaft as he slid smoothly inside her. She closed her eyes and surrendered herself to the glory of what he was doing, of what they were doing together. Her gasps were muffled into his shoulder, his harsh pants against her neck, as Falk moved with almost lazy rhythm, each time a little deeper. Julia felt her body respond and suddenly she wanted to cry out, but she clenched her teeth, forbidding the sound of such weak wantonness to escape.

Holding on tight to Falk's shoulders, her nails digging into him, her cheek pressed against his rough jaw and her eyes closed, Julia thought this must be the most wonderful sensation on earth. He was so deep within her that she knew not where he began and she ended. They were one.

Suddenly it became even more wonderful, as Falk withdrew slightly and then thrust faster, cradling her buttocks between his hands, faster and faster, the bed shuddering and creaking. Shock waves filled her belly and expanded, until she burst with sheer delight and she clutched at him, exploding again as he, with a husky growl, filled her with his life-giving fluid.

As soon as his pounding heart had slowed Falk drew a deep breath and eased himself out of her. He stroked strands of damp hair from her face and kissed her brow. 'Now,' he whispered, 'my lady knows.'

Her rosy cheeks deepened with colour and she lowered her eyes. 'Aye,' she replied, her voice husky and shy. Her hands pushed at his shoulders, to ease his weight from her slender frame, and reluctantly he rolled away. He would have preferred to hold her in his arms, but he knew well that after lovemaking she preferred a distance between them. It had taken them many months to reach this point. How much longer before she finally surrendered, body, heart *and* soul?

They slept late and Julia was awakened by the disturbing noise of someone shouting.

'Sander!'

She squinted her eyes open and watched Falk pacing about the chamber and snatching at his clothes. She rolled her eyes and turned away, pulling the covers up over her head to block out the sounds.

'Damn!' exclaimed Falk, 'I promised the Duchess to present you at court this morning and 'tis now nearly midday. Sander! Where the devil is that boy?'

She heard the splash of water and then Falk's footsteps approach the bed, and stifled a cry as his hand slapped her on the backside.

'Come, wife. The sun is too high in the sky for lying abed.'

Julia opened her eyes and glared at him through the tangle of her hair, which had dried to an unruly mass during the night. She stretched and sat up slowly, holding the covers to her nakedness, her eyes avoiding Falk, who strode about as equally naked but unabashed. He dipped his head in a bucket of water, exclaiming at the shock and shaking off the frigid water.

'I pray to God I have not wed a lazy wench,' he warned as he towelled himself dry.

Julia snorted disdainfully and burrowed down even deeper into the warm comfort of the bed. Then she gave a cry and started with fright as a strong arm snaked around her waist and the mattress sagged as Falk knelt upon the edge. Laying his hand flat against her belly, Falk pulled her backwards across the width of the bed. He threw off the covers and rolled her over beneath him, kissing her mouth, her cheeks, her neck, before lingering on the softness of her unaroused breasts.

From the corner of her eye Julia spied Sander as he came in the door bearing a tray. She squeaked and pushed at Falk's chest. Seeking the cause for her alarm, Falk glanced over his shoulder, and shouted, 'Get out!'

Sander exclaimed his apologies and backed from the room, almost tripping in his haste and snapping the door closed behind him.

'Now...' Falk gazed down at her trapped beneath his body '...where were we?'

Julia dug the heels of her palms into his chest. In the broad light of day she cringed at the memory of her wanton abandon, fearing that she had given too much of herself. Her eyelids lowered and no answering smile touched her lips. At once, Falk was aware of her mood.

'What is this?' he asked, his hands still. 'Were you not well pleased last night, my lady?'

'Aye,' Julia murmured, 'but one quick tumble does not a marriage make.'

'A quick tumble?' There was a dangerous note in his voice. 'I had thought it was more than that.'

'Then you are mistaken. 'Twas naught but my curiosity to...to know.'

He smiled then, his thumb absently stroking her cheek. 'I did not fail to notice your knowing. Indeed, I think I bear the scars still upon my back.'

Her blush deepened, but as he leaned down to nuzzle at her neck, she stiffened and determinedly clenched her thighs together against his questing knee. 'This morn I wake to find myself ashamed.'

'Why?'

'I acted like a harlot, whilst my countrymen lie either dead or captive at the hands of Normans.'

''Tis no fault of yours.' His hand slid down to her hip, the sweet memory of their ecstatic union urging him on. 'Have you forgotten so soon you are my wife? And mine for the taking.'

'Nay, but neither can I forget how I came to be your wife.'

'You talk in riddles, English. Come now...' he lowered his voice persuasively '...wrap your arms and legs around me the way you did last night.'

'And if I refuse? Would you use your strength to force me?'

He coloured beneath the tanned hue of his face, 'I confess that from the beginning I have had to use the advantage of my male strength, but what choice did I have? That our marriage be celibate? I may not be the perfect husband that you dreamt of, but married we are and I, for one, intend to make the best of it!'

Julia stared at him for a long moment, her voice a mere whisper. ''Tis not a perfect husband I seek, but...'

'Tell me.' His dark eyes sought hers, as she tried to avoid his gaze and he had to hold her chin with his fingers. 'What manner of a husband do you want?'

'One that I may honour, and respect.'

'And I am lacking both?'

'You—' Julia bit her lip, stamping down on the twinge of pain that flickered in her heart '—you are Norman.'

'God's teeth! I have killed men for less insult than that!'

'Then 'tis well I am not a man.'

'Aye...' his fingers tightened on her waist '...that I have noticed, English. A reluctant wife I would persuade with kisses, and a reluctant whore with coins, but as you wish to be neither, then I will not bother.' He stared down at her, and with a curse he rolled away, moving to sit on the edge of the bed and snatch up his chausses from the floor. 'Get dressed!'

Julia sat up, pushing back her dishevelled hair, 'I have nothing to wear.'

For a moment they contemplated each other, their emotions spinning on the air between them, then Falk rose from the bed and shouted for Sander. His squire came to the door and looked in cautiously.

'Find my lady some clothes...' Falk tossed a bag of coins to him '...and be quick about it!'

Julia sat cross-legged with the covers drawn to her chest while she watched as Falk dressed and latched on his sword. Silently he bowed to her, his gaze rigid, and left the room. She heard the outer door open and close in Sander's wake and she breathed a sigh of relief to be alone. Quickly she climbed out of the rumpled bed and washed in cold water left over in the tub still placed before the grey ashes of the hearth. Within her a heady mix of fear and excitement brewed at the prospect of what this day might hold.

Sander returned, bearing two silk kirtles, both blue, but one a shade as dark as night and the other a bright sapphire, close matched to the colour of her eyes. He had also managed to procure for her fine linen undergarments and a girdle of white brocade worked with an intricate design of delicate silver thread, as well as a hairbrush.

Gratefully Julia accepted the bundle from Sander and chose the sapphire-blue gown to wear. He turned away while she dropped her towel and shrugged on a shift, which, although not new, seemed clean enough. Then she donned the blue kirtle, struggling to reach the lacings at her back and under her arms to attach the sleeves.

'My lady,' offered Sander tentatively, stretching out a hand to help—hesitating, not daring to touch her without permission.

'Thank you, Sander.' Julia presented her back and smiled, answering his French with her English but satisfied that they understood each other well enough. 'I think I have need of a maid, but where would I find one?'

Just then Falk returned, walking in to find his squire with his hands in Julia's armpit. He paused in mid-stride, one brow raised. Instantly Sander dropped his hands and stepped sharply away.

'What goes on here?' asked Falk quietly.

Julia met his glance boldly. 'Sander was kind enough to help me dress, as I have no maid. And do not look at the boy so, for he has done nothing improper.'

'Indeed?' With a jerk of his head Falk dismissed his squire from the room and came to Julia's side. His big fingers grasped the fragile cord beneath her arms and pulled hard, deftly tying a bow and attending to her other sleeve with the same ruthless efficiency.

Julia stifled a gasp as her body was tugged about like a rag doll, suspecting that it would take little to spark the tinder within Falk, causing a fireball to erupt. She stood with head bowed, staring at her feet, as he lifted the white and silver girdle from where it lay upon a coffer—remarking that Sander had not been shy to spend his coin—and settling the girdle about Julia's hips, adjusting it slightly so that it sat evenly.

'Thank you.' She reached for the hairbrush and began to tug at the snarls of her wild hair, but again Falk took command and retrieved the brush from her hand. 'Does a knight not have better things to do than brush a lady's hair?'

'Be quiet,' growled Falk, his hand on top of her head and holding down the roots while he brushed out the curling tresses. 'I did not think my touch was so unbearable to you.'

Julia flushed, and clenched her fists at her side. She could think of no reply that would not goad him, but even her silence seemed to fan his ire. He continued to brush her hair until it gleamed and crackled, and she was desperately aware of his tall frame just an inch from her back. He handed her an ethereal square of cobweb-pale gauze and a gold circlet adorned with three pinnacles. 'Braid your hair and cover it, for 'tis only I who shall look upon its glory.'

With fingers that trembled slightly Julia obeyed, and then he led her from their chamber and down many corridors and stairways to the great hall.

William sat upon a dais richly adorned with a crimson damask canopy and swags lined with ermine. At his side was Matilda, seated upon an ornate chair identical to her husband's and yet her tiny size made it seem enormous. Several clergyman and local barons stood at William's shoulder, and two clerks armed with parchment and quills sat close by. The dais was ringed by knights who were the king's own personal bodyguard, and their gleaming array of weapons left no doubt that William was well protected even in his own hall.

His face was stern as he sat in council on the many, mostly petty, disputes and grievances brought to his attention.

The hall was lined with a throng of people, and some now turned as Julia and Falk entered, gazing upon them with open curiosity. As they walked up the length of the room Julia noticed some hostile glances from several ladies, and she glanced up to Falk, but he stared straight ahead as they approached the dais and he announced their presence to a courtier.

While they waited Falk drew Julia to one side, her hand tucked through his arm. She looked about, recognising some faces from the journey, amongst them the plump matron and her two daughters.

'Who is that lady?' asked Julia of Falk.

He scanned about. 'Which one?'

'The plump one, with the yellow gown and the two girls who are so tall.'

'Ah. That is Lady Magda de Bohun and her daughters Alys and Bettina. She is Flemish, but her husband holds lands near Caen. Why do you ask?'

'She was kind to me at Hastings castle.'

'Then I am glad, and will give her my thanks. I believe she speaks a little English and may well prove to be a friend.'

They were joined then by Ruben D'Acre and Falk warmly greeted his comrade-in-arms. Intro-

ductions were made as Ruben brought forwards his
new bride, Carina, the youngest daughter of the
Count of Arromanche, a shy, plain girl with
mouse-brown hair and hazel eyes, but her manner
was sweet and clearly she was as devoted to Ruben
as he to her. Julia was disappointed to find that she
spoke no English, but smiled at her encouragingly
despite their inability to communicate with each
other.

Out the corner of her eye Julia noticed Ruben
suddenly jab his elbow in Falk's ribs, and she followed his livid glance curiously. Amongst the
moving, chattering crowd stood a tall woman,
quite still. Julia caught her breath at her beauty,
for her face was a perfect oval, nose delicate and
straight, full lips crimson and her eyes and hair
were a rich, dark sable that complemented the
milk-pale lustre of her skin.

'What is she doing here?' asked Falk.

Ruben shrugged and murmured, 'Beware, she's
coming this way.'

Falk swore beneath his breath.

Julia sensed the coiled emotions within him and
she felt the thick muscles of his forearm tense beneath her fingers. She too stiffened as she noticed
that the beautiful stranger approached them. Her
voice was very soft and low when she greeted Falk
and swept an elegant curtsy. He spoke to her in a

cool tone, and then a smile of satisfaction spread across his lips as he made the introductions.

'May I present Lady Vernice,' and in French, 'My wife, the Lady Julia.'

Her shock was obvious, as her beautiful red lips parted on a sharp indrawn breath, her nostrils flared and her dark eyes widened. For a brief moment she stared at Julia and then she pointedly ignored her and her face became a blank mask as she conversed with Carina D'Acre. After a few moments exchanging idle pleasantries she again turned to Falk, bestowed upon him a slow, seductive smile and then turned and swayed her hips as she walked away. Julia looked after her with her brows raised in surprise, dumbfounded by the French woman's rudeness. She turned her gaze upon Falk. 'Who was that?'

He laughed, with bittersweet enjoyment. 'No one.'

Julia was greatly tempted to stamp her foot and shout, but calmly she persisted, 'Tell me again her name.'

'Lady Vernice. Although some would say she is no lady.'

'Is she a relative?'

Falk smiled wryly and gazed after the dark head. 'Aye, you could say so.'

She dug her nails into his sleeve until he winced. 'I would know why it is everyone is staring and sniggering behind their hands.'

Falk looked about, and saw some truth in her words. 'She is nothing. A woman I once foolishly betrothed myself to in my youth.'

'Did you love her?'

'Aye, I did.'

This information did not sit well with Julia and her gaze followed the elegant figure of Lady Vernice, a slight frown marring her brows. There was no chance to enquire further as a courtier swept them towards the dais and announced them to William. Matilda sat up very straight in her chair, and her glance swept over Julia from head to toe in a narrow-eyed inspection worthy of any general surveying his foe upon the battlefield.

William came straight to the point. 'Is she breeding yet?'

Falk bowed, with a smile, thankful in that instant that Julia could not understand a word. 'Nay, sire.'

'I had expected good news long before now, Falk. I trust you know how to go about the business of begetting a babe, or have I kept you so long upon the battlefield that you have forgotten?'

'Nay, sire, I have not forgotten, but I find myself enjoying the task your Majesty has set me so greatly that I am reluctant for success.'

Guffaws met this bawdy comment and Julia looked about with eyes narrowed suspiciously, wondering at the conversation. William was quick to notice her puzzlement. ''Tis high time she learnt to speak our language. Matilda, what say you?'

Matilda inclined her head in agreement, a smile hovering slyly about the corners of her mouth. 'I will speak to Father Gerard and put him in charge of her instruction.'

Not by the merest flicker of the tiniest muscle in his face did Falk betray his apprehension, for Father Gerard had a fearsome reputation for his pious rages. He glanced sidelong at Julia, and wondered if she would cope well with the fierce priest.

William was not one to indulge in idle conversation and Falk withdrew, taking Julia with him. The midday meal was announced and they were given a place above the salt, beside Ruben and Carina D'Acre. Julia found herself to be ravenous and was grateful for the meat and bread that Falk cut for her, but found the wine too strong for her taste and settled for mead.

She ate silently, thoughtfully, as Falk and his companions talked and laughed over the many courses. He paused once and pressed upon her a variety of sweetmeats and honeyed fruits, unaware of how isolated she felt. Julia wished, again, that she could understand the French tongue. At last the meal came to an end, but she was denied the sanctuary of their private chambers as Falk went off to the barbican to practise the art of warfare, so beloved by Normans, and Julia was escorted by Carina D'Acre to the ladies' bower.

Afternoon sunlight streamed in through the thick panes of a high, large window, a group of ladies seated below to catch the warmth of the sun's golden glow. Matilda had gathered about her the wives, daughters and sisters of her husband's most important vassals; some of them were now either widows or fatherless and would shortly be leaving for the Abbey pour Dames at Caen, a nunnery, where they would live out their days in frugal piety.

Carina made the introductions and Julia curtsied politely to several matrons, all seated with their embroidery. Some inspected her with avid curiosity, others seemed little interested in yet another Saxon, their doubts about the wisdom of William's policy of integration through marriage only to be whispered out of Matilda's earshot.

Lady Vernice was seated by the fireside and Julia could not hide the coolness of her regard as she barely inclined her head towards the other woman. Dark eyes regarded her with an equal frostiness.

'So, you are the one Falk chose to make his wife?' Her English was perfectly spoken, if the accent a little rough.

Before she could check herself Julia replied, 'I have that privilege.' She was rewarded by the obvious bristling resentment displayed by Lady Vernice, but she heeded Carina's restraining hand on her forearm. As they walked away Carina whispered something and shook her head with a frown, her meaning, if not her words spoken in French, clear to Julia that Lady Vernice was not to be trifled with.

Throughout the long day Julia brooded over this meeting with her husband's former lover. A small part of her was dismayed and awed by the woman's obvious beauty, and yet Julia was sure that it was not flawless. Had Falk himself not spoken of her with utter contempt? Surely she had nothing to fear from this...rival? She glanced across the bower at Lady Vernice, seated beside the fire with Matilda, and wondered why it should bother her in the least if Falk decided to reacquaint himself with his former betrothed. Why, he would then leave her alone, wouldn't he? Julia exclaimed as she stabbed her forefinger with her embroidery needle, and sucked the tiny drop of blood with a fierce frown.

Supper that evening was another banquet, yet for Julia proved long and tedious. Afterwards a band of musicians struck up a chord with their lutes and drums and tambourines, and soon many were dancing. Julia refused Falk's arm, reminding him that she did not know the steps to these Norman dances. Lady Vernice was quick, far too quick, thought Julia sourly, to offer to take Julia's place and with many eyes upon them Falk could not refuse without breaking a knight's sworn oath to be always courteous to a lady.

Julia watched them as they circled the hall, her arms folded over her waist and brows lowered, thinking that she had never seen a woman more beautiful, nor one that she so disliked. Lady Vernice moved with elegant grace, her chin lifted on a swanlike neck as she smiled up at Falk. Was it her imagination or did Falk seem mesmerised by those sable eyes? Indeed, she did not like the way they looked at each other; did not like the way Falk held her fingers in his hand or moved his tall frame with easy familiarity as they danced in perfect unison together.

She was greatly tempted to plead a headache and ask Luc or Thierry to act as escort to her chamber, but just then the carole came to an end and Falk returned to her side. She did not look at his face, but noticed that he drank a cup of wine very quickly and then linked his arm through hers.

'Come, let us retire.'

Gladly she fell into step with him, glancing back over her shoulder to cast a look at Lady Vernice, who returned it with one of triumph that only caused Julia more uncertainty. When they reached their bedchamber Falk had scarce closed the door behind them before he caught Julia in his embrace and kissed her passionately, walking her backwards to the bed as his fingers nimbly worked on the lacings of her gown. When she felt the edge of the bed against the back of her knees he had already stripped her down to her shift, and tumbled them both upon the soft mattress. His kisses were tempting, but she feared that a dark-haired beauty had fueled his ardour and Julia gripped Falk's wrist. She stayed his hand as it moved to slide the straps of her shift from her shoulders.

He raised his mouth from her lips and paused to gaze into her eyes. 'You do not want me, my lady? Are you...unwell?' he asked delicately.

Julia blushed. 'Nay, my lord, I am not unwell, but there is a matter I wish to discuss with you.'

'Can it not wait?' He kissed the corner of her mouth, her chin, behind her ear, his fingers cupping her breast and his thumb toying idly with her nipple.

She struggled to control her ragged breathing as excitement danced along her skin and she resisted the urge to press closer and lift her hips to him. She looked away from the dark intensity of his eyes and forced herself to speak clearly. 'Nay, it cannot wait.' Determinedly she removed his hand from her breast and held it between her palms.

'What is it, then?'

'Lady Vernice—'

'Oh God!' He sat up and raked his hand through his hair.

Julia followed, staring up at him, 'Tell me about her.'

'Nay! She is best forgotten.'

'Is she?' Julia reached out and grasped his face between her two hands, forcing him to turn back and look at her, 'Is she forgotten, Falk? Or does she still hold a place in your heart?'

At that he laughed out loud. 'You have nothing to fear, little wife.'

'Once you loved her enough to want to marry her! And I do not believe that love dies easily. Why did you not then make her your wife?'

'Because she married my father!'

His words caused Julia to gasp with shock. She opened her mouth to speak, but he laid his finger on her lips and admonished, 'Be silent. I do not care to speak of that she-devil again!' He placed his hand flat between her breasts and pushed her down upon the bed, the fragile linen of her shift tearing beneath his hands as impatiently he bared her body.

Julia gave a cry of protest, which he silenced with a hard kiss. He was angry, very angry, and she feared his lovemaking would be brutal. She tore her mouth free from his and beat her fists upon his back.

'Do not take your anger out on me, Norman! It was not I who betrayed you!'

'Nay,' he snarled, his biceps bulging as he gripped her wrists and struggled to subdue her, 'but it seems that you and she are much alike! Teasing a man's lust and then acting the ice-maiden when bedding fails to suit your plans!'

'My refusal would not stop you from bedding me!' she retorted.

'Aye, it would, English. I am not a savage beast who enjoys rape. You wish me to stop?' His grip had gentled now, his lips softly brushing the taut peak of her breast. 'Then I will do so. Say the word.'

Julia gasped as his hand slid between her thighs, and she arched her neck, staring up at the canopy of the bed as he touched her intimately, his kisses burning a path across her ribs. Again he murmured an enquiry, asking if she wanted him to stop. After a few moments, as desire broke a hot sweat across her skin, she shook her head and placed one hand behind his neck, pulling him down to her. No more words passed between them and afterwards, when Falk was asleep, Julia lay awake staring at the fire

flames and wondering how she would find the answers to her many questions regarding Lady
Vernice, for she would never dare to ask Falk
again.

Chapter Ten

The next morning Julia was eager to seek out Lady Magda and make discreet enquiries, but her ambition was thwarted as immediately after breakfast a lady-in-waiting escorted her to the priest assigned to teach her French.

An ornate gold cross worn about her neck had given Julia her first indication that Matilda was devoutly religious, and indeed the chapel was very grand, leading off from a cloistered garden where a dozen monks and priests had their chambers. Here Julia was met by a small man, wiry of build and his greying hair tonsured. His features seemed to have the ageless complexion of those devoted to God, but his eyes were bright and shrewd and looked Julia over swiftly as she made her curtsy.

'I am Father Gerard,' he spoke in English, his voice surprisingly firm and deep. 'You may sit at that table there.' He pointed to a scarred oak table against one wall of the cloisters passage and facing out on to the garden. 'Do you know your letters, child?'

'Aye,' replied Julia, sitting down on the cold wooden bench and raising her eyes to his, 'I can read and write as well as any priest, but I am not a child.'

Colour suffused Father Gerard's smooth cheeks and he glared at her for a moment. 'I see. You are a Saxon?'

'Aye.' Julia lifted her chin proudly.

'And who is your husband?'

'Falk de Arques.'

'Ah. A noble warrior. For his sake, and for my Duchess, I will overlook your...pertness. This once. Now, let us begin, for you have much to learn.'

Father Gerard soon came to realise Julia's quick intelligence and he found himself enjoying her lively company. Many others feared him and said nothing worth listening to, but this young Saxon woman refused to be intimidated and her lively mind was of great interest to a man surrounded by mundane creatures who had no imagination, no truth, and certainly no intellect. He sensed in her an honesty that would not allow herself to save her own skin if it meant telling a lie, and a trusting innocence that believed in every word she was told. God help her at court!

* * *

A bell rang at midday, and Father Gerard released her to eat dinner. 'But do not linger and return as soon as you are finished, for we are making great progress and should press on.'

Julia would have preferred to go to the ladies' bower and seek out Magda de Bohun, but there were probably many days ahead of her when she would be confined to the bower. The sooner she could understand their chatter the better!

In the great hall she looked for Falk and he greeted her with a kiss and a smile as he sat down on a bench at one of the many trestle tables set up for the noon meal. 'Greetings, wife. How has your day fared?'

'I am learning to speak your tongue, Norman.'

'Indeed? And what can you say?' he asked as he helped himself from a platter of fresh bread.

Julia coloured a little. 'Why, nothing yet. A language is not learned in one morning!'

He glanced at her, and asked carefully, 'And your teacher, Father Gerard, he is agreeable?'

She shrugged, seeking not to speak ill of a holy man, who at times seemed to have the impatience of the devil himself, and finally she murmured, 'He is very wise.'

'Indeed.'

'And you, husband, how has your morning been?' She endeavoured to keep their conversation going, as often they seemed to share little more than…bedsport, as Falk would call it. She turned her attention to her food, hoping he would not notice her blush.

Falk shrugged, his vast shoulders making more of a statement than her own delicate bones, and she sensed his boredom as he reached for his knife and sliced for them both a generous helping of roast pork. 'I have this day taught Sander how to wield his sword without falling from his horse.'

She laughed. 'A brave accomplishment.'

'A miracle, I would say.' Falk grinned, chewing on his meat as his eyes roamed over her face. He wondered if he could persuade her to eat quickly so that they might retire to their bedchamber for the rest of the dinner hour.

Noting his perusal, Julia touched a finger to her cheek, 'Is something wrong, my lord?' She dabbed at a possible speck.

'Nay.' He laughed, and leaned forwards to kiss her mouth, his hand sliding to her thigh.

Julia blushed fiercely. His comrades laughed and made ribald comments about newlyweds, until Falk silenced them with a glance. Firmly Julia removed his hand from her leg and placed it on the table. 'There is a matter I wish to discuss with you, my lord.'

'Aye?' His eyes narrowed in suspicion, remembering the subject she wished to discuss before, but his smile was both amused and mocking of her flustered state.

'Indeed. I find myself wondering what my daily routine will be. Is it to be spent sewing and gossiping with silly ladies? After all, I am used to running my own keep and would like to be usefully occupied. In the infirmary or some such place.'

'Ah.' Falk pretended to ponder this seriously, chin in one hand. 'Mayhap you might go to the smithy and sharpen my sword blades? Or we might train you to be an archer in the forefront of William's army. I have experience of the accuracy of your aim.'

Knowing full well that ladies were not permitted to train for war or work in male-dominated trades such as smithing, Julia clucked her tongue with annoyance. 'You do not take me seriously!'

'What,' he asked gently, lowering his gaze to her own with all seriousness, 'might I suggest? Matilda is the one you must speak with, not I. She decides what occupations her ladies might while away the hours with.'

Julia snorted her loathing, mocking his words. '*While away the hours*. They strike me as an idle, spiteful lot!'

'That may be so, but—' he warned, his smile now gone '—do not make enemies.'

Julia thought that this advice came too late, as she glanced across the table and found Lady Vernice surveying her with cool regard. Deliberately, Julia turned to her husband and laid her hand on his forearm, as she asked, with a deliberate flutter of her eyelashes, 'And if I had enemies, my lord, my knight, would you slay them for me?'

Falk laughed. 'Of course.' He lifted her hand and kissed her dainty fingers, his voice lowering. 'Have you eaten your fill, my lady?'

'I think so.' Julia glanced at her trencher, and then shivered as he leaned closer and whispered in her ear.

'Then let us go to our chamber and…rest. I have some time to spare before I am needed in the bailey.'

His fingers curved about her hip and Julia felt a hot stab of excitement low down in her body, as well as another fiery blush. ''Tis the middle of the day, my lord!'

'All the better. I can see your face when you—'

Julia coughed abruptly and then tugged at his sleeve, 'My lord, look at that cake. Does it not look tempting? Why, I am so hungry still, be so kind as to cut me a slice.'

They stared at each other for a moment, he with a frown, she with an overly innocent expression. Then he laughed and murmured that the night was still to come, and reached for the honey cake, cutting them each a thick wedge.

After the meal they parted company, Falk returning to his combat training and Julia to her lesson with Father Gerard. She thought she knew the way, but took a wrong turn and found herself in the corridor near the private chambers of Duke William. She retraced her footsteps, pausing to admire a tapestry along the way, went down a spiral of stairs and came out in a passage that she hoped would lead her to the cloisters.

Suddenly a door burst open and a female serf stumbled forwards, crying out as a woman shrieked and rained blows upon her shoulders with a wooden hairbrush.

'*Imbécile!*'

Julia halted, the sound of that voice familiar, a frisson of anger burning along her spine. She ran forwards and shouted at Lady Vernice to stop, trying to protect the serf from the blows that were aimed at her, and several landed on her outstretched arms.

'Stop it!' shouted Julia, more loudly, and reached out and grabbed Lady Vernice by the wrists. 'What do you think you are doing? Stop this at once!'

Vernice swore at her in a most unladylike fashion, drew a deep breath and hurled the hairbrush at her servant with a vicious force. The maid yelped as it thudded against her back, turned as she was into the protection of Julia's arms. Vernice spoke to her sharply in French, turned on her heel with a flounce of her velvet skirts and slammed the door of her chamber in both their faces. The maid began sobbing and Julia patted her and spoke to her in gentle tones.

'Come now, all will be well. Are you hurt? Shall I take you to the infirmary?' Julia sighed crossly then. 'You probably do not understand a word I am saying.'

'Oh, no, no, my lady.' The young maid straightened and grabbed at Julia's hand, kissing it fervently several times. 'I understand. I speak the English very well, for my father was a Saxon. Thank you, my lady, for your kindness.'

Julia smiled and straightened as she helped the maid to tidy her hair and wipe her tears, adjust her dress, giving her a chance to calm down. 'Is the Lady Vernice your mistress?'

'Aye, but no longer. She has dismissed me.' Tears started anew and streaked down her plump young face. 'I am to leave the castle before nightfall.'

'But why?'

'She did not like the way I brushed her hair.'

'Pish!' snorted Julia, quick to take her opportunity, 'I have need of a maid. Come with me, and you shall be my own personal handmaid.'

The girl gasped, eyes wide as she dropped to her knees and began kissing the hem of Julia's gown.

'Oh, do get up!' Julia implored, exasperated with this typical display of Norman emotion. 'I do you no great favours, for my lord is not a rich man and our chambers are humble. There is little I can offer you besides three meals a day and a pallet before the fire, and that must be shared with my lord's squire.'

'I make no complaint.' The maid beamed, her fair curls bouncing as she rose to her feet.

'Come then, I will show you to our chambers.' As they hurried along the corridor, Julia asked, 'What is your name?'

'I am Emma.'

'Emma. 'Tis a pretty name. I am Lady Julia, wife to Falk de Arques.'

'I know.' A flush stole over her cheeks, 'Lady Vernice has complained about you from noon till night.'

'Has she, indeed?' Julia raised her eyes heavenwards and gave a silent prayer of thanks for this godsend, linking her arm with young Emma as they walked. 'What did she say about me?'

'Well...' Emma hesitated a moment, but when urged not to be afraid of speaking honestly, she continued, 'She says you are skinny and ugly and a stupid Saxon, and that you will not hold your husband's attention for long.'

'Indeed!' snorted Julia, opening the door to their chamber and ushering Emma in.

'But, my lady, I do not think so!' Emma exclaimed. 'I think you are the most beautiful and kindest lady I have ever met!'

'Thank you.' Julia smiled and drew the maid forwards as Sander rose from his stool by the fire, where he sat repairing the leather strap of Falk's sword belt. 'Sander, this is Emma. She is to be my own personal maid and I wish you to be kind to her and find her some work to do while I am out. Several of my lord's shirts need repairing. How is your needlework, Emma?'

'Invisible, my lady!'

Julia smiled again, wondering if this enthusiasm and devotion might become just a little overwhelming. Hopefully, as Emma settled down, it would soon adjust to normal proportions.

'I must return to my lesson with Father Gerard and will see you both later.'

She managed to find her way back to the cloisters, but Father Gerard was annoyed at her lateness and his mood did not improve as the afternoon wore on. Finally, after a particularly rude outburst, Julia set aside her quill, rose from the bench and curtsied with slow dignity.

'You will excuse me, Father. I fear we are not good company for each other and I have a pressing matter to attend to.'

'Sit you down! I have not given you leave to go!'

Julia's eyes were very cool and very blue as she regarded him. 'I am not a slave, nor a prisoner. I may come and go as I please, and at the moment it pleases me to go!'

She turned then and walked away, her back very straight and hands folded tightly together.

'If you go, do not think to come back, madam!'

Well, that suited her just fine, thought Julia. She had no need to endure rudeness and spite from a man who was supposed to be holy. Her footsteps tapped across the flagstones as she made her way back to the great hall, intent on finding Falk and informing him of their new servant before some-one else did.

She knew well that it was not etiquette for a lady to be seen in the training yards of men, so she sent a pageboy with a message and waited impatiently, chewing on her thumb knuckle while she rehearsed a pretty speech regarding Emma. She could not bear to see the poor girl thrown out on the street, and she thought it nothing less than a gift from God to find herself a serving-maid who spoke English, and had knowledge of so much that Julia wished to learn! Please, she prayed, please let Falk be agreeable to keeping her!

It was some while before Falk appeared and when he did she led him to a quiet alcove and explained to him what had happened. Standing with his hands on hips, hair damp with sweat and his clothes stained from the dusty yards, his frown deepened as her words registered.

'Nay! I cannot keep two women, and especially not one who has come from Vernice.'

'Hush!' Julia glanced over her shoulder as others in the hall stared at them curiously. Her voice was low and urgent as she pleaded, 'Please, my lord, I beg of you. I need a maid to help me dress. 'Tis not fitting that you should do so, and besides, if you are called away, for William is ever fond of his wars, what will I do? She speaks English, and is so sweet, and will be no trouble at all.'

Gazing down at her, Falk sighed, and retreated before this onslaught of female logic. 'Very well. But any trouble and she is gone in an instant.'

'Of course.'

'And you will teach her to keep her tongue between her teeth. I will harbour no spy and if I hear she has carried tales to that—that—'

'She-devil?' Julia supplied helpfully.

'Aye. I will beat her backside until her nose bleeds.'

Julia smiled, knowing full well that this dire threat would never come to pass. But she murmured the right words, for men were ever determined to be the master.

'What manner of a girl is she?' Falk asked.

'My lord?'

'Is she clean? I will have no pox or whores beneath my roof.'

'Falk!' Julia was shocked, 'She is neither of these things. She is quiet and biddable and pretty and plump. Fair haired and blue-eyed, but plain and wholesome. She will not be given to lewd behaviour.'

'Lewd behaviour, eh?' His arm circled her waist as he drew her close in a tight embrace, his voice suddenly soft and caressing, 'What know you of such things?'

'Falk, we are watched!'

'Can a man not kiss his own wife?'

'In public, in broad daylight? Nay, I should think not!'

He laughed, and kissed her anyway, deeply and thoroughly, before leaving her with a flushed face and weak knees as he returned to the bailey. Julia hurried to her chamber, eager to talk with Emma and glean what information she could of the high-and-mighty Lady Vernice. She set Sander the task of finding another pallet for Emma to sleep on and then took her new maid into her bedchamber and showed her the coffer where she kept her gowns and personal effects.

'I know there is little, at the moment, as most of my things are either in England or stolen.'

'No doubt my lord will soon replace them, my lady. There is a very good market in Rouen, and the cloth merchant has some fine materials.'

Julia nodded, uncomfortable with the idea of being dependent and beholden to her Norman husband even for the clothes upon her back. She searched her mind furiously to find a suitable beginning to her quest. Seating herself in a chair beside the cold hearth, she handed Emma her hairbrush.

'Let me have a demonstration of your skills.'

'I have little skill, my lady.' Emma trembled, her eyes enormous and fearful.

'I tease you, Emma. Brush my hair for me, nice and gently, for I find it soothing to my thoughts, and I have many.'

Obediently, Emma moved to stand behind the chair and carefully unbraided Julia's hair, drawing the brush through the shining tresses with soft, slow strokes. 'My lady is troubled?'

'Aye.' Julia sighed. 'I hear that once upon a time Lady Vernice was betrothed to my husband.'

'It is so. Ten years ago.'

'What happened?'

'I was only a small child, but I do know that my Lord Falk was very much in love with her. Lady Vernice was not content to have the penniless bastard son, when she could have the rich noble father.'

'How cruel! Was my lord very upset?'

'Aye. He was but eighteen years old then, and he joined with William to be a knight.'

'And how old was Lady Vernice?'

'Why, she was twenty-three, being older than him.'

Five years older than Falk! A beautiful older woman, and she had humiliated him by marrying his father. How that must have hurt! But was it his pride, or his heart, that had suffered the most? A sudden thought occurred to her and she asked, 'Why is she at court now and not at home with the Count?'

Emma leaned forwards and whispered in conspiratorial tones, 'I cannot say for sure, but the Count has aged in the last few years. He has run to fat and laziness. They have no children of their own, but there are two sons from an earlier marriage to the Lady Agnes, who died twelve years ago. The sons do not like Lady Vernice and there are always arguments and much shouting. She says the Count suggested a visit to court to allow tempers to cool, but I think my lady has come to court to find a lover!'

Julia gasped and sat up so quickly that her hair snagged on the brush and she yelped with pain.

It was too much to hope that her acquisition of Emma would pass unnoticed. In the hall, after supper that evening, Lady Vernice cornered Julia in Falk's temporary absence when he was called to a meeting with Duke William, and Julia found herself caught in a steely grip upon her arm.

'So, you have taken another of my cast-offs,' hissed Lady Vernice in Julia's face, all pretence of politeness gone.

Her knees quaked and her heart hammered, but Julia shook off the biting fingers and replied, 'I have need of a maid. One unexpectedly became available and, I must say, I am well pleased with her.'

'Is that so? She has cost me a penny or two to feed and clothe over the years. I shall require compensation.'

'But you had already dismissed her.'

'So?'

Julia shrank before that malevolent glare and whispered, 'Then you had best speak to my husband.'

'I will.'

At once Julia saw her folly and regretted giving Vernice any opportunity to have dealings with Falk. She watched Vernice walk away with grave misgivings in her heart. They had been in Rouen only two days and already she was caught up in a whirlwind of events. How she longed for the peace and quiet of Foxbourne!

A week later sunshine beat down upon the knights stripped to the waist as they practised their swordplay, shield defence, mounting and dis-mounting a destrier on the move—all the arts that made the Normans famous as fighting men.

Falk, bare-chested and his hair damp with sweat, parried in a mock sword-engagement with a younger knight destined to be one of William's finest cavalrymen. The men circled each other in a wary crouch, arms upraised as their practise swords glinted in the bright sun.

They were interrupted by a courtier upon a foam-flecked, snorting horse, riding up in a flurry of dust and bearing a message that summoned Falk to his king. Falk sheathed his sword and lifted his helm, sweat and dirt leaving an outline from the nasal bar imprinted upon his face. He wiped the back of his hand across his brow and squinted up at the courtier. 'Tell his Majesty I will be there anon.'

'I beg my lord's pardon, but King William was most insistent that you come now. At once. He said...' the courtier screwed up his face as he tried to remember the exact words '...'twas a grave matter and you were not to worry about the stink of—of honest sweat.'

A sudden chill struck Falk. Donning only his deerskin tunic and tossing his shield to Sander, he ran to Drago and vaulted upon his back. Galloping across the meadow and into the bailey, Falk's spurring fear was that something had happened to Julia. Had she fallen down a stairwell and broken her neck? Or taken ill with a summer fever? There was much sickness about at this time of year. Or…or she had run away…she had been so downcast of late, pale and listless.

Drago snorted an angry protest as he was yanked to a sudden halt in the stable yard. Throwing his reins to a boy, Falk ran off in a whirlwind of kicked dust and straw towards the castle entrance, leaping up the steps three at a time.

His booted feet thundered on the stone floors and his sword clanked at his hip as he ran up stairs and along corridors until at last he came to William's receiving chamber. The double guard let him pass and a courtier announced his presence to William before the door had even closed behind him.

William looked up from where he was seated at a massive table. He was surrounded by a sea of parchment maps; letters from all manner of royalty, his vassals, and even one from the Pope; the remains of his noonday meal, and a debris of items collected over the years. On either side of him stood his most trusted and accomplished war-lords—William FitzOsbern and Roy de Montgomery—as well as noblemen such as Rudolf de Tosny and William de Warenne, whose wealth was useful. The tableau broke slightly as Falk strode forwards to stand before his king. The men looked up and there was a hint of a smile upon their faces. It could not be bad news, thought Falk, but still his bow was stiff and an answering smile did not meet his chiselled lips.

In his usual brisk manner William wasted no time in getting straight to the heart of the matter. He turned to a scribe, who took up one corner of the table, surrounded by ink and quills and curls of waiting paper, and demanded he read out a letter, for William could neither write nor read. At the end he gave congratulations and his orders, and then dismissed Falk as he returned to study the maps of northern England, as yet not fully under his supreme control and threatening to upset his tenuous hold upon a hard-won kingdom.

Falk bowed again, and withdrew. Outside the chamber he stood for a moment, thoughtful upon his news and wiping away the sweat and dust that scratched his eyes. Then, with a grim smile, he turned on his heel and headed for Matilda's bower, where the ladies of the court would be gathered.

When he entered the bower, all eyes turned to him and abruptly the female chatter and lazy strumming of a harp stopped. Like plump pigeons surveying the hawk that hovered over them, the ladies sat still, watching, waiting. Some were coy and cast their eyes back down to their sewing, a few swept openly lustful glances over Falk's muscular torso, bare and bronzed, clad only in the deerskin tunic.

'What is this, my lord Falk?' enquired Matilda imperiously, dropping her quill upon the letter she wrote, and rising to stand before this bold intruder.

Falk bowed to the tiny woman, his clenched fist held to his heart in a gesture of respect and loyalty.

'Forgive me, your Grace, but I seek my wife, the Lady Julia.'

'Ah, yes. I know well which one is *your* wife. The Saxon, who cannot, or will not, speak French.' She watched as his black eyes swept about the room in search of Julia, her own rather bright and relishing, like a cat toying with a mouse. 'I have sent her from my sight, as she did try my patience verily.'

'Your Grace?'

'I asked for her help to embroider a new tapestry for Bishop Odo, that will record our great victory at the Battle of Hastings. She refused and spoke to me most rudely in her Saxon tongue. I had cause to slap her face for such impudence.' Matilda noted his fists, which had relaxed after the first salute, now clench. 'I see this displeases you, Falk. Do you then love this girl so very much?'

'As your Grace knows, we were not wed for love. It was an alliance at his Majesty's behest and no words of love have yet been spoken.' Falk replied stiffly, his gaze not meeting hers.

'But 'tis surely what is in your heart, for have we not all seen how your eyes follow her? A firm hand, my lord.' Matilda turned then, bored, seeing that he was too well disciplined to vex any sport out of him. 'I have sent her to the chapel to pray upon her sinful nature. You may find her there.'

With a flick of her dainty fingers he was dismissed and Falk bowed, stepping backwards as he withdrew from Matilda's royal presence.

The chapel was on a floor below and Falk now hurried down the connecting stairs. He hesitated a moment with his hand on the door ring. Julia would be in a mood fit to curdle milk and he wondered, with a slightly wry smile, if he should don his chain mail before approaching.

Murky sunlight beamed in through a row of arched windows set in the outer wall. Emma looked up as soon as she heard his footfalls. With a jerk of his head Falk indicated that she should leave, and she scrambled up and flew on quick, light feet to the door. Julia did not turn as she knelt at the front, before the ornate marble altar, her back slim and straight, her braided hair bright as a flame in the glow of afternoon sun, her gown a dark blue pool about her.

Falk advanced, holding the hilt of his sword in one hand, so that it would not clank, and brushing back his hair with the lean brown fingers of the other. As his shadow cast itself upon her Julia looked up, and he saw at once her tear-blotched face and the red imprint of Matilda's fingers upon her cheek.

'I thought it must be you,' said Julia, her lips pursed in a grim line.

'How so, my lady?' he asked, gently.

'I recognised your stink.' She wrinkled her nose delicately. 'Have you no shirt, Norman?'

'It lies somewhere out in the meadow, for I had a message summoning me to King William and at first I was concerned…about you.'

Julia laughed harshly. ''Twill take more than a slap from a poxy French—'

'Julia!' he commanded, his hand clamping over her mouth as he glanced swiftly over one shoulder at the deep shadows of the chapel. Although deserted, it was well known that castle walls had ears everywhere. 'Hold your tongue, wife. 'Twill do you no good to vent your bile. Besides, I have news that may sweeten your mood.'

Julia clawed at his hand, spitting out the salty, dusty taste. 'Nothing would please me except to be gone from this hellish place.'

'Then God has seen fit to answer your prayers, although at a high price, some would say.' Without further ado he told her plainly, 'My father has died of a fever.'

'Oh.' Julia tried to adjust her pout to a suitable expression of sympathy, not altogether succeeding and adding, 'I am sorry.'

'Do not be. I am his bastard and he gave little thought or care to me or my mother, being the vicious son of Satan that he was.' He remembered well his mother's lonely struggle to provide for him. 'But both of his legal sons have died with him and I have been named as his only heir. As my wife, you are now the Comtesse de Arques and we will soon be leaving Rouen to take up residence at the family home, a fortress in the north that is called L'Espérance d'Arques. Have you learned enough French to know the meaning of such a name?'

'Nay, but no doubt you will tell me.'

He grinned, never annoyed by her impudence that had already earned her one slap that day. 'It means Hope of the de Arques.'

'Fascinating. And I suppose I should be grateful for this honour.'

'I do not seek your gratitude,' he replied, gruffly. 'Will you kneel there all day, or are you waiting for me to pick you up?'

She cast him an indignant flash of her eyes. 'I was told to stay here, upon my knees, until Father Gerard came to fetch me.'

Falk settled hands on hips and surveyed the deserted chapel. 'I see him not and thus make prior claim upon my own wife. Come…' he put his hand to her elbow and drew her up from the floor '…we will celebrate our good fortune.'

Julia rubbed her aching knees and swayed slightly, feeling all of a sudden light-headed. At once his arm went around her waist, but she pulled back, insisting she was well. 'Do you not wish to pray for the departed souls of your father and brothers?'

His eyes narrowed and he cast a sceptical glance to the altar. 'Nay. 'Tis a waste of time to pray for those damned to hell.'

''Tis an unchristian thought.'

'Nay. An honest one.' His glance skimmed over her pale face. 'Is that not what you value in a husband? Honesty?'

Suddenly Julia burst into tears and she covered her face with both hands as she wept uncontrollably.

'Julia—' he took her in his arms and pressed her face to his chest, stroking her hair '—will you not tell me what is troubling you? And do not say there is nothing, for you have not been yourself this week past. What is it? Tell me, please.'

Julia shook her head as she sobbed weakly.

His voice was very soft as he stooped over her, his lips close to her ear. 'I had thought we had crossed the hurdle of—of your…acceptance…that is…that you enjoyed making love with me…what I am trying to say is…I know it is not your monthly time, but you will not let me touch you. Why?'

At that Julia could no longer bear to contain her woe and tore herself from his arms, standing back to stare up at him and exclaim, 'I saw you!'

'What?'

'I saw you and Lady Vernice, in the garden, kissing.'

'What!'

'Do not try to deny it, Falk! I am not blind or mad, I know what I saw! I have heard a rumour that Lady Vernice has come to court to seek a lover, and I think she has found one! My husband!'

'Julia!' He shook her by the shoulders as her voice rose hysterically. 'You talk nonsense! Who told you that I was Vernice's lover? For I will cut their tongue out for such a lie!'

At that Julia sobered and grimly closed her lips, for she could not reveal Emma's name and condemn her to Falk's wrath. Emma was her only friend and confidante and she could not bear to lose her.

'What you saw was not I kissing Vernice, but she kissing me. And if you had waited a moment longer, you would have seen me thrust her away and tell her that I would not betray my wife!'

Julia hardly dared to believe that her anguish of the past week could be set aside by a few simple words. But she wanted to believe him, and she slowly raised her watery gaze to his, sniffing and hiccuping as the storm of her tears subsided.

'Don't cry,' he said gently, his thumb wiping the teardrops from her cheeks. 'It is you I wed. It is you I shall cleave to.'

He did not speak the words she longed to hear, but it was enough, for she did not know herself if she could speak words of love to him. That he was faithful was more important. With a small cry she flung herself into his arms and clung to him.

Chapter Eleven

In the grey light of dawn, a few days later, Julia stood at a window in the great hall and looked out upon the busy preparations being made for their journey. She could not say she was sorry to leave Rouen, but neither did the prospect of a strange castle, three days' journey north, stir even the slightest excitement within her. Mayhap her gloom had much to do with the fact that Lady Vernice was to accompany them, for she was newly widowed and reluctantly returning home. Alas, she had formed an attachment with Gilbert de Slevin and, as William had assigned him to duty as a hearth knight, he too was to ride with them, although Julia had begged Falk to persuade him not to. Falk had said he had little influence over whom Vernice chose as her companions, none at all when it came to an order from William. He was powerless to interfere.

'My lady?'

Julia turned at the sound of Emma's soft voice.

'Aye?'

'My lord Falk is ready to leave and bids you to come down to the bailey.'

Emma held out her mistress's cloak and fastened it about her throat with an oval clasp of patterned gold, gifted to her by Falk. She arranged the twin braids of Julia's hair outside the dark brown folds of heavy, fur-trimmed wool, and waited.

With a sigh Julia left the window and the hall and went downstairs. As she emerged on the steps she noted that the breeze had a nip to it and she glanced up at the heavy clouds, praying that it would not rain.

Across the yard Falk left Hervi and came to her side. Julia noticed at once that he wore armour, and that all the knights who were to accompany them and serve Falk as their liege lord were similarly equipped. Her eyes flew to his in alarm, but she bit back her question and her worry. All around the busy commotion had come to a halt and the yard was quiet, except for the snort and stamp of horses, the jingle of harness.

Matilda and William had left the day before for England, where Matilda would be crowned Queen and she had announced her expectation of giving birth to another child. There were few gathered now to watch the new Comte and Comtesse de Arques ride out of Rouen, and so it was Julia that the knights now looked to as their lady. They waited expectantly as Falk took her hand and led her to Snow, lifted her up into the saddle and handed to Piers and Luc, who rode at her side as her own personal bodyguards, the banners of de Arques—a dark azure shield decorated with three argent crosses, one at each corner, and in the centre the distinctive sable outline of the castle L'Espérance. There was no other quite like it, and at the bottom was written the motto of the de Arques—*Ah qu'il le bon, le bon Dieu*—'How good he is, the good Lord.'

A cheer went up, as the banners were raised and fluttered on the wind. Then a great noise erupted of clanking armour and excited talk as the knights mounted up and the cavalcade moved out of the bailey and clattered across the drawbridge. At their midst rode a woman who was too young to appreciate the title of dowager comtesse, and who was far too ambitious to settle to obscurity in a convent, whiling out the days of her widowhood. Let them cheer for the Saxon, she thought bitterly, but it will not be for long!

They rode north into the Seine-Maritime district, through countryside rich and lush with pastureland for sheep and cattle, fields with their summer harvest of wheat and barley, through deep forests of beech and elm and oak. As the day brightened the sun glinted silver on steel helms and chain mail, spears and spurs, quite a dazzling sight. Sometimes the villagers came out of their rustic homes to stare, to point, some eyeing Julia and her unusual colouring suspiciously; and they could be thankful that the whisper of 'witch' did not reach Falk's ears, or he would surely have cut out their tongues.

Near the village of Clersy they came across a farm of lavender, the fragrant flowers growing row upon row to the horizon. Julia begged that they might pause and purchase several large sacks, mindful of the fact that it would soon be winter and a snowbound keep could become foetid with unclean rushes upon the floor. She had a mind to make vast quantities of lavender soap, for the Norman knights did not seem overly fond of bathing and sometimes their stench quite brought the nausea to her throat.

After a brief stop for the noonday meal and to water the horses beside a cool stream, they entered a valley devoted to apple orchards. A faint memory stirred in Falk's mind, dredged from his long-ago harsh youth, and he sought out a farm famous for its cider. He purchased six barrels and also a dozen freshly baked apple cakes spiced with cinnamon and sweetened with honey. A neighbour, sensing an easy profit from the new baron, ran to bring his wares to sell—honeycomb. Julia was eager to purchase everything he had, for the honey would be well used for baking and the wax of the comb could be made into candles, a precious commodity.

Falk grumbled about the sudden lightness of his purse, but secretly he was pleased at her interest in their domestic welfare, when little, of late, had seemed to interest her at all.

The convoy continued its slow journey over hill and dale. Julia, her maid Emma and the Lady Vernice were the only women of the party, alongside Falk and the five Angevins, four knights and fifty men-at-arms who came from William but who would serve Falk. They made camp for the night in a meadow edging a convent, where a welcome meal was bought and eaten in the refectory, and they shared with the nuns the delicious apple cakes. Falk and Julia, and Vernice, had rooms there for the night, while the others would sleep in tents; except for Emma and Sander, who had pallets outside their door. The Angevins would take turns to sleep—during the dark, quiet and dangerous hours of night two of them would always be awake and watchful.

In the morning, which dawned bright and clear, Julia stood at the open window of their small, spartan room and brushed her hair, watching as Falk moved about in the nearby field, talking to his men, checking tack and weapons and that no one had slipped away during the night. She could hear his deep voice, but not his words, but she did not fail to notice the respect and eagerness to please that he commanded, from even the highest-ranking hearth knight, Hugh de Monceux.

A frown creased her brow. Why, with each passing day, was it so difficult to summon the long-abiding hatred and resentment that had been with her since the moment they had met? Nothing had changed. She was still Saxon and he was still Norman. She was still bound to him by force, and he still owned her as he surely owned everything else within sight, whether it be horses or armour or honey or sacks of lavender. She felt so unsettled…so uncertain. What did the future hold? And what of Vernice? Was she to live with them? And who, indeed, would be mistress of L'Espérance, for Julia was certain that Vernice would not be willing to relinquish her position of authority. With a sigh she tossed her brush to Emma, who hovered anxiously, waiting to pack the last of her mistress's belongings and aware of the men who waited for them.

In the courtyard Vernice was already mounted, but Julia paused to thank the nuns for their hospitality and received a kiss and embrace from each one. Then Piers lifted her up on to Snow and they rode out, to join with Falk and the rest of the column as they trooped out of the meadow and on to the track that led north.

The day mellowed and Julia refused to allow Vernice's snide comments and whispered conversations with Gilbert spoil her pleasure. She rode along in a dreamy state, her eyes often skimming over the treetops and fields and the bright blue sky, but always returning to the dark-haired man who led them upon his black destrier.

'Emma?'

'Aye, milady?' The maid nudged her palfrey up closer to Julia.

'What is the French word for sky?'

'*Le ciel*, milady.'

Julia repeated this out loud several times, 'And…what is the word for tree?'

'*L'arbre.*'

'And…birds?'

'*Les oiseaux.*'

'And…horses?'

'*Les chevaux.*'

'And how do you say…my husband?'

'*Mon mari.*'

'*Mon mari.*' Julia murmured this as she looked at Falk.

He had not donned his helm and her eyes rested on his broad shoulders and on the smooth column of his strong, tanned neck. She remembered how his skin and his muscles felt beneath her hands as she held on to him when they… Just then Falk turned his head and looked back. His dark gaze collided with hers and Julia blushed, as though her naked thoughts were exposed for all to see. He smiled at her, his eyes warm and lingering. Julia smiled too, and lowered her gaze with a demureness so charming that Falk felt a rush of heat to every part of him that was male. He spurred Drago, and the great warhorse leapt forwards, taking him away from sweet distraction.

That night they spent at the home of a vassal loyal to William, his castle small, dank and gloomy but a bed was offered to the three nobles, whilst the rest of their party camped in the bailey. Their host was a large, ebullient man of Viking descent, Cedric de Ware, and his sense of humour was bawdy and his voice booming. His wife seemed long-suffering and sat unsmiling through most of the evening meal. Julia followed in Vernice's wake and begged an early retirement, pleading a genuine exhaustion after two days in the saddle and taking with her Emma, who already had cause to complain about Cedric's wandering hands.

As their host plied him with more wine, and talked on and on, Falk let his mind wander back to that moment during the day when his eyes had met Julia's. It remained clearly in his memory, specially marked because it was the first time she had smiled at him in such a manner. He longed to go upstairs to see what else lay behind her shy smile, but he could not leave the table without appearing rude or insulting. Besides, he wanted to keep Gilbert de Slevin firmly in his sight at all times.

When at last Cedric fell asleep in a drunken stupor and had to be carried away to his own bed by several sturdy serfs, and Gilbert had retired to his bedroll before the hearth, Falk bounded up the stairs to the solar.

And found Julia blissfully asleep. Between Emma and Lady de Ware. Falk retreated to his own blanket before the hearth in the great hall, surrounded by Sander and the five Angevins. For a short while he listened to the wind whistle about the rooftops and raindrops hiss amongst the fire ashes, forcing from his mind all thoughts of his distant wife, until at last he too fell asleep.

In the morning, descending to the great hall, Julia found Falk already gone, out into the cool morning to rally their departure.

She stood by the fire and sipped on cold milk, then set it aside as nausea wafted up again from her stomach. Pursing her lips, Julia thought some fresh air might be all she needed, for the smoky, dank hall was surely not good for anyone's health. Vernice made a rude, caustic comment about the rough conditions, but on this occasion Julia could not help but agree with her.

On the steps she met Falk, as he shouted an order over his shoulder, striding swiftly. He collided with her, murmured an apology and caught her shoulders between his two hands. Setting her steady upon her feet, his dark gaze swept over her pale face and the shadows beneath her eyes.

'You are well?' he asked, concerned, sensing that indeed all was not well.

Julia nodded. 'It is just my stomach that is unsettled. Perhaps something I ate. Or just tiredness.'

Falk nodded, in an abstracted manner, his eyes going again to the packing-up as he watched carefully his knights preparing to move out and embark on the final leg of the journey. He turned to Julia with a smile then and promised her, 'Just one more day and then we shall reach journey's end. Would it please my lady to be mistress of her own keep?'

She did not voice her burning question about who, indeed, would be mistress of L'Espérance, or what would become of Vernice. She smiled up at him. 'Aye.'

He stroked her cheek with the back of his hand, something passing between them as their eyes dwelled deeply on each other. Then Falk was called away and the moment passed.

* * *

As soon as their fast was broken they mounted up and waved goodbye to Cedric de Ware and his lady. As Falk prepared to wheel about an impatient Drago, the horse's eyes rolling in the direction of Snow as she headed with dainty steps under the gateway, Cedric caught the destrier's bridle and leaned in close to speak in hushed tones to Falk.

'Have a care, de Arques, for that Flemish devil over the border has taken a penchant to Bethune forest. 'Tis a perfect spot in that narrow gully for an ambush.'

Falk nodded, taking his warning seriously. 'I thank you for the advice, sir, but fear not, I have had many years practise in watching my own back.'

'Your guard is loyal?'

'More loyal than my own kin. I would trust them with my life, and, more importantly, I would trust them with my wife's life.'

Cedric nodded sagely, his jowls quivering. 'And 'tis a double duty.'

'What?'

'Your wife is with child, is she not?'

'Nay!' For a moment Falk looked utterly startled, and then confused, his gaze flicking to the swishing grey tail of Snow and her white rump, and the slim back of Julia riding elegantly side-saddle, 'At least, she has said naught of it to me.'

Cedric laughed, and slapped Drago affection-
ately on the neck. Drago snorted and tossed him a
warning glare. ''Tis always the way, lad. He who
makes the babe is the last to find out.'

'How can you tell?' questioned Falk, still looking in the direction of Julia. 'What is there about
her that makes you think she is with child?'

'Why, naught, lad. I happened to hear her vomiting this morn in the garderobe and knowing you
are newly wed, and a fine specimen of virile manhood, 'twas not difficult to work out the cause of
her malady. Now, away with you, and good luck!'

Falk raised his hand in salute, spurred Drago
and cantered off to join the head of his party. As
he passed Julia, he glanced at her swiftly, a frown
marring his handsome face.

That afternoon, as they approached Bethune forest, Falk sent two knights on ahead as scouts,
heeding Lord Cedric's advice. They returned to
say the way ahead was clear, but still they entered
the forest cautiously. Falk called for absolute silence. The only sounds were the jingle of harness
and the muffled footfalls of the horses as they
stepped on the mossy path.

With practised ears the knights listened to the
other sounds all around them, peering into the deep
gloom between the trees. But all they heard was
the twitter of birds, the snap of twigs caught be-

neath hooves, the shiver of a breeze rustling through the leafy branches, and the creak of saddle leather. There was nothing to betray the presence of an ambush party and it was with relief that they emerged from the cool shadows of the forest.

Aware that they had several miles to cover and only an hour or two, at most, of daylight, Falk quickened the pace. He was keen not to be caught out in open country when dusk fell. The afternoon faded quickly into evening, the pale sky tinged pink on the wide horizon. Swallows swooped low and the shadows deepened when at last the banks of the River Bethune were sighted. They rode through a valley green with beech and elm, and then clattered across a humped-back stone bridge and through a small village that brought them before the formidable walls of L'Espérance de Arques.

Julia craned her neck to catch her first glimpse of the castle that would be her home. On their last night in Rouen, which now seemed so long ago, Falk had described to her the home he had been sent to as a boy of twelve, on the brink of adulthood, when his mother had died and there had been no one else to care for him. Although he had not lived here for many years, he remembered clearly all the details. He told her it was built of stone on a high outcrop of rock, overlooking a bend in the slow moving waters of the River

Bethune. Originally the site had first been settled by the Romans and they had built a fortress here of which only the high flint walls that ringed the outer bailey still remained. This outer bailey was wider than the meadow surrounding Foxbourne and there was space enough to train an entire troop of cavalry and a dozen archers.

The castle itself, within the cradling walls of the inner bailey, was far advanced in design to many other castles in Normandy, thanks to a long-gone but intelligent ancestor. It had four round towers attached to a square keep at its centre, a deep well fed cleanly by an underground spring, kitchen and herb gardens, storerooms, armoury, stables and a chapel.

Falk cursed beneath his breath as they rode beneath the portcullis of the inner bailey unchallenged. He wished they had arrived earlier in the day, when the shadows were not so dense. Anything could leap out from them. He had the nasty feeling they were sitting ducks. The knights followed him cautiously, eyes narrowed, one hand on their reins and the other gripping sword hilts. Falk halted, but did not yet dismount. For long moments he sat in the saddle and glanced about. Drago stood rock still and steady, blowing softly when he longed to snort, aware of his master's tension.

It dawned on Falk that there was almost a deserted air about the place—no flags, no lights, no sentry. While he had not expected adulation from his father's family, he had at least expected… something…an acknowledgement that he, Falk, was now their baron.

'Piers, Luc, Alun, Thierry?'

'Aye!' the men replied in unison.

'Stay with the Comtesse.'

At his command the four Angevins closed ranks about Julia, as well as Emma and Vernice riding close at her side.

'Sven and Thorn, take the gate. The rest of you, come with me.'

Falk dismounted and the yard rang with a hiss of steel as he drew his sword and the knights were quick to follow suit. He ran up the stone steps that led to the massive entrance hall door, standing now unbarred and open. Falk approached cautiously, peering inside.

At this time of the evening he would expect the hall to be bustling with activity, as servants prepared the evening meal, set up trestle tables, tended to the hounds and the noble family that had, perhaps, been out all afternoon hunting or hawking or tending to the estate.

But this was not so and all was quiet.

In the dark gloom of the great hall he looked around. A fire in the hearth burned sluggishly, untended, and chained to the far wall several hounds now yapped with desultory interest that spoke of neglect. A hundred memories of long ago rushed at him at the sight of the familiar hall—the rafters, the fireplace, the banners and antlers displayed upon the panelled walls, all little changed despite the many years. Falk fought off his memories and concentrated on the facts that now presented themselves. He ordered one of his men to light several rush lamps so they might see more clearly what was before them.

Three human forms lay slumped across the dais and high table reserved for the use of the lord and his family. At first Falk feared the worst and he prodded a nearby body with the toe of his boot. With a groan the male serf rolled over, cursing, and now Falk lowered his guard as he caught the stench of wine fumes. Swearing far more volubly than the snoring serf, he barked out several commands that sent his men swarming over the keep, as he realised that matters were seriously amiss.

Outside Julia stretched her aching back and dangled her foot from the stirrup, the reins hanging loosely upon Snow's withers as the mare stood quietly, neck stretched low, tired.

Seeing that Julia made to dismount, Emma protested, 'Milady, the master bid us to wait here!'

'Oh, stuff and nonsense! I hear no clash of steel.' Julia looked around the courtyard and up at the impervious walls of the keep. 'The place seems quiet as a grave. I am sure that if there was trouble of any kind the ''master'' will have sorted it out by now. Besides, my backside aches from this saddle and if I do not quickly find a place to empty my bladder 'twill be too late.'

'Aye,' said Vernice, 'it has been a long journey and I for one seek a soft bed and a decent meal.'

The women dismounted, despite the fact that Emma muttered under her breath and railed in sharp French at Piers as he tried to force them back. Seeing that Julia was determined, the four Angevins swiftly dismounted and fell into step about the three women; besides which, Piers had a soft spot for Emma and he did not want to ruin his chances with her by entering into a quarrel. They formed a tight guard about Julia, Emma and Vernice as they crossed the churned ground of the yard and mounted the steps that led up into the keep.

Inside the hall, as her eyes accustomed themselves to the gloom, Julia exclaimed with surprise, for it was a scene of some mayhem that greeted her gaze. Two knights were throwing buckets of water over the slumped figures sprawled upon the dais. Her husband clutched the tunic of one bleary-eyed serf, whose nose he had already bloodied with an angry punch and at whom he shouted, 'Tell me the truth, you lying whore-son!'

'Falk!'

'What?' he roared, turning impatiently, but not relinquishing his hold.

Julia blinked, her features setting stubbornly and hands going to hips as he glowered at her.

'I thought I told you to wait outside!' Falk then spoke sharply in French to the Angevins, rebuking them severely and promising dire punishment. They shifted uneasily, eyes downcast.

'Do not chastise them,' Julia interrupted his tirade, 'for 'tis not their fault but mine. I am in desperate need of...' Julia glanced about and then lowered her voice to a whisper that only he could hear '...of the privy. Now, Falk, what goes on here? Let go of that man. 'Tis no way to begin your lordship with such a display of violence.'

Falk swore viciously and thrust the serf away from him with such force that he staggered and collapsed to the floor. 'I will tell you what goes on here. That Flemish bastard Hans Van den Bogaarde has walked in and helped himself. And these—these miserable excuses for serfs did nothing to stop him. Instead they took advantage of the broken cellar door and have drunk themselves into a stupor. And, to make matters worse, Van den Bogaarde has abducted all the female serfs. There is no one to cook or clean.'

'I see. But what of your father's knights?' Already Julia strode to the rear of the hall and began rolling up her sleeves, calling for Emma to follow, but quickly Falk overtook her and blocked her path.

'The knights have either died, fled or thrown in their lot with Van den Bogaarde. Where do you think you're going?'

'To the kitchen, of course. We are all hungry—'

'Nay. My wife is not a serf to scrub and cook.'

Julia tilted her head and looked up at him. 'Then who will, my lord?'

He took her elbow and led her away. 'I do not know, but not you. Emma, do what you can and my men will help you.'

Piers stepped forwards and gallantly offered his services to Emma, following her to the kitchen, and throwing a grin over his shoulder at the others.

Julia opened her mouth to protest, arms akimbo, and met Falk's scowl. He said softly, 'Be silent now, for I am in no mood to argue with you and if you do I may be tempted to beat you.'

'Try, Norman, and you'll be sorry!'

As their eyes met, each knowing that he would never lay a violent hand on her, they smiled and the trials of the day seemed suddenly to lessen. Falk took her hand. ''Tis what I am most fond of in you, wife. Your spirit.'

'My spirit?' Julia tossed her head with a smile, a wicked sparkle in her eyes, 'I have not heard it called that before.' She stood on tiptoe and reached up to kiss him, her hand on the back of his neck urging him to oblige her by stooping down. Then she pressed her mouth to his, the tip of her tongue just skimming his lips.

Falk was taken by surprise, for she had never voluntarily kissed him before. Aware that his knights watched, and grinned, he set her determinedly aside, but held her hand to keep her close by, his fingers slotted one between each one of hers in a possessive yet tender clasp.

The mood in the hall had lightened considerably, just as Julia had hoped, for she had no wish to live in a hall ruled by violence. Aware that now the daylight had all but gone, Falk took command and quickly gave his orders.

'Luc, go tell Thorn and Sven to secure both the outer and inner gates, for I want no surprise visitors in the night. Make sure you leave at least two sentries on each. Hervi, get these lazy sons of...' he saw Julia watching him and amended '...sons of dogs on their feet and have them kindle the fires and light tallows, and then see what state the armoury is in. Sander, see to Drago and Snow.' Here his glance skimmed over Vernice hovering by the hearth, and he included her horse in his instructions, before adding, 'See the wagons unloaded and then help Emma in the kitchen.'

The knights were quick to obey, Julia observed, as they each went in their bidden direction. She watched her husband's face as he spoke in French, and an odd light lit in her breast and fanned curious warmth through her limbs. She had little idea of the meaning of his words, but she was held in awe by the deep timbre of his voice and the strength of his command.

'Now…' at last he turned to Julia '…what was that about the privy?'

Julia smiled weakly, lowering her eyes in some confusion, suddenly feeling as gauche as a child. She gripped his hand tightly as they climbed the stairs, leaving behind the noise and bustle of the hall, but no sooner had they rounded the first bend in the spiral staircase than Falk stopped, and set aside his tallow light upon a ledge.

'My lord?' Julia looked up, a question creasing her brow.

Falk stooped and drew her up to the step upon which he stood, his arms clasping her slim back tight and pressing her close against him. His head descended and his mouth found hers. He kissed her deeply, slanting his head first this way and then that, his jaw working rhythmically as he opened her mouth and tasted her with his tongue. He groaned, and Julia responded. Her arms slid up and around his neck, enjoying the scrape of his stubble upon her cheek and the feel and taste of him as he kissed her hungrily.

It seemed he would never stop and Julia drew several breaths through her nose, aware that his hand clasped and supported the back of her head as his onslaught bent her slender neck. Then his mouth broke free and he kissed her cheek and her throat, murmuring, 'I have wanted to do that for two days now.'

He pressed her back against the wall, his hand curving over her breast and Julia could feel the hardness of his arousal thrusting against her belly. He groaned again and reached to pull up her gown, but Julia stayed him with one hand upon his chest.

'My lord, would you take me upon the stairs like a common serf?'

'Aye!' He laughed, desperate to find relief within the honey-soft core of her slender body.

'Nay,' admonished Julia, pushing him back with two hands, 'I will not let you. Besides, if you do not show me the privy now I fear my lord will be making love in a puddle.'

'My apologies,' Falk murmured, suddenly remembering his manners. He resisted the urge to kiss her again, and offered his hand. 'Come.'

It seemed very dark and cold ahead of them and Julia made a small sound of doubt. He held the tallow light higher and looked down at her as she clambered up behind his lithe form. 'There is naught to fear,' he assured her, 'If I remember correctly 'tis just here, along this passage.'

Julia held one hand to her nose at the stench that now assailed her senses. Falk swore and promised that the serfs would clean the garderobe with their tongues on the morrow.

'A brush and lye soap will work far better.' Julia suggested. Then Julia's eyes widened in alarm. 'Is there any danger of sickness?'

'I would not bring you here if there was even the slightest danger. Now, get on with it for I have no desire to stand all night in this foul hole.'

'Well, then, turn your back.'

He laughed. 'You jest, wife.'

'Nay, I do not. 'Tis most…private.'

He sighed and turned away.

'Not so far,' complained Julia, 'I cannot see.'

'Hell's teeth, woman!'

Julia grumbled about his rudeness, but she realised that she now trusted him so completely that she even allowed him to accompany her on such an intimate chore. When done, Falk took her hand and led the way down a short passage, at the end of which they came to a solid door. He opened it upon a chamber of such dank blackness that Julia reached for his arm, pressing close against his armoured bulk.

'Do not fear,' he murmured, smiling slightly at her anxious face, 'my men have checked every room in the castle and there is naught here but ourselves. For the moment.'

They entered the chamber and Falk lit candles on a wrought-iron stand and knelt before the hearth to tempt the kindling there laid into flames.

'This was their chamber,' he said over his shoulder, 'My father and—'

'The she-devil?'

His eyes met hers and they exchanged a smile.

'It does not please you?' Julia sensed his mood was not a happy one.

'Nay, it does not.'

'We could, mayhap, sleep elsewhere.'

'Where? In the hall with my men? With Vernice and de Slevin?'

Julia looked up sharply, 'Do you think they…?'

'Aye.' He swore and kicked at the brickwork of the fireplace. 'And I'll wager she did not wait until she became a widow.' He glanced across the room at the vast four-poster. 'But the bed looks comfortable, and big. We could do some fine rolling around and I have a mind to teach you that it is not always the man who lies on top.'

'Falk!' Julia blushed fiercely, and he laughed.

She turned away, to hide her confusion at all the pleasant and exciting emotions suddenly at war with her long-held resistance to him. She advanced to the ornate tester bedstead of dark, carved oak and hung with dusky-rose brocade.

'Do you think,' she asked, 'he died in this bed?'

Falk rose from the fireplace, satisfied with the flames that crackled there, and unlatched his sword belt. 'Nay,' he lied, not looking at her, 'I believe he died in the chapel.'

Julia sighed with relief. 'I do not think I could sleep in a dead man's bed.'

Tongue in cheek, Falk crossed himself, behind her back, and asked forgiveness in a swift, silent prayer for his untruthfulness, and then moved on quickly. 'Help me remove my armour, for Sander is busy tending to the horses.'

She turned away from her pensive contemplation of the bed and came to stand before him in the orange glow of firelight. At his direction she helped him to remove the heavy weight of his hauberk, dropping the chain mail with a hissing slither upon the floor. His sword he had already discarded and now, standing unfettered by steel, he reached out for her, his two hands upon her waist drawing her near, as he murmured his desire for her, his fingers working loose the ribbons of her braid.

The door creaked as it was thrust open and Emma came bustling in with an armful of linen to make up the bed. They sprang apart, just before Emma peered around the pile of her burden, and the maid did not notice the ribbons upon the floor, nor the guilty look upon their faces.

'My lord, Hervi bids that you come at once to the armoury.'

Falk cleared his throat, his eyes lingering and regretful as he looked down upon Julia. 'Very well.' He kissed her cheek. 'Until later.'

When he had gone Julia went to stand by the fire, gazing thoughtfully into the flames as Emma dumped her load of linen upon the bed and, taking out one small square, began to wipe away the dust that clung to every surface.

'Emma, where is Lady Vernice?'

'She is in the hall ordering anyone who would listen.' Emma angled diligently into every curlicue and twist of the ornate bedposts, 'But do not fear, my lady, I hear from Piers that the master will see her gone to the nunnery at Caen.'

'Indeed? And if she will not go?'

'Piers says the master will make her—' here she paused dramatically to draw breath '—*and* he says my lord Falk will run his sword through the abbess if she refuses to take her.'

'Oh, Emma, you talk nonsense. It will not come to that.' Julia rolled her eyes and pressed one hand to her jumping heart at such a dire thought.

'We must pray that it does not, for William and Matilda are pious supporters of the convent and my lord will find himself in terrible disfavour, if not the dungeon, if he should do such a thing.'

Emma seemed to seriously believe what she had been told and Julia was mindful to have words with Piers for teasing the innocent Emma so shamefully.

Satisfied that she had dusted the room as well as could be, Emma turned to the bed and began sorting out the linen. Julia came to her side, one hand upon the maid's shoulder staying her as she stared for a long moment at the grey mattress. Her mother had once warned her that men did not view the telling of truth in quite the same manner as women and Julia could not imagine a Norman baron being left to die upon the cold stone floor of his chapel.

'We have brought our own mattress from Rouen?' she asked Emma.

'Aye, milady.'

'Then take this one out and burn it!'

Chapter Twelve

There was much work to be done that night in putting the castle to rights, preparing a meal to feed sixty people, unloading the wagons of their personal possessions, scouring the rust from armour and tending to the horses. By the time Falk stumbled to bed, Julia was fast asleep. Remembering his conversation with Lord Cedric, he gazed upon her tenderly and did not awaken her. Quietly, he undressed and climbed into the bed, turning to lie against the curve of her body. She felt so soft and warm. He closed his eyes, idly fingering a long, silky strand of red-blond hair as his body relaxed after the rigours of the day and at last he too fell asleep.

Dawn came too soon. Sander, at Falk's prior bidding—fearing the warm comfort of a bed shared with Julia would tempt him to linger—came banging on the door. Julia sat up, startled, pushing her sleep-dishevelled hair from her face, her eyes roving wildly about, noticing at once that Falk had left their bed.

'My lord, is aught amiss?'

Falk shrugged on his tunic and braies and then shouted for Sander to enter, turning his back to Julia as he told her, his firm voice brooking no argument, 'I am going after Van den Bogaarde.'

Julia felt a start of alarm. 'Nay, Falk! You do not know how strong he is. If—if it came to a fight, who knows what might happen?'

He smiled a slow, dangerous smile. 'I hope that it will come to a fight, for I intend to take back what is mine and teach the dog a lesson.'

'But, Falk—'

'I am a soldier. It is what I am trained to do.'

Seeing that she could not dissuade him, her mind turned to other thoughts. 'Am I to remain here? Alone?'

'Aye. I cannot take my wife in to battle, but I promise that you will not be alone.' He spoke curtly, holding up his arms as Sander lifted the bulk of his chain mail hauberk over his head, 'I take only Hugh de Monceux and Hugo Fitzpons, along with thirty men-at-arms and, of course, Sander. The rest I leave here with you. You have command of this keep and, as Comtesse, your every word will be obeyed as though it were my own.'

'What of Vernice? Will she be agreeable to this vast plan?'

He snorted in derision. 'What she thinks is of little importance. She abides on sufferance beneath my roof and on my return I will make arrangements for her to remove to the nunnery at Caen.'

'And Gilbert? Is he to ride with you?'

'Nay. I leave him here, for I would not care to have his blade at my back. Hervi will keep an eye on him, have no fear, and for all his lecherous tendencies he is still a good soldier and I must leave you well defended. But I leave also de Bohun and de Lacy. They are trustworthy and you may look to them for assistance.'

Fully dressed and armoured, he latched on his sword and came then to stand beside the bed. He held out his arms and Julia shifted over, sitting up on her knees to place her own arms about his neck and hug him tight, despite the dig and pinch of his metal armour.

He turned his head and kissed her, his hands moulding themselves to the round shape of her bottom and pressing her close. He breathed in her scent, his lips moving tenderly on her lips, her mouth clinging to his as he lifted his head. Her hand on his neck urged him back down and he stooped to kiss her again, and again, until at last he tore free from her embrace and forced himself to step away, taking a deep breath and raking back his dark hair with one hand.

'When I return, my lady, we will finish these kisses,' he murmured, 'to our mutual satisfaction.'

And with that he bid her adieu and strode purposefully away.

Listening to his footsteps clattering down the stairwell, Julia glanced to the window. But it was shuttered with oilskins and she knew that she would not be able to watch him from there as he mounted Drago and rode out. For a while she snuggled down into the warm spot where he had lain beside her in the bed, breathing in his male aroma and picking a few dark chest hairs from the linen. How long? she thought. How long before he would return and she could run and tell him of this new feeling that had budded within her and would blossom into something wonderful…if he so wished?

She listened to the sounds of his departure, stifling the bereft feeling within her. With Falk out of the way there was work to be done, and she would make him proud to call her wife and this gloomy, massive pile of stone home. She shifted her position in the bed and glanced across the room at a table standing in the middle. Upon it lay a bunch of keys.

Quickly, Julia threw back the covers and jumped out of bed. For a moment, the room swayed alarmingly and her heart jumped as again that wave of nausea rose up like a churning wave from her stomach and swamped her senses. It passed, after a few moments, and Julia did not care to dwell upon it. She dressed in her oldest gown, the brown wool she had worn on her journey from Foxbourne, and donned both linen apron and wimple, tucking her hair away. Rolling up her sleeves, she set off with a determined stride downstairs.

In the hall she greeted Gabriel de Lacy and Roelf de Bohun (a cousin to Lady Magda) and they looked up with some surprise as she passed on to the kitchen, calling loudly for Emma. First order of the day was to tend to the hounds. She ordered them at once unchained, fed, watered and let out into the bailey. She set the youngest of the three serfs, a lad who went by the curious name of Grenouille, to look after them, impressing upon him the importance of not only keeping them well fed and watered but given some exercise and plenty of affection. He seemed happy to do her bidding and displayed some fondness for the mixed pack of golden mastiffs and grey wolfhounds; the dogs too seemed not averse to Grenouille.

Satisfied, Julia gave her attention to the second most important task of the day, which was to inspect the kitchen, check the storeroom and make an inventory. Armed with quill, parchment and ink, Julia scraped open the lock on a massive door at the rear of the kitchen, and pushed the heavy door open upon creaking hinges.

There was a dank smell, and Julia sent Emma, hovering at her elbow, to fetch a lighted tallow. When the maid returned she held it up high while Julia entered and perused the shelves. There was salt, in a clearly marked, well-sealed box—she opened it and was pleased to find that it was not damp, nor riddled with crawlies. Closing the lid, she wrote it down as the first item on her list, and then moved on to inspect pepper, dried herbs, cinnamon and nutmeg, recording each item diligently.

Julia was pleased to find earthenware jars of preserved apple and apricot, garlands of dried onion and garlic hanging from the rafters, a round of hard yellow cheese and a block of yeast wrapped in muslin. Upon the floor stood several barrels of wine and a large sack of flour. The flour was good, and as soon as her inventory was concluded Julia set Emma to baking bread, assisted by the three sullen serfs who had been so drunk upon their arrival.

They were suspicious of the new baron and his wife, having been poorly treated by the previous lord, and neither were they keen to do women's work. Julia managed to overrule their complaints with promises of a boon and a day to make merry, and soon had them scouring the cobwebs from every corner and cleaning out the dirty rushes.

The morning passed swiftly and Julia had scarce time to pause for a bite to eat. While she chewed on a crust of bread and a piece of cheese, one wary eye upon Vernice and Gilbert as they cozened together beside the fire in the hall, she asked Emma about the serf she had set to be their houndsman, Grenouille.

''Tis a most curious name he has. What does it mean?'

'My lady, it means frog.'

'Oh.' Julia stared at their subject, and could see why, by his rather protruding eyes and odd-shaped mouth, but he reminded her of Ham in far-off England and she promptly announced, ''Tis cruel! I shall call him Oswin. Aye, make it known, Emma, that I do not wish to hear such an unkind name used again.'

'Very well, my lady. I shall tell them.' Emma sighed. Nothing was going to be easy with her young mistress.

It was afternoon before Julia set about inspecting the hall and the chambers above stairs. There were four (the largest had been commandeered by Vernice), but all were sparsely furnished with just a bed and one or two coffers, a chair. Clearly any tapestries and rugs had been stripped from the floors and walls, for there were dusty, pale patches in every room. There was certainly not a single item of silver, or any musical instruments, or the simple, basic comforts of a keep that she had always been accustomed to having, such as warm furs, parchment and ink, books.

This then was her domain and she would venture no further—the armoury, the stables, the well, the meadow and archery butts, all this was male territory and she had no doubt that de Lacy and de Bohun, and Hervi as Falk's captain, would take excellent charge.

By eventide Julia could no longer find for herself work to occupy her time, and she changed her dirty gown for her dark blue kirtle. She brushed her unruly hair and descended to the hall, where Vernice, so beautifully dressed in maroon velvet and a girdle of gold brocade, her hair smooth and gleaming, made her feel skinny and ugly indeed.

Gilbert rose as he heard the tap of Julia's footfalls upon the flagstones. He greeted her in French, and bowed with grave courtesy. Julia stood stiffly, her expression cool as she hid her revulsion and from the corner of her eye saw the Angevins ringed about the hall. If Gilbert so much as stepped one toe out of line, she had only to call out and five swords would be drawn to his throat. Gilbert too seemed to know this, for he was the model of propriety.

Reluctant to reveal just how much French she had learned from the forceful Father Gerard—with whom Matilda had insisted she resume her lessons—and from listening to her husband and maid talking constantly in that language, Julia simply inclined her head and went to take her seat. Also sitting with them were the two senior knights, Gabriel de Lacy and Roelf de Bohun. Thankfully, these gentlemen seemed adept at polite, meaningless conversation, and as they both knew Vernice and Gilbert well from William's court at Rouen, Julia was not required to be the life and soul of the party. Indeed, as she cast sidelong glances at Vernice flirting with the roguish Roelf, Julia wondered if they knew each other rather too well.

She accepted a goblet of wine from Sir Gabriel, aware of the watchful gaze of Lady Vernice as she lounged in her chair beside the hearth, which she seemed to have occupied for much of the day.

'Lady Julia...' Vernice leaned forwards '...did my Lord Falk say when he would return?'

'Nay.'

''Tis a day's ride to Van den Bogaarde's place over the Flemish border,' supplied Sir Roelf, 'but I have no doubt Falk will strike swift and hard. Fear not,' he addressed his words to Julia, 'he will

not linger. In a few days he will be back. Maybe
sooner.'

Julia smiled. 'Thank you for your confidence.'
She did not want to think about what Falk was
doing, for she abhorred violence and she trembled
to think of what might happen to her husband if
he was not successful in his mission. She rose
then. 'Excuse me for a moment, while I see what
provisions the kitchen has made for the evening
meal.' She doubted whether Vernice would be satisfied with a simple fare of cold meat and hard
cheese.

The evening was an ordeal. Julia had little appetite, a pounding headache and felt sick to her
stomach. She sat in the chair that would have been
Falk's and endured the presence of Gilbert to her
right and Vernice to the left as best she could.
Gilbert, she noticed, was little pleased as Vernice
flirted with Sir Roelf and he drank more than he
ate, but at least he seemed to have little interest in
her.

Toying with the base of her goblet Julia enquired, at a suitable moment and as casually as she
could, 'What are your plans for the future, Lady
Vernice?'

Vernice blinked slowly, her eyes like a predatory and clever cat. She covered Julia's slender
hand with her own beringed fingers. 'Why, my

dear, I do not know. Of course, I may return to court, but at the moment I could not leave you here alone, amongst all these men—' here a wicked laugh '—I will stay and keep you company until my lord Falk returns.'

Julia gritted her teeth and resisted the urge to snatch her hand away. She smiled politely. 'That is not necessary, Lady Vernice, I assure you.'

Without looking at either of them, Julia was quite sure that Gilbert and Vernice exchanged meaningful glances over her head, for both were considerably taller than herself. Again, she longed to have Falk's solid bulk at her side, for reasons that were fast becoming many!

'But of course it is necessary, silly child! Why, you cannot even speak to these serfs in their own language.'

'I have Emma, and Hervi, to translate for me.'

Vernice laughed, a hollow sound. 'Anyone would think that I was not welcome.'

Aware that she was close to breaking all the rules of etiquette and hospitality, Julia was silent. After all, Vernice was a widow, and a relative. Much as she longed to be rid of her, it would not be viewed in a favourable light to act too harshly against her. She would have to be patient, and play the game Vernice was intent on amusing herself with.

After the meal, pleading a headache and retiring
early to her chamber, Julia poked viciously at the
logs crackling in the fireplace and remembered the
way Vernice had said 'my lord Falk'. My lord Falk
indeed! He is not yours, thought Julia, and kicked
her foot against the stone hearth with some force.
Never yours!

She had to find a way to be rid of her and Julia
sat down to ponder this as Emma brushed out her
hair. After some moments of careful thought she
realised that she had to establish exactly what were
Vernice's intentions. Did she covet Falk, as the
new Comte de Arques? Or was it indeed Gilbert
de Slevin that she had become enamoured of? And
what of Gilbert? Did he have a passion for the new
widow, or was it a passing fancy that would
quickly pall as she no longer possessed a fortune
at her fingertips? She would need to establish
Gilbert's intentions as well, and there was only one
way to do that.

Lying alone in bed that night, trying not to think
of Falk and how he fared, she pondered upon her
plan of action and knew that she had to be very,
very careful if all was not to go horribly amiss.
Then her thoughts drifted, to the castle, and to the
nearby village and its peasant inhabitants. Surely
they belonged to L'Espérance and it was her duty
to care for them as surely as she did the serfs
within the castle walls? On the morrow she would

pay the village a visit and introduce herself. It had always been her way at Foxbourne to be on good terms with the vassals, for then she earned their respect and their loyalty, and a happy vassal produced his tithes without complaint.

The following day Julia had Snow saddled and she rode out, with the five Angevins as her guard and most senior of the serfs, Marteau, as her guide. They clattered across the humped-back bridge and down a narrow lane overhung by a canopy of tree branches grown so close together they formed a tunnel. Sunlight shone in dappled patches and the ground was soft underfoot, masking their hoof-beats.

'What is the name of this village?' asked Julia of Marteau, and when he did not understand her faltering, strangely accented French, Hervi asked for her.

Marteau shrugged. 'Le village du chateau de L'Espérance de Arques.'

As they approached Julia saw at once the signs of neglect in the tufted straw roofing the small huts in which the peasants lived. It seemed the village with no name had no master either. She saw the broken implements lying useless against the walls, and she saw fields of pristine countryside that should have been cultivated to bear crops of wheat and barley. There seemed to be no vegetable patches and almost no livestock—how these people managed to survive she could not imagine. Julia saw too, the look of hopelessness and distrust in the pinched, sallow faces that stared at her horse, but did not dare raise to stare at Julia, surrounded by her well-fed, well-clothed and, indeed, well-armed guardsmen.

Shame, and anger, ignited within her breast and swept over her from head to toe in a fierce wave. Julia wasted not a moment in giving her instructions to Hervi.

'We will care for these people, Hervi. See to it that their roofs and their implements are repaired. I do not know if we have seed for them to plant crops and vegetables, but if not we will go to the nearest market town and buy it for them. Cows and pigs and chickens too.'

'My lady, 'tis summer, too late for planting,' Hervi argued.

Julia held up her hand. 'I will not sleep with a full belly while these people starve. If they cannot grow their own fodder, we must provide for them in the meantime. Tell them what we will do.' And seeing that these people would be too proud to accept charity, 'And tell them that one-third shall be a tithe to the Comte de Arques, and the rest is for themselves. Tell them that Falk, their baron, is an honourable man who will care for them in peace and war.'

Hervi acquiesced and did as he was bid, his voice raising as the peasants murmured and shuffled. As they took in Julia's instructions they turned to one another with looks of disbelief, daring now and then to take a peek at their new Comtesse and seeing that no whip was raised to them for daring to look upon her. Hope stirred.

As they prepared to turn about and return to the castle, an old woman, bent over and struggling to walk with the aid of a gnarled staff, came shuffling forwards and grabbed hold of the hem of Julia's gown. At once Alun shouted and made a move to kick the old crone away, fearing for Julia.

'Nay, Alun!' Julia stayed him, 'Let us hear what she wants.'

The old woman's dialect was impossible for Julia to understand, and while she spoke she tugged forward a small child, a boy of no more than eight years. He was dirty, his black hair matted and his clothes ragged, but when he glanced up Julia gasped, holding a hand to her mouth. The boy's eyes were Falk's, very black, and his nose was Falk's, very straight, and his square chin too was familiar. Uncertain, Julia looked to Hervi and he told her, with some embarrassment, ''e is one of the Comte's *enfant naturels*.'

'What!' Julia looked about to see who could be the mother of Falk's child.

Hervi guessed at her distress and told her quietly, 'Not your 'usband, but 'is father, *le baron décédé*.'

They ascertained from the old woman, in a long, tortuous conversation, that the boy's mother was dead and she, the grandmother, could no longer care for him. There were no other children in the village, for the few there had been had all died of the fever at the same time as the Comte and his two sons. The grandmother now asked if Julia would take the boy in, as page mayhap, and raise him within the relative safety of the castle.

'Aye,' said Julia, needing little more than a moment in which to give her answer, 'aye, we will take him.'

'My lady, is theez wise?' questioned Hervi. '*Votre mari*…'e will not want 'is father's bastard.'

'Nonsense! Falk is fond of children. We will take him. Pick him up and put him before you, Alun, and see to it that he is properly washed, clothed and fed.'

Julia then wheeled Snow about and cantered back in the direction she had come, to the castle she was quickly learning to call home.

That afternoon the sentry shouted from his lookout high upon the south tower and with hope in her heart Julia paused, as she crossed the bailey from the herb gardens, and raised one hand to shield her eyes from the glare of the late afternoon sun. Hervi came out from the armoury and ascended to the tower. Scarce able to wait a moment to hear if it was Falk, she picked up her skirts and ran to the tower entrance. Her feet made a patter as she raced up the spiral stairs, and emerged breathless upon the battlements, leaving a trail of scattered herbs in her wake as they bounced and fell from the basket hung upon her arm.

Seeing the expectant look upon her face, Hervi said in his rough, slow-spoken mixture of French and English that it was only a tinker with a few pots and pans and wooden spoons to peddle. Her disappointment bit deep. 'Twas no easy task being left with the charge of a castle this size, and so many people within! Why, Foxbourne seemed naught more than a hen-house in comparison. Every moment of the day someone came nagging at her elbow about something and, although she relied heavily upon Falk's knights for assistance, she was weary.

Only a few days later, on a bright blue morning, another uninvited guest arrived at the gates of L'Espérance de Arques. This time, however, he was entirely welcome and Julia, with arms and legs and braids flying, ran to embrace Father Ambrose. Laughing, she drew him into the hall, sat him down and clapped for Emma to bring him refreshment. Then, kneeling at his feet and holding his plump hand to her cheek, as though she hardly dared to believe his existence before her very eyes and holding on tight lest he vanish like a hazy dream, she bombarded him with questions.

'How come you to be here, Father? How is Mother? Did she get my letter about Falk's inheritance? Obviously she did, or you would not be here! And Foxbourne? How long will you stay?'

He laughed, patting her head, his bulk heaving beneath the rough brown wool of his monk's habit, his tonsured head bowed to look upon her much-missed face. 'I am on pilgrimage, child. I will meet with a party of Benedictine monks in Rouen and together we will journey to Jerusalem. Your mother is well, and sends her love. Foxbourne still stands.'

'Oh Father, Father! How glad I am to see you.'

'Is all well, my lady?' Father Ambrose looked about, an enquiry in his eyes. 'Your husband…?'

Julia proceeded then to tell him the whole tale, her voice lowering as Vernice and Gilbert came into the hall. 'I pray that he will soon be home.'

Looking shrewdly over this pair, Father Ambrose patted her hand and accepted the tray of bread and cheese and wine that Emma brought for him. Introductions were made and Vernice made known her desire to hear mass.

'Perhaps on the morrow,' Julia told her coolly. 'Father Ambrose has had a long journey, most of it on foot. I am sure he must be weary.'

'I am never too weary, my child, to do God's work. There is a chapel?'

'Aye. 'Tis a pretty one, with stained-glass windows and a marble altar,' said Julia, 'I will see to it that all is made ready for you, Father. Sit you there and enjoy your meal. There is no need for haste.'

Flashing a glance at Vernice, she rose to her feet and hurried to the kitchen to fetch candles and chivvy Emma into bringing a broom and a cloth to clean the dust and cobwebs from the chapel. Although the day was yet newly begun, climbing the stairs Julia felt tired already, nauseous, and she wondered again what strange malady had befallen her these weeks passed, that she could not seem to shake. She vowed to make herself a tisane of camomile and mint to ease her digestion.

Falk had made camp a mile from the stronghold of Hans Van den Bogaarde and sent ahead two scouts to spy out the lie of the land and Van den Bogaarde's fortifications. It was late evening when they returned and beginning to rain, but Falk was eager to hear their report and then swiftly made up his mind to press his advantage of surprise and a greater number of men. He gave orders that a tree trunk suitable as a battering ram be cut down and that the men were to take their rest until the early hours of morning. Then he sat before the fire outside his tent, watching as Sander prepared food.

He chafed at the delay to take food and rest, for his blood was hot for revenge and the need to return home to his young wife, left alone amongst knights that she barely knew. He remembered how Julia had hugged him goodbye, had been eager for his kisses. Did he even dare to think of love? He could not wait to find out, and ascertain as well whether he was to be a father; Julia seemed unaware of any babe and had certainly made no mention of such to him. Mayhap he would be the one to tell her! Falk chuckled out loud, and then coughed and narrowed his eyes to the horizon as his squire, Warren and Hugo looked at him enquiringly.

With a heavy sigh, Falk stood up and paced, glancing across the meadow at his men as they sat about preparing their weapons, checking bowstrings and shields, talking softly to one another. There was an air of excitement as they anticipated the coming fight, for they had trained many hours to bear arms, to win a quarrel by force of those arms, and they were spurred on by the knowledge that Falk de Arques led them. It was his serfs, his silver, that had been stolen and they saw it as their privilege to win it back for him.

The camp settled down as men practised the art of sleeping on rough ground, in the open, for only a few short hours; some, like Falk, did not sleep at all, but kept their nerves taut and ready. Past the witching hour of midnight Falk gave the command to rouse his men and mount up. They moved off slowly into the dark rain-spattered night and crept up like silent ghouls upon the sleeping household of Van den Bogaarde.

Falk did not hesitate. He did indeed strike hard and fast, in the way that William had taught him—without mercy. His intention was that the name of de Arques would be remembered and feared.

At the end, there was only a handful of women and children left screaming and sobbing in the mud and rain as their hall blazed to the ground. Falk ensured that his own female serfs were bundled into a cart brought along for this purpose, the other cart loaded up with his looted household goods. He took nothing that was not his by right. He rode off again into the night as suddenly as he had arrived, his face and hands blackened with the grime of battle, his sword stained with Hans Van den Bogaarde's blood, truly never to be forgotten by those that watched wide-eyed as he departed.

As dawn broke he drove his men onwards without pause for rest, determined to reach L'Espérance by nightfall.

* * *

Julia groaned, and rolled again towards the bucket Emma held as she knelt beside the bed. The maid murmured soothingly and wiped Julia's brow and mouth with a cool, damp cloth, but to little avail. Her mistress continued to writhe and moan, clutching at her stomach, her shift soaked with sweat.

'Send for Father Ambrose!' cried Julia, 'And write a letter to my husband, for I fear I am dying.'

Emma clucked her tongue at this nonsense and smiled with a wisdom far beyond her years. Julia looked up sharply, frowning at her maid.

'You do not believe me, Emma?' she asked indignantly, 'Why, I have some strange bloating decease. My bodily functions have ceased and I can hold down naught.'

Emma had been reluctant these weeks past to make it plain to her mistress, who could, at times, be short-tempered, the exact nature of her malady. But now, with a heavy sigh, she saw no other course.

'My lady,' said Emma cautiously, 'did your mother never explain to you the symptoms of a babe?'

Julia stopped in mid-groan and lay still, and then jerked upright, exclaiming, 'What!' Her hands went at once to her slightly rounded belly, staring at it in awe and confusion. 'A babe!'

Emma smiled. ''Tis a common effect of coupling.'

'Emma! I will not have crude talk.'

The maid shrugged, pouted and muttered something in French about high-born ladies and their temperament. Then she stood up and put aside the bucket. 'My lady will have a little dry bread? 'Twill ease your bile.'

Julia nodded and chewed thoughtfully upon a crust. A babe! Falk's babe. A little son, with black hair. He would be sweet and strong, like his father. Julia sank back against the pillows, her arms thrown above her head as she stretched languorously. Oh, how pleased Falk would be with this news! She could not wait for him to come home. Throwing back the covers, Julia swung her legs out of the bed and announced, 'Quickly, bring my gown, for I would go now to the chapel and pray upon my knees for my lord Falk's swift return home.'

News of Julia's impending motherhood spread throughout the castle and celebrations were called for. Embarrassed, Julia accepted the many congratulations from Falk's knights, blushing heartily at their knowing looks. Even Vernice offered her a cool cheek and a hug, but Julia sensed her displeasure by her curt tones and pursed lips.

Mindful of her condition, Julia spent the day quietly, seated in a chair beside the warm fire crackling in the hearth of the great hall. She bent her head and concentrated with unusual diligence upon Falk's tunic as she repaired a rent beneath the arm.

Across from her sat Gilbert. She could not openly criticise his presence and suggest he move his carcass elsewhere. Now and then, beneath lowered lashes, she cast him covert glances, trying to decide what, exactly, it was about his face that she disliked. It was not so much the hideous scar that twisted his one cheek, for Falk too had scars. Gilbert, at first glance, was quite handsome, perhaps even more so than Falk, for her husband was dark and his features hard—courtly beauty was based upon the golden, blue-eyed good looks that Gilbert possessed. Was it perhaps the thinness of his small mouth, hinting at a cruel streak? Or the close-set eyes and arched brows that she thought rather devil-like?

Quickly Julia looked down, placing another careful stitch in Falk's tunic, as Gilbert stirred and glanced her way. Then she forced herself to bestow upon him a smile and make polite enquiry as to how he fared. He looked taken aback at this unusual display of friendless from a woman who had made no secret of her hostility towards him, but Gilbert was unshakeable in his conviction that all women desired him.

'I make no complaint, my lady,' he replied cautiously, glancing to where stood Hervi and Luc, ever watchful.

'We are fortunate to have such fine weather at the moment.'

'Indeed.' His lips twisted in wry amusement at her clumsy attempt to make conversation with him. 'My lady looks very well this morning.'

Julia did not feel in the least well, but she inclined her head with a small smile of thanks. 'I would be grateful if you could spare some time to exercise Snow for me. I fear that…' Julia blushed '…in my…condition…I will not be able to ride for some little while.'

''Twould be my pleasure to ride my lady…my lady's horse.'

Her cheeks were flagged with hot colour, aware of Gilbert's penetrating gaze as he sought to take advantage of her tentative olive branch. How to broach the subject of Vernice? Julia sought desperately for words. Then the object of her affliction entered the hall, sashaying with a sway of her hips and the soft swish of velvet on the flagstones. Vernice laid her hand possessively on that knight's shoulder, while leaning down and whispering in his ear. Gilbert laughed and looked at Julia with such a burning gaze that her blush deepened, but Vernice ignored her and seemed little interested in Julia's reaction to Gilbert. Or did she think her so 'skinny and ugly' that no man in his right mind could possibly have any interest in her? Julia pursed her lips and stabbed her needle with unnecessary force through the fabric of Falk's tunic.

A feast was planned for the evening meal to celebrate Julia's good news and she retired to her chamber in the afternoon to rest and refresh herself. On waking, she took a bath and had Emma brush out her hair until it gleamed like burnished copper, twisting a rope of tiny seed pearls through two thin braids on either side of her temples. She dressed in her midnight-blue gown and placed her girdle carefully over her hips.

This evening she would shake Lady Vernice out of her conviction that she was the only attractive woman residing at L'Espérance. If she failed to be jealous of Julia's attentions to Gilbert, then she would know that Vernice had only one goal in remaining beneath their roof—Falk.

During supper Julia smiled at Gilbert often, allowed him to cut meat for her and fill her goblet with wine. She was careful not to overplay her hand, her eyes often downcast, but even so she caught the stares of the five Angevins and knew that her attentiveness to Gilbert caused consternation and would no doubt be reported to Falk. This notion caused a slight tremor in her hand, for she knew well that Falk was easily goaded to jealousy and would not appreciate her little flirtation, even if it was to the purpose of ridding them of Vernice. Truth to tell, she was not at all sure that she was going about the business in the right manner, having never flirted with a man before in her life. But judging from the narrowing of Vernice's coal-black eyes as she too noticed, and pondered, Julia's behaviour, she ventured to guess that she was not entirely unsuccessful.

After supper someone struck up a chord upon the lute, and someone else tapped a drum.

'My lady, would you do me a great honour and dance with me?' Gilbert held out his hand to her.

'Thank you, but I do not know these Norman dances well.'

'I will be happy to teach you. Come. Do not be afraid. Let us enjoy ourselves this evening.'

Julia smiled up at him, and took a deep drink of wine to steady her nerves, before placing her hand in his and allowing him to lead her down from the dais and out onto the floor. Truth to tell, Gilbert was an accomplished teacher and Julia had always been fond of music and dancing. She was soon whirling around the hall, laughing and enjoying herself very much indeed.

Chapter Thirteen

The rain poured down in icy sheets, gusted by a relentless wind. The horses plodded with necks hung low, ears and tails twitching as they flicked at the stinging drops. Falk chivvied his party along, anxious now to be home before dark.

They came out of Bethune forest and into the village, at last on familiar territory. Here Falk noticed the wisps of smoke from the small group of huts, the newly thatched roofs, the freshly hoed patches of ground behind each hut, the three goats and two cows tethered beneath a newly built byre.

Clattering across the humped-back bridge, Falk glanced over his shoulder and checked that the females that rode with them were still following safely, before spurring Drago into a controlled canter as the walls of L'Espérance reared up out of the misty gloom. The gates were barred, as he expected, but when Thorn, on sentry duty, leaned out of his tower and peered at the arrivals, he gave a great shout at seeing who it was. Quickly the gates were opened, and the Comte de Arques was welcomed home.

Falk dismounted swiftly, amidst the clattering noise of his men at arms. His glance went at once to the keep. There was a fierceness about him that the lust of battle had quickened in his veins, and he was powerless to rid himself of it. Only Julia could do that. With her gentle smile and tender touch. He needed to lie in her arms and make himself forget the men he had so ruthlessly killed. Quickly he gave his orders for the female serfs to be taken to the kitchen and tended to and for his wagon load of silver and tapestries and furs to be unloaded. Then he ran lightly up the steps and entered the hall.

Falk looked about, his arrival unnoticed. It was a merry gathering, he noted with some surprise, with music and laughter and dozens of candles lit all about the hall. Two couples were dancing in the middle of the hall, edged by the other knights as they sang, clapped hands in tune to the beat of a drum, or took deep draughts of their wine. Falk walked slowly forwards, hands on hips, a frown lowering his brows and making his face, already stained with dirt, cuts and bruises, a frightening sight. He saw that Vernice danced with Roelf de Bohun and that Gilbert de Slevin danced with someone. He could not see her face. And then the couple turned, as Gilbert twirled his partner about and a swirl of red-blond hair flashed through the air. Laughter rang out. Her feet pattered across the flagstones as she danced, smiling up at Gilbert...and for a moment Falk could only stare, before his battle-lust overboiled into rage.

His wife! By God! His wife was dancing with Gilbert de Slevin, smiling at him, holding his hand, allowing him to put his other hand upon her waist!

A bellow of fury erupted from Falk. At once the music ceased, the dancers came stumbling to a halt and all seemed to move so slowly. Julia turned, her eyes wide as she gazed upon Falk.

Gilbert's laughter had quickly subsided as Falk stormed into the room. Cursing loudly, he grabbed Gilbert by the scruff of his tunic and ripped him from Julia's side. Julia screamed, shocked by this brutal behaviour, horrified by Falk's blackened and bloodstained appearance. There were many others who joined in with cries of consternation. They one and all stared at Falk, his sword hissing a silver song as he drew it from the scabbard latched to his waist, staring at the dark grime upon his face and hands, the blood-rust edging his blade. Gilbert held up his hands in a gesture of surrender, his eyes wide open in surprise, for he wore no sword.

'Arm yourself, de Slevin, for this day we settle the score! My wife is mine and I share her with no other.'

'Falk!' Julia approached him, 'We merely danced, my lord, believe me.'

With an angry snarl Falk thrust her aside. 'You, madam, I shall deal with later.'

Hervi and Gabriel rushed forwards. Their loyalty was unquestionably to Falk, but they could not stand by and see their lady ill-treated. They caught Julia before she fell to the floor, and she looked to both men, eyes wide with fear and doubt.

'What goes on here?' asked William Fitzpons, now arriving and barging into the group gathered about the hall, still others crowding in the doorway behind him. But no one answered as all eyes were turned upon Falk. He lunged forwards and slashed at Gilbert's tunic, leaving a rent across his chest and a thin streak of blood that provoked cries and a babble of consternation. Falk stood glowering at the man he had challenged.

'Come on! Let us settle this once and for all!'

'I will not fight you, Falk,' replied Gilbert grimly, his hands still raised, 'I have done nothing wrong. I merely dance, in public, with the Lady Julia, with her full consent. She was not forced.'

'Indeed?' Falk swivelled his menacing glance to Julia, his tone the growl of a savage beast. 'I will teach you the meaning of fidelity, wife.' Again Falk lunged at Gilbert, slashing his sleeve. 'Find your sword, de Slevin, for I am well in the mood for teaching lessons.'

At that Julia conquered her fear with anger and she shook free of the supporting hands beneath her elbows and rushed at Falk, grasping at his sword forearm. 'Stop this! I will not have fighting in my hall!'

Falk threw her off, with an angry snarl. 'Get out of my way, woman!'

'You will not do this, Falk de Arques!' shouted Julia, rushing at him again. 'I demand that you put down your sword at once!'

Falk swore, maddened beyond all good sense, and raised his fist to strike at her. But the Angevins, watching and waiting for their moment, sprang and caught his arm before the blow could fall, all five of them protecting their lady, and protecting Falk from the folly of his rage. It took all of them to wrestle from his grasp his sword and there was much shouting and scuffling and the thud of fists as Falk fought them off. At last they had him subdued, and Julia stared with horror at her husband. Then, with a small cry, sickened to her stomach, she turned and ran from the hall.

All night Julia tossed and turned, sometimes pressed against the warm, plump body of Emma, who loyally remained, sometimes lying alone, weeping, on the edge of the bed. In the early hours she fell asleep out of exhaustion, one hand propped beneath her cheek and the other pressed to her swollen, aching eyes.

*   *   *

In the morning Falk woke first. His heart pounded at the queasy lurch of his stomach and the instant surge of memory. He lay wrapped in a bedroll before the hearth of the great hall, close about him the barricade of the Angevins. He remembered that they had prevented him from going to his wife in her chamber, for fear of what he might do to her, and forced him to sleep the night here.

He was tempted now to go to his bedchamber and awaken Julia, and indeed he rose and climbed the stairs, but his hand trembled upon the door ring and he could not bear to even look upon her. What would she think of him now? He, who had killed a dozen men in cold blood and was ready to kill another before her very eyes, in her own hall? He, who had raised his hand to her and would have struck her, surely knocking her to the ground with the force of such a blow, hurting her, damaging her lovely face. He turned abruptly away and went downstairs.

Last night he had washed in a barrel of steaming water, but this morning he felt the need to wash again. He scrubbed and scrubbed, washed his hair twice and had the serfs toiling back and forth as they filled the bathing tub with copious amounts of hot water. Meticulously, he cleaned beneath his nails with the point of his dagger. Dried and dressed again, he broke his fast in the kitchen and drank cold milk and ate some bread, then he went up the spiral stairs of the north tower and stood alone upon the battlements, seeking fresh air to clear his mind. But he was so filled with disgust and misery that nothing could take it away, and he looked out at the dripping trees, the grey river, and the sullen sky that promised more rain.

It was here that Vernice found him. Any woman with a grain of wisdom would have flinched and turned away from the raw emotions imprinted upon his face. But Vernice merely sashayed to his side and placed her cool hand upon the corded muscle of his forearms, folded across his chest as he leaned against the stone wall.

She smiled up at him. 'Take comfort, my lord. You did as you thought right.'

His glance was piercing, his voice cold as snow. 'Madam, I wish for no comfort from the likes of you.'

Vernice shrugged. 'Your silly little wife has made you angry. But that will pass. What you need is a woman, a real woman, not a simpering child.' She leaned provocatively into him, her full red lips pouting.

Falk felt his bile rise. Julia would have taken careful note of his sharp breath, his lowered brows, the flexing of his muscles, but Vernice seemed ignorant of these warnings. He eyed her with distaste, still leaning with his deceptively nonchalant stance upon the wall. Clearly, Vernice had formed the idea that she now had a chance to pick up where they had left off many years ago, but Falk realised that he could never love this vain, selfish, brittle creature, and doubted whether once he ever had. But he knew the advantage of being rid of her and so told her softly, 'Pack your belongings and be ready to depart before noon.'

'What!' Vernice exclaimed, 'This is my home. You cannot force me from it.'

'This is no longer your home. Julia is mistress of L'Espérance and I urge you to pack and be ready to leave, lest I be tempted to throw you from my gates with nothing more than the clothes upon your back. Now, be gone from my sight, for I have had a taste of your ''comfort'' in the past, and found it not to my liking.'

Shortly after she had left him the five Angevins came, elbows stabbing one another in their haste as they pounded up the stairs, eager to speak with Falk. For a long moment he did not turn and face them, but continued to stare out at the bleak landscape, seeming to be untouched by the damp wind as he stood uncloaked. Then, at their coughs and shuffling, he turned with one brow raised in silent enquiry.

'My lord, we wish to speak with you.'

'Well, then, speak.'

'My lord, last night…forgive us, but we had to stop you. You were not yourself.'

'And about the Lady Julia. My lord, she has done nothing deserving of your anger.'

Falk's shoulders stiffened, and he half-turned, 'I never thought for a moment that she did.'

There was silence, a heavy, brooding silence. Then, ventured Thierry, 'Will you not now speak with the Comtesse and satisfy yourself as to what occurred?'

'Surely,' implored young Piers, 'you cannot think that my lady would ever do more than smile and dance with another man? Why, 'tis madness! She is faithful only unto you, milord.'

Luc agreed. 'She would not give him, or any man, the time of day.'

'Will my lord come now and speak with the Comtesse? The sound of her weeping does sorely plague our ears.'

Falk turned his back to them. 'I shall be the one to decide to whom I shall speak, and when. Hervi, take ten men and escort the Lady Vernice to the convent at Caen. Do not return until she is safely there and make it clear to her that in the future she will not be welcome beneath my roof.'

'Aye, milord.' Hervi smiled and bowed before departing to ready his men.

The others shuffled off with him, leaving Falk alone to brood in silence.

* * *

The castle settled into a hushed state of anxious waiting, its lord and lady far distant from each other. In her chamber Emma brought Julia fresh-baked bread and cheese to break her fast. There was a jug of wine and Julia's tongue curled, her stomach heaving. 'Take it away!'

She did not even bother to dress, but sat in her shift, curled up in a chair beside the fire. Having failed to persuade her mistress to eat, Emma went off to tend to her chores, leaving Julia alone to nurse her tears.

How could Falk think I would betray him? asked Julia of herself a hundred times. Over and over the phrase beat through her mind, until she thought she would go mad. Near midday the door opened and, without looking up, Julia murmured, 'Go away, Em. I want no dinner.'

'Is that so, my lady?' said Falk, his deep voice vibrating about the room and causing Julia to sit up with a jerk and raise her eyes to him, fearfully.

He closed the door and strode across the room, halting to stand before her as she sat in the armchair with her knees drawn up to her chest. He reached out and stroked his thumb across her flushed, tear-stained cheek. His hand fell away and his eyes glanced down to his boots. 'I am sorry.'

'Oh, Falk!' Julia leapt to her feet and flung her arms about his neck, tears spilling from her eyes.

'You frightened me. I have never seen you so angry...so—so wild.'

'Last night I killed many men...slaughtered them without mercy. When I returned to find you in Gilbert's arms, laughing and dancing with him...I could have killed you too. I raised my fist to you.' He spread his hands and stared at his feet, head hung low in shame, 'Such a beast am I.'

Desperately she dragged his face towards her, looking up into his eyes. 'Is that why you have avoided me? And I thought it was because you feared I had been unfaithful!'

'Nay!' he cried hoarsely, 'Nay, my love, I did not think that. It was my own self I feared, that I would be repugnant to you. The barbarous Norman ever willing to fight and slay.'

'You are Norman, aye, but not barbarous. You are a man of honour and you had to do your duty, no matter how hard it was and how brutal it may seem to others. I do not judge you. I love you. I love you!'

Slowly, his arms went about her waist, hardly daring to believe the words he heard. His head lowered and he pressed his face to her soft cheek, rasping her skin with the stubble upon his chin and jaw. For a long moment he could not speak, his throat working soundlessly as deep emotions welled up and all but strangled him. He felt her small hand at the back of his neck, smoothing his hair, and he felt the slenderness of her fragile body pressed tight against him.

'Falk?' Julia drew back, uncertain, frightened at his lack of response.

He cleared his throat then, and murmured huskily, 'My own dear wife, I love you too. Have you not known? Since that first day at Foxbourne, when I cut off your hair, I have loved you.'

Julia leaned back in the circle of his arms and stroked his cheek. 'Forgive me. I have fought you every step of the way. It has taken me long to see what a fine and honourable man you are.'

He laughed at this praise, hardly able to understand how he deserved it after his behaviour.

'You are!' Julia insisted, 'And you are so brave, so strong, so handsome, so—'

Falk held up his hand, 'Enough. My head will be so swollen I'll scarce be able to stand.'

''Tis not your head that is swollen, my lord,' murmured Julia mischievously, as she pressed against him, 'Kiss me, Norman, kiss me now.'

Falk stooped and lowered his head, his mouth finding hers. At the touch of his lips upon her lips, Julia felt heat surge through her. Her breath came in quick, sharp gusts through her nose, as he slanted his head, drinking his fill of her sweet mouth. Quickly her fingers fumbled to remove his clothes and his own fingers slid the shift from her shoulders.

He groaned, and slid his hands over her smooth curves, pausing on the swell of her breasts and the round firmness of her belly. As he kissed her neck, she murmured, 'Falk, I have something to tell you.'

For a moment he stiffened, wondering what news she had and preparing himself for the worst. She smoothed the palm of her hands over the muscular width of his broad shoulders, revelling in the feel of him as he leaned over her. One hand slid round to his chest, exploring the expanse of solid muscle, the sprinkle of fine dark hairs, following the thin line with her fingertip, downwards. She felt so dizzy with pleasure that she shook her head, and arched back her neck. In a husky whisper she told him of the babe she carried.

'I know.' He grinned.

'You know?' exclaimed Julia, leaning back in his embrace and staring up at him.

'Cedric de Ware dropped a hint a week ago. I wasn't sure back then, but I have only to touch you to know that my son quickens in your belly, for you were reed-slim and now there are curves to fill my hands.'

Julia laughed. They both laughed, and then he scooped her up into his arms and carried her to the bed. Placing her down gently, he knelt beside her, looming large and powerful and masculine as he eyed her delicate body. Then he lay down and his hand slid between her knees.

'I wanted to tell you,' Julia gasped, shuddering with intense pleasure at his hand sliding higher, 'but had no chance.'

He silenced her then, returning his mouth to her lips, kissing her deeply as he continued to explore and tease and cherish her body, and she shyly touched him too.

When, at last, he rolled over and covered her body with his, Julia cried out as she gave all of herself to him—her whole body, her whole heart.

'I love you, my Lady English.'

'Oh, Falk!'

He gave an exclamation of triumph as he drew from her that victory.

'Say my name again. Tell me that you love me,' he commanded hoarsely, as he moved his hips in a languorous rhythm of exquisite pleasure and she clung to him.

'I love you, Falk!' Julia sang his name with joy, over and over and over.

* * * * *

HISTORICAL ROMANCE™

LARGE PRINT

A CONVENIENT GENTLEMAN
Victoria Aldridge

The bank won't lend Caroline Morgan the money she so desperately needs until she gets herself a husband.

Caro finds Leander Gray, the younger son of an aristocrat and the only eligible man in town, collapsed in a local bar. He grudgingly agrees to a paper marriage and Caro is left wondering what she's got herself into. But when the gambler turns gentleman her feelings begin to change…

New Zealand
Love rush – Gold rush

A VERY UNUSUAL GOVERNESS
Sylvia Andrew

Edward Barraclough's happy bachelor existence is thrown into a spin when he is forced to look after his two orphaned nieces. Employing the right governess is vital and as unassuming and a little dowdy as Miss Petrie may appear, he suspects she's neither so humble nor respectful underneath!

Independently wealthy Lady Octavia Petrie is on the verge of confessing that Edward's mistaken her for someone else. Then, in a moment of sheer madness, prompted by his cynical attitude, she finds herself accepting the temporary position.

MILLS & BOON®

Live the emotion

HIST0904 LP

HISTORICAL ROMANCE™

LARGE PRINT

THE WIDOW'S BARGAIN
Juliet Landon

When her Scottish home is invaded by a dangerous band of reivers, Lady Ebony Moffat's first thought is to keep her young son safe. For his sake she is prepared to make a bargain with the men's leader—her body for her child's life.

Sir Alex Somers is intrigued. In a reiver's guise he has raided Castle Kells, seeking out traitors at the behest of the King of Scotland. Alex means no harm to the boy. But with his desire for Ebony so intense, he can't help but be drawn by her offer…

Robert the Bruce
…Scottish borders, raiding parties, endangered lovers…

THE RUNAWAY HEIRESS
Anne O'Brien

Miss Frances Hanwell effects a daring night-time escape—in the Marquis of Aldeborough's carriage! Mistaking her for a kitchen servant, Hugh only realises his grave error the next day. With scandal imminent, a reluctant marriage seems the only course of action.

Reluctance turns to respect when Hugh uncovers the brutal marks of the unhappy life she's been leading. Suddenly, he will do all in his power to protect her…especially now, as an unexpected inheritance threatens to take Frances from him…

MILLS & BOON®

Live the emotion

HIST0204 LP

THE MYSTERIOUS MISS M
Diane Gaston

The Mysterious Miss M is a living male fantasy – alluring, sensual, masked. But when Lord Devlin Steele finds himself responsible for her – and her child – he comes to know the real Maddy: the loving, passionate woman who drives away the nightmares of the Waterloo battlefield.

But the aristocratic soldier can't support his new family. He will only inherit his fortune on marriage to a suitable lady – and Maddy is far from suitable. With the dangers of London's underworld closing in, how can he protect the woman he has come to love?

THE SOCIETY CATCH
Louise Allen

Miss Joanna Fulgrave is regarded as the perfect society catch, although the only bridegroom she'll consider marrying is gorgeous Colonel Giles Gregory. But her marriage hopes are dashed when it seems Giles is about to propose to someone else – and Joanna's family have already found her another match!

Fearing her family may force her into a loveless marriage, Joanna flees. Giles is hot on her trail, determined to catch her and bring her home safely – but will he be as determined to make her his bride. . . ?

MILLS & BOON®

Live the emotion

HIST1104

HISTORICAL ROMANCE™

LARGE PRINT

THE NOTORIOUS LORD
Nicola Cornick

To sensible Rachel Odell, Cory, Lord Newlyn, has always been her friend and now, suddenly, she's aware of him as a man – an exceedingly handsome man. But he is her complete opposite, an adventure-seeker…and a rogue. It dawns on Rachel that throughout the summer Cory has been waging a slow, deliberate campaign to seduce her – but why? Is it because Cory has a secret agenda, or is it simply that he wants to claim his best friend as his bride…?

BLUESTOCKING BRIDES

The ladies of the Midwinter villages are about to be shocked, scandalised and…seduced!

FALLEN ANGEL
Sophia James

Nicholas Pencarrow, Duke of Westbourne, is intrigued by the woman who saves his life and then vanishes. Every attempt to make contact with this beautiful mystery lady is politely rebuffed.

Brenna has a dark secret she must keep buried, so she has built a respectable, uncomplicated world about herself where she avoids all male advances. Although, against her better judgement, the determined man keeps breaking through. Could she risk harming Nicholas's reputation by lowering her guard just once?

MILLS & BOON®

Live the emotion

HIST1204 LP

HISTORICAL ROMANCE™

LARGE PRINT

BELHAVEN BRIDE
Helen Dickson

When Anna Preston was introduced to her estranged family at their Belhaven estate, London's glamorous set became her new milieu, with never-before-dreamt-of trips to Paris and the French Riviera. There was now even a chance of a place at Oxford.

Thrown headlong into this exciting new world, she needed a solid rock to cling to, and this she found in Alex Kent. Having escaped the revolution in Russia as a boy, Alex was an impressive – if enigmatic – man. He sought to protect Anna from the perils of her new life, but even he couldn't keep her from the dangers that come with falling in love…

THE HEMINGFORD SCANDAL
Mary Nichols

Jane had broken her engagement to Harry Hemingford and sent him packing after his scandalous behaviour. So why was he back now, just when Mr Allworthy had proposed? Her suitor was undoubtedly a good match, but had she ever really fallen out of love with Harry?

Was safety really more important than the joyous happiness she found in Harry's arms? Perhaps Society's opinion should just go hang!

MILLS & BOON®

Live the emotion

HIST0105